First Base

Chicago Heartbreakers
Book One

Ally Wiegand

First published in Great Britain in 2024 by

 **embla books**

Bonnier Books UK Limited
4th Floor, Victoria House, Bloomsbury Square, London, WC1B 4DA
Owned by Bonnier Books
Sveavägen 56, Stockholm, Sweden

A CIP catalogue record for this book is available from the British Library.

ISBN: 9781471416927

This book is typeset using Atomik ePublisher.

Embla Books is an imprint of Bonnier Books UK.
www.bonnierbooks.co.uk

To my mom—for teaching me that I can do anything I set my mind to

MAGGIE

How could you not be romantic about baseball?

It's a game of failure and perseverance. A game that starts when the flowers first bloom and ends when the leaves fall from the trees. Fathers bond with their sons over their favorite teams, and those sons begin to form their own dreams of walking between those two white lines to a roaring crowd of fans. For several hours, you can forget about the world around you and lose yourself between three outs. There are heroes and villains, Davids and Goliaths. For non–sports lovers, it's a game you can fall asleep watching, wake up thirty minutes later, and not have missed a thing. The perfect pastime.

Years ago, I had been one of those kids with their dad. My father and I bonded over the game he grew up loving. From the moment I could walk, he had me at my very first Cougars game with a foam finger and a little souvenir baseball helmet full of ice cream. I had sat in this very stadium eating a corn dog and watching some of the greats run around the bases while fans screamed their support. Everything about it was magical. It was the first place where I imagined wanting to capture a moment forever with the camera my mother got me for my birthday when I first got into photography. The process of trying to get just the right shot that would encapsulate the memories and the feelings from a moment was exhilarating.

There had never been another feeling like a baseball game for me. The energy that danced through the air was unbeatable. It could make even the most unlikely sports fan cheer as the rookie hit a home run on his very first at bat of his career. Or when two brothers faced each other for the first time ever in the major leagues. It was a game that brought people together and could have the entire stadium sitting on the edge of their seats, waiting for the next big play or groaning when their favorite team lost.

I mean, how could you not love baseball? There truly is something in it for everybody.

Those moments at the baseball field with my dad felt like a foreshadowing to where I am now. That very first camera that I used to capture my first action shots helped me realize what I was good at. The days spent at the ballpark, just me and him, were the catalyst for my interest in working in the sports industry. It is a masculine industry where women are forced to work twice as hard to prove they deserve their place. Even in the jobs behind the scenes that women dominated, men still seemed to question our ability to showcase the magic of baseball. Those days spent in the stadium with my dad allowed me to understand what brought fans back to the field game after game.

The week prior to Opening Day always brought chaos, and to say that things were a little hectic around Renaissance Field would be an understatement. With Opening Day arriving in two short days, the grounds crew was working tirelessly to make sure the field was perfect, box office workers were getting ready for season ticket holders, the players were tweaking their form to prepare for the first pitch, and the media teams were rallying the fans with as much excitement as they could make around the big day.

Which was exactly why I was here bright and early for a practice at six in the morning, camera in tow. My boss, May, had called me an hour before to ask me to be at practice to grab some shots for the social media pages, much to my dismay. She had woken me up from a hot dream that included me and a popular actor on a romantic date in Mykonos. Those dream dates are the only sort of romance I've had in the past four years, and I consider those hours asleep with me and Mr. People Magazine's Hottest Guy of the Year sacred.

However, even when I did get a call out of the blue to come shoot a practice I wasn't already on the schedule for, I still went. Not because I knew I had to, but because I knew I wanted to. I loved my job. It was like I had entered a fever dream the moment I signed my contract with the Cougars almost three years ago and I had yet to wake up.

Did it pay the bills? Sure.

Was I going to get rich off it? No.

But did I love coming to work every day and photographing a sport I was excited about with players that were easy on the eyes? Absolutely.

Did I want more? Yes.

What *more* was, I didn't know, but it had been itching some part of the back of my brain for some time now. Like something was missing.

I nodded at some of the grounds crew as I passed them in the tunnel that opened out onto the field. The second the world went from complete darkness to the seats rising around you with neon lights peppering the top concourse was easily my favorite view of the entire park. The sound of a bat hitting a ball cracked across the stadium, the empty seats amplifying it. Some of the media team was already set up in the stadium seats behind home plate, but that wasn't my destination.

"How do you always beat me here?" I asked my best friend and fellow photographer, who was already taking pictures of the team like she had been here for some time already.

"Because you always stop to get coffee, no matter how late you're already running, Maggie. And you always take the bus, which we know is not the most reliable." I glared at my friend as I pulled my camera out of its bag. She knew how cranky I could get if I didn't get my caffeine in the morning, and she knew why I refused to drive my car through the city anymore. But she still had to remind me of my faults every morning I was late, which was most mornings.

Olivia Thompson and I were complete opposites, which was probably why we had gone from just coworkers to best friends after only a week of knowing each other. Olivia's auburn hair was always perfectly tamed, while my brown curls were a frizzy, wild mess. She was never found without a full face of makeup, while I was lucky to remember to put on sunscreen at the end of my skin care routine. We fit together like two puzzle pieces, perfectly filling the gaps that the other one lacked. She was the Amy Poehler to my Tina Fey. The Thelma to my Louise. The Laverne to my Shirley.

We were both hired in the same season almost three years ago now. Together we have covered some of the biggest moments in the league. The two of us work together like a well-oiled machine, never needing to tell the other where to line up to get the second angle. We never corrected each other and always trusted one of us would get the shot in the end.

Outside of work, Olivia was like my Mr. Miyagi. Without her, I would be sitting on my couch every night eating ramen, drinking wine, and watching yet another rom-com. She was the life of the party, and quite literally she would drag me every weekend to said event.

"Anything interesting happened yet?" I asked as I started to walk toward the third-base dugout to get a closer shot of the guys taking practice swings at home plate. This was my favorite practice of the entire year. The nerves were high, but not as high as the excitement. Most of the players had found their place on the team and joked freely. Morale was normally at the highest point of the season and so was the hope of winning it all, last year's result forgotten. It was the promise of new beginnings and the potential for anything to happen this season. A fresh start.

"Actually, yes," Olivia replied as she carried her camera attached to the long monopod over her shoulder. I raised an eyebrow at her in surprise.

How could I have already missed something good? It was six in the freaking morning.

"Remember May telling us about the Cougars picking up that hotshot Tommy Mikals?"

"The one who has a different girl on his arm every night as he leaves the clubs after games?" I asked.

"That would be the one."

"What about him?"

"He's here." My eyes darted around the field, searching for the newcomer. There was our star pitcher, Adam; my favorite player, Jamil;

and then my eyes landed on someone I didn't recognize playing short-stop. He was tall with broad shoulders and had a full sleeve of tattoos on perfectly muscular arms. He wore his hat low over his eyes, and his pants were stopped around his knees, which I've always thought was much better than long pants. He carried himself with a confidence that came from years of experience, years of always coming out on top. But even with the skill he showcased, his antics off the field tainted him for most of the league. When San Diego let him go, most of the other teams wouldn't touch him with a ten-foot pole, too afraid of the media scandals that would follow him. Chicago must have thought his cheap price and high skill level were worth the risk of a few scandalous photos splattered across the tabloids.

A *GQ* model wouldn't hold a candle to him. I turned to snap a few shots of him as he went to field a hard-hit ball up the middle to try to cover the fact that I was totally eyeing him through my camera.

There were a few perks to my job, I had to admit.

He's hot, I mouthed at Olivia. She nodded emphatically in response. The two of us couldn't deny that we definitely appreciated the eye candy we got to stare at every day at work. It would be a shame not to appreciate beauty when it was walking right past you in a pinstriped uniform with sweat glistening on its muscular body.

I kept my camera lens on him as the next player came up to take some practice swings. Tommy took off his hat to wipe at some sweat that had accumulated on his forehead, revealing a head of perfectly messy brown hair. It should be illegal for a man to look that good during physical exercise.

The crack of a wooden bat hitting a ball echoed again around the stadium, and I watched through my lens as Tommy turned to look in my direction. His eyes widened like he was watching a car crash in slow motion, and then I realized he was looking right at me.

"Maggie!" I heard Olivia yell. "Protect the camera!" I glanced up to see a foul ball sailing toward me, and I had barely enough time to dive out of the way, camera in hand. My shoulder took most of the fall; a bruise would most likely be there tomorrow. But I luckily kept my camera from hitting the ground and myself from being demolished by a baseball.

"You okay?"

Standing over me was Mr. GQ Model himself. Of course I had to notice that his eyes were the brightest blue I'd ever seen. It was like I was trapped in a trance, unable to look away from his face. His smile reached all the way up to his eyes, and it felt like if I looked directly at it, I'd be blinded. All of the air felt like it had been sucked from my lungs as I stared up at him. After a few seconds passed where I had yet to respond to his question, he raised a worried eyebrow.

As I realized that he was probably wondering if I had a serious head injury, I quickly fumbled around with my camera and reached up to place my hand in the one he had extended out toward me, letting him pull me to my feet. He yanked me upward as if I were as light as a feather, practically sending me flying face-first back into the ground.

"You okay?" he repeated, since I hadn't answered him the first time. This time, his voice had softened as if he realized I was struggling to form a coherent sentence. His eyes seemed to search my entire face, looking for any signs that I had been injured. If I had known I was going to lose all dignity today in front of one of the most attractive men I'd ever seen, I wouldn't have run from my apartment to avoid missing the bus. I nodded, not trusting that I would open my mouth only for no sound to come out. There was no need to embarrass myself any further. I'm not sure why I did it, but I found myself squeezing his hand to reassure him that I was fine and was surprised that he squeezed it back. The corners of his eyes squinted as he gave me a closed-lip smile. The moment had to have lasted a minute at most, but it felt like an eternity with the two of us standing there before he let go. Tommy started to walk backward, his eyes still on mine, before he turned to jog back to his position.

"Smooth," Olivia told me after Tommy was far enough away. I flipped her off behind the screen of my camera.

The head coach called the team to pick up the stray balls, which was Olivia's and my cue to walk onto the field to get some casual pictures of the guys. Most of the older players that knew us posed, hoping to get some new shots for their social media.

"Maggie!" Jamil waved at me as he tossed a few baseballs in from the outfield. I waved back at him, laughing as he struck a pose with one of the outfielders and motioned for me to take a picture. When I pulled my face back from the viewfinder, I noticed Tommy looking at me curiously. I ducked back behind my camera, not wanting to get stuck staring at him blatantly again.

"Why did it have to be him?" I whispered to Olivia.

"Because you have the worst luck," Olivia replied. She wasn't wrong. Life hadn't dealt me the greatest of hands these past few years.

"Hi, ladies." Jamil walked over to me and Olivia and slung his arms around our shoulders. I winced when his hand pressed into the spot on my shoulder I had just landed on. His smile was electric and much too enthusiastic for this early in the morning. He came to the club the same year that I did. We bonded one night over leftover concession-stand hot dogs, slushies, and a mutual feeling of struggling with a new chapter in our life. Jamil listened to me as I told him how my new job felt like I was starting over. It felt like as soon as I left college that door was completely shut, and I had taken a leading role in an entirely new story. Jamil shared his feelings of imposter syndrome, that season being his first year on the big stage, and that night he had gone zero-for-three at the plate. His golden retriever energy and the earnestness with which he listened to my sadness sealed Jamil's place at the top of my list of favorite players on the team.

"Jamil." I let him squeeze us into his sides before he took off running toward the team. He turned back around when he got halfway.

"You haven't drunk enough of your coffee yet, Canon." I rolled my eyes at his familiar nickname for me. He coined it after that night we first met, when he realized he never saw me anywhere without my camera. When he first gave the nickname to me, I remember thinking how corny it sounded, which I had voiced to him constantly at the beginning. After a while, it grew on me, but I would never admit that I secretly loved it or I'd never hear the end of it.

"What are you trying to say, Jamil?" I yelled back at him as I turned the camera to snap a few shots of him.

"He's trying to say you're always cranky at morning practices," Olivia jumped in. Part of me wanted to argue, but we both knew that if I did, she had a list of times on her phone when I had been less than pleasant to be around that was longer than a CVS receipt. She had started it halfway through our first season together after I failed to remember a single time I had acted like I'd woken up on the wrong side of the bed. From then on, she always had actual proof to prove me wrong.

The morning went by as it normally did. After Olivia and I took all of the pictures that May had requested, we scammed one of the grounds crew into getting us some of the doughnuts that they always had in their shed, and we relaxed in the stadium seats behind home plate to work on our tans as we waited for the practice to end.

The entire time my eyes followed Tommy. After a quick search, I found hundreds of articles about him and confirmed my earlier conversation with Olivia that he was, in fact, a ladies' man. There were whole Reddit pages dedicated to his escapades.

Even so, I couldn't help but watch the way he moved on the field. I glanced back down at my phone and found that it was evident the confidence he exuded on the field didn't stop once he walked off the dirt. I quickly scanned a few tabloid articles detailing wild nights at clubs that involved hookers, drugs, and lots of alcohol. Everything in those articles was screaming at me that he was exactly the type of player that I kept at arm's length. One of the last articles had pictures pulled straight from his personal social media account, and I made a mental note to remember the username for later.

"Maggie? Did you hear me?" I snapped out of whatever trance Tommy had me in for the second time today.

"What?" I asked, noticing that she was packing her stuff up.

"Were you daydreaming about Tommy Mikals?" Olivia wiggled her eyebrows mischievously at me.

I shook my head adamantly. "Absolutely not."

Olivia leaned over to whisper in my ear as we passed the media team on our way out of the stadium. "You've got to admit he's gorgeous."

I hated that I couldn't tell her that she was wrong. Because Tommy was *drop-dead gorgeous*. The kind of gorgeous that I was sure would have groupies fawning over him as he left the stadium after games. The kind of gorgeous that was far out of my league. But I knew that if I even admitted to her that I found him attractive, she would get her hopes up that I was finally coming around to dating again. Or at the very least, was open to talking about things like that.

"Hold on." I stopped in the middle of the tunnel. "I left one of my bags. I'll meet you at Burt's later."

Olivia rolled her eyes at me. It was typical that I forgot something at least once a week. I turned back down the tunnel and walked out onto the field, only to see Adam, Jamil, and Tommy walking toward me. My camera bag was slung over Adam's shoulder. He held it out like an offering when he saw me, a knowing look on his face. He had saved my camera more times than I wanted to admit. Before a couple of years ago, something like this never would have happened. But after college, it seemed like my mind was skipping around far too often, never reliable enough anymore. I used caffeine like a crutch to try to keep my mind sharp enough to remain in the present and not dive back into a hole where it felt like my thoughts couldn't reach.

"Mags, you forgot something," he called out. I hustled over to the three of them to grab it, ignoring the look on Jamil's face. It screamed *I told you that you haven't drunk enough coffee yet.*

"Thanks, Adam." I turned to try to make a quick escape. I didn't trust myself to my own devices around Tommy Mikals after our first encounter, and I especially didn't want to look like I was drooling over him in front of Adam and Jamil. I knew I'd never hear the end of it.

"Mags, have you met Tommy yet?" I cringed as I heard Adam call back out to me. "Tommy, this is one of our team photographers, Maggie Redford."

I spun back around, pasting a smile on my face as I made eye contact with the Chicago Cougars' new player. Just like before, it was like the air in my lungs evaporated on sight. My stomach swooped like I was a passenger on a roller-coaster ride as I struggled to regain my breath.

"It's nice to officially meet you. Glad you're okay." Tommy stuck his hand out to me after he realized that I wasn't going to be the first one to say something. I was beginning to wonder if I had seriously wronged someone recently and this was karma catching up to me.

"Nice to meet you officially, too. Good luck this season." I tried to use that as my opportunity to escape, but cursed as I heard Jamil call out to me again. *Damn him and his chipper morning attitude.* I only wanted to put space between myself and Tommy Mikals and his brilliant blue eyes and sexy smile.

"Canon, are you and Olivia going to go to the club tonight? We're celebrating Opening Day."

I looked at Jamil over my shoulder and gave him a small smile. "You know my answer to that, Jamil."

"I'm always hoping one time you'll surprise me." Jamil returned my smile before I turned to walk as fast and far away from Tommy Mikals as I could. I tried to ignore the fluttering that had started in my stomach from the moment I had looked up into his eyes after I'd nearly been annihilated by that baseball. I hadn't seen anyone look at me like that for a long time. Those butterflies felt like they were at war with the sadness that came to the forefront of my mind at the feeling.

———

It was the first day of college and as per usual, I was running late. I had even set five extra alarms to avoid this exact moment: me running across campus looking like a scared, lost first-year. Some senior was probably filming me from the window of their dorm, and I'd find the video later on some account online.

As I came running around the corner of the hallway my class was supposed to be in, I saw a guy with sandy-blond hair that curled around his ears. He was staring at a piece of paper that had been taped to the door, and he was startled when I came barreling closer. When I realized that he was standing in front of my classroom, I put on the brakes and pulled up right next to him.

"Here for English 111?" His voice was like butter. It was rich and made every other voice I'd ever heard seem dull. Whoever he was, he clearly wasn't from the Midwest. He had a thick East Coast accent.

"Yes," I told him, between sucking air into my lungs and trying to focus on the piece of paper he had been reading.

"The professor canceled class today. Said we'd start on Wednesday." Some of my worry at the thought of being late to my first college class less- ened. *"You okay?" The guy was looking at me with an amused expression*

on his face. Which was probably from the sweat that had started to accumulate on my forehead from the run across campus.

"Oh, yeah. Just a little morning exercise." I watched as his eyes crinkled before he let out a small laugh. When he looked at me again, it was like I could practically see the sparks shooting around in the air between us.

"I'm Luke." He stuck his hand out toward me.

"Maggie."

TOMMY

The Cougars were my last chance at redemption.

All of my poor decisions as a young kid who got access to a massive amount of money, alcohol, and women for the first time in his life had finally caught up to me, almost effectively ending my professional baseball career. I wasn't proud of any of those decisions. I was the epitome of young, dumb, and stupid. By the time I finally realized what road I was going down, it was too late for my career with San Diego. They cut me, wanting to put distance between themselves and the reputation I had made for myself. The moment that the general manager walked up to me to tell me to pack my bags and leave the clubhouse, it was like I had come back up to the surface, finally able to breathe again. From then on, I promised myself I would stick to the path that younger me would have been proud of taking. I was lucky that I was even starting my eighth season in the league. I hadn't gone to college. I joined the draft right out of high school and didn't have a degree to fall back on. I needed to focus on baseball and proving that I still deserved to be taken seriously.

But life seemed to be tempting me once again.

I watched Maggie Redford hurry back down the tunnel, her camera bag clutched tightly to her chest. She didn't glance back at us. Her steps were hurried, and if I didn't know any better, I would have guessed she was trying to put as much distance between herself and us as she could. My eyes followed her until she disappeared farther into the stadium. It wasn't until she was long gone and I was in the locker room that I realized my chest had grown tighter, as if she had wrapped a string around my rib cage and pulled.

The second I saw her at practice this morning, I was instantly intrigued. I had watched between swings the way her eyes roamed the field, looking for the next angle. She walked around the field like there was nowhere else she was more comfortable being. When she smiled at her coworker, I was like a magnet, completely drawn to her.

It had been over a year since my last relationship. At the time, I had thought it would be the relationship that would make me a monogamous man. But instead, I had my heart eviscerated. During the year after San Diego had let me go and the Cougars had signed me to a contract, I had been completely celibate. I hadn't wanted to risk potentially losing my career again to women that weren't worth my time. When I looked at Maggie, my brain had to remind other parts of my body that I had sworn off women.

Her smile had me rethinking all of my rules.

Maggie was unlike any woman I had ever seen. She was an explosion of energy. Everything about her felt like it was turned all the way up—forcing you to notice her—but what I found even more interesting was that she didn't seem to know that about herself. The moment I stood over her, offering her a hand after her close call with the foul ball, it was like she had morphed into a scared animal, unsure of what to do or where to go. The confident girl with the dissecting eyes was gone.

Her light brown hair was wild and big, curling out in every direction. When she smiled, it was like she was grinning with her whole body. Her eyes crinkled at the corners, and her smile seemed to take up half her face. When she looked up at me from her spot on the field, cradling her camera, I struggled to remember to breathe. Her eyes were like bright emeralds, the kind that gem investors would pay millions for. She was all soft curves and feminine lines. Basically, the complete opposite of any other woman I had ever dated before.

Back in California, it felt like I had a different model on my arm every weekend. I was used to the type of girls that picked at their salads when I took them out to dinner and cared about the labels they and their dates wore. At the time, it had felt like a symptom of a glamorous lifestyle, like something that came with the turf. But when my own habits had taken a turn for the worse, it felt like none of the people I had surrounded myself with cared if I ended up dead on the side of the road. All they cared about were how many likes they got on their latest photos on social media and if they were wearing something more expensive than the person next to them.

When the wool had finally been removed from my eyes, I realized I needed to turn my life in a completely different direction. I had worked my entire life to be where I was now, and if I continued dating and spending time with the people I had been, all of that hard work would be for nothing.

"Oh no, man." Jamil pulled me back into the present. "No chance."

"What?" I asked as we continued toward the player parking lot, thoughts of Maggie still hanging around the corners of my mind.

I had been nervous when I first arrived at Renaissance Field. I was expecting the entire team to hate me from my previous history. But luckily, Jamil and Adam had taken me under their wing, and as soon as the team realized that they had accepted me, the rest fell into line. I was immensely thankful to them for that and for their friendship. They were the type of guys that I should have surrounded myself with earlier in my career, rather than the guys that used their name and image for a flashy lifestyle.

"I saw the way you just looked at Maggie Redford," Jamil continued. "I'm sorry to tell you that you have absolutely no chance with that woman. She's locked up tighter than Fort Knox."

"There's nothing to worry about. Women are not my priority right now."

Jamil slung an arm around my shoulder and pulled me in closer. "I hear you, man. We may actually have a real shot at the playoffs this year. Especially since Adam over here has been throwing lasers this off-season."

Adam rolled his eyes at Jamil's comment but flashed me a smile. He had quickly become one of my favorite people on the team for his laid-back personality and dad-like tendencies. He was the first person to introduce himself to me at an early team event. It was like he had adopted me as his son. Adam was getting toward the end of his career and typically avoided any antics that happened among our teammates, sticking to the role of mentor.

"Keep your mind focused on the season and you'll be fine," he told me.

"Are you going to go out with us?" Jamil asked as we all stopped in the middle of the parking lot.

"I don't know." I rubbed the back of my neck, my hands messing with the longer strands of hair. "I've got to be careful with being seen out like that. I'm on a short leash with the Cougars, and I don't have an agent to bail me out anymore."

"You're still going to rock without an agent?" Jamil's eyes widened.

"I can't bring myself to get another one after what happened before," I told him.

"Well, if you change your mind and want to do something, the family and I are having a movie night tonight. I can shoot you our address if you decide you want to stay in." Adam started to back away toward his extended SUV made specifically for hauling around multiple little monsters.

"Thanks, man," I called after him.

"We're not going to do anything crazy, I promise. It's the only night during the season I will actually go out." Jamil started walking toward his car. "I better see you there!"

I shook my head at him as I watched him hop into his sports car. He rolled his window down before he pulled out of the parking lot and pointed at me. "I'm serious!"

"Send me the address," I called after him. He'd better be telling the truth that they weren't going to do anything crazy. The second bottle service started or women with little-to-no clothing came near, I was gone.

My car was one of the last ones in the parking lot, and as I started to make my way toward it, ready to go home and take a long shower, my phone went off. I dug it out of my pocket, expecting it to be Jamil sending me the address to the club tonight, but I saw something else that I wished I hadn't seen.

> Dad: Make sure you work on your hands drifting at practice. We can't have you keep missing the inside half of the plate. The Cougars will bench you faster than San Diego did.

My jaw clenched as I read the text. I didn't bother responding. I locked the screen and tossed the phone on the passenger seat next to me. My dad had started sending me text messages about my hitting form after San Diego dropped me. It was his way of showing his disapproval for the decisions I had made that led to my dismissal from the team. All of the work that I had done in the off-season to still be desirable enough for a team to pick me up after everything that had happened with San Diego didn't seem to matter to my dad. The only thing he could focus on was the fact that I had let alcohol and women distract me from our previous shared goal.

When those texts started, all I could think about was when I was a kid and how excited I would be to dissect my practices with him when I got home. After every game in high school, the two of us would chat over dinner about different at bats or plays I made in the field. It never felt overbearing then. At that time, we both had a shared vision for my future success. When my professional baseball career was almost lost, it seemed like my dad didn't know what to do with me or how to talk to me. It was as if we only had baseball as a commonality. My camaraderie with him felt almost like a phantom limb, the pain always there, reminding me of something that I had lost. I was beginning to wonder if professional baseball wasn't *our* shared dream anymore, but only his.

Even with how I felt, there was still a massive part of me that wanted this season to end well, to give my dad something to be proud of again. If I didn't, I was worried I'd always be a failure in his eyes, and the thought of that made my chest tight, like a million pounds of pressure had been put on top of me.

My mind flashed back to Maggie and her brilliant emerald eyes. If there wasn't so much weighing on this season for me, she would have been the type of girl that I would have wanted to get to know. The type of girl that I probably needed. But right now, she was a risk I couldn't afford. A distraction that I didn't want.

However, I knew as much as the next guy that if I focused solely on this season for the entirety of it, I would be burned out before the All-Star break. That was the very reason why I saved the address that Jamil sent me into my favorites. An under-control night out would give my brain something else to think about besides every swing I took at practice today. My phone buzzed in the seat next to me again, and I saw my dad's name flash across the screen on my dash, notifying me that he had sent another text. I backed out of the parking lot, leaving the phone face-down next to me.

MAGGIE

The breath I had been holding slowly passed through my lips once I was safely outside the stadium, waiting for the bus. A heavy weight seemed to press into my chest as I battled with the overwhelming emotions that wanted to restrict every part of me.

The moment that I had looked in Tommy Mikals's eyes and felt those same sparks I had the first time I met Luke, it was like my entire world had been tilted off its axis. As if all of the carefully constructed walls I had put in place for the past four years to protect my heart had started to crumble, and that terrified me.

It had been almost four years of sorting anything that reminded me of Luke into a folder that I had shoved to the recesses of my mind. I had gone this far without having to revisit any of those feelings I had placed inside that folder. But the moment that Tommy had looked at me like I was *interesting*, like I was someone who was worth knowing, those feelings I had shoved away with the intention of never revisiting came pushing their way back to the front of my mind. Which was exactly why I decided I would be avoiding Tommy for the rest of the season. He was a distraction that I didn't need.

My breath was still coming in rapidly, and the breathing routine my therapist taught me came to mind. After the accident, my parents had made me start sessions. I wouldn't talk to them about what had happened, and all they wanted was for me to talk to somebody. Simply sitting in that room with the therapist had been one of the hardest things I had ever done. It made me feel weak, like I wasn't mentally strong enough to cope by myself. But after a few sessions, I realized that talking with a professional displayed my strength more than not coping on my own.

I went through the familiar steps of counting my breaths, using the realty ad across from me as my anchor point. After a couple rounds, I was able to fully function again. In my mind, the safest thing to do was to keep Tommy at a distance. There was no denying I found him attractive. I couldn't force my body to think otherwise, but I could minimize all interaction with him with the hope of never seeing him look at me like he did today. I didn't deserve to be looked at like I was someone worth knowing. If Tommy knew the truth about how broken I was, that look would have been one of pity and not interest.

The bus pulled up in front of me, and I swiped my card, smiling at Renarda, the driver, as I did.

"How are you today, Miss Maggie?"

"Opening Day is in two days, Renarda. Can life get much better?" Renarda had been driving the route from my apartment to the field for the past three years, and the two of us had grown an easy friendship. She never questioned why I always chose the bus, and her easy smile always put me at ease on the rides.

Olivia was absolutely right that the bus was not the most reliable means of transportation, but she also understood why I preferred it. The main reason being that I didn't own a car anymore because I couldn't afford to buy a new one. The other reason was as simple as not trusting myself to drive anymore. The bus got me safely from one place to the next, and I didn't have to feel responsible for anyone else's well-being.

But right then it didn't matter if I got home by bus or hot-air balloon; I wanted to be in the safety of my apartment where there wasn't an attractive man making me feel things I hadn't felt in a long time. My mom always told me I shouldn't run from my feelings, but it had worked well for me so far in life, and running from Tommy Mikals's smile was exactly what I needed to be doing right now.

The bus dropped me off around the block from my apartment. I didn't live in the nicest building in the city, but it wasn't the worst either. The paint was peeling off the walls, the gas for the stove and heat didn't always work, and sometimes Mrs. Adams across the hall played her soap operas too loud. My view out the back of my apartment might be of garbage, but it had its perks too. It was in a nicer neighborhood, and I had never left my apartment feeling like I was concerned for my safety, which said a lot for apartments in the city. Greg, the owner of the coffee stand on the corner, always gave me a free coffee whenever I stopped by to see him, and my entire street was full of street performers, which always provided entertainment.

Would I live somewhere else if I could afford it? Probably.

Of course I had dreams of seeing trees and the sky out of all of my windows, but that was a luxury I couldn't currently afford. I had to settle for my small, dark apartment that had very little natural light and always had the background noise of Mrs. Adams's television.

I left my keys on the counter in the kitchen before I dropped down onto my sagging couch. My mind was still playing through the series of events that had happened since I had woken up this morning. After fifteen minutes had passed, I finally concluded that I wasn't going to be able to think of much else. The only solution I could think of that would help get Tommy Mikals out of my head was allowing myself to think about him. So I pulled out my phone and searched for his personal social media page with the username I saw earlier.

The first photo was a rather artsy shot of him standing in front of The Bean in Millennium Park with a subtle announcement of his trade to the Cougars. It had been posted a couple of weeks ago and was the only photo of him in Chicago. I continued to scroll through his feed. There were photos of the ocean in California, of him surfing, and of him playing for his previous team in San Diego. But there were no photos of him with any women or at any parties for the past year. In fact, there was almost a distinct moment where Tommy's entire feed changed from the partying scene to outdoor activities.

It was rather odd that Tommy seemed to have dropped out of the party scene and the public eye, but his image was still plagued with head-lines of him with women and alcohol. I knew there were recent tabloid articles that included pictures of him with women dangling off his arm as he left various nightclubs. But it was clear that Tommy must have been making an effort to not further the narrative in his own space.

Farther down Tommy's feed there was a period of time when the only girl on his arm was a tall, thin, blond woman who was beyond gorgeous. I tapped on one of the pictures to find the woman's handle before clicking over to her page. Her name was Sutton James, and she was a very attractive model. I wouldn't say that I was surprised to find that Tommy had dated a model. It seemed that he had run in the same circles as plenty of famous celebrities and beautiful women. But as I scrolled through Sutton's page, it was like every trace of the two of them had been erased. In female lingo, that typically meant the breakup had been bad. I flipped back over to Tommy's page and scrolled even deeper, thumbing through pictures of him chugging from a champagne bottle, pictures of women perched on his lap, and pictures of him looking like a completely different person than who I saw today.

After I had firmly reminded myself of who Tommy Mikals was, I closed my phone and threw it down on the couch next to me. He was a player. Someone that broke hearts so often, he forgot that he even did it. He was used to girls throwing themselves at his feet. He probably even had a list of girls that he'd hooked up with in every city he'd visited with his old team.

Tommy Mikals was the exact opposite type of guy I should be attracted to and not who I needed in my life right now. He should not be giving me the same feelings that someone like Luke had. Only after feeling like I had firmly refiled that folder in the back of my mind did I allow myself to finally relax. I couldn't allow myself to pursue any ques-tions around him clearly trying to change his image, because if I ended up realizing that he was someone who had simply made some poor deci-sions when he was young, dumb, and stupid . . . well, then I couldn't use any of those articles as valid reasons to stay away from him.

My hand found my phone again and dialed the number I had had memorized since I was a kid.

"Maggie!" My mom's voice filled my ears and took the edge off all the anxiety that had built up inside me.

"Hey, Mom. How's your day?"

"It's good. Your father is still working, and I managed to get a little bit more done on my painting." My mom created beautiful works of art for a living. Growing up, most of my memories consisted of her in an old pair of paint-splattered overalls, a paintbrush tucked in the pocket and a bandana covering her hair.

"I can't wait to see it."

"How was practice today?"

"It was good." I wasn't sure what else to say. It wasn't like I could say, *Hey, Mom, I think I met someone today that I could see myself liking.* That would set off more alarm bells than me not having gone on any dates for the past four years.

"Did something happen?" Leave it to my mother to have a sixth sense for when something wasn't quite right with me.

"Just a normal day," I told her, trying to push the attention away from anything being off with me.

"It's two days before Opening Day and you're telling me it was just another normal day?"

I let out a sigh when I realized that she wasn't going to let this one go. It wouldn't hurt if I told her part of the truth.

"Met the new guy on the team this year."

"Tommy Mikals?" my mom asked.

"How did you know that?" My eyebrows raised in surprise. My mom was not normally in tune with professional baseball. That was reserved for me and my dad.

"Your father was talking about it this morning." I heard a sink turn on over the phone. "What's he like? Is he as bad as all of those news articles say?"

A part of me hesitated as I thought about how to answer that. "He seems nice so far. Not at all like I thought he'd be."

That seemed safe enough to tell her.

"Is he as hot as he looks in photos?"

"Mom!" I groaned at the thought of my mom and me both finding the same guy attractive.

"It's just a question," my mom replied absentmindedly.

Tommy's bright-blue eyes flashed in my mind. Along with the tattoos that stood out against tan skin on his arms during practice. And how his hair curled out perfectly from his baseball hat. Even the reminder of these small details seemed like they could take my breath away. I had never felt like I could be intoxicated by someone before. I cleared my throat, trying to break through some of the heat that had started to build inside me at the thought of Tommy.

"He's better in person," I mumbled, hoping she didn't read too much into me actually admitting that.

"Are you sure you're okay, sweetie?" My mom's voice dropped to a soft whisper. Every part of me hoped she was only circling back around and not that she had picked up on the very real attraction that I felt toward Tommy.

"Absolutely," I told her.

"Okay, well don't forget we have family dinner coming up soon."

"Of course. I'll see you guys then."

My mom told me goodbye before the phone line went dead. Even if I didn't feel like I was ready to admit to my mom that I was physically attracted to someone, just hearing her voice seemed to put some of my worries at bay.

I had a few hours before I would need to catch a bus that would take me to Burt's to meet Olivia. All I wanted to do was sleep, but I knew that was the last thing I needed to be doing. I had finally gotten to a place where I didn't feel like I wanted to spend all of my free time asleep, and I didn't want to go back.

So I did the next best thing and turned on an episode of *Sex and the City* to allow myself to get lost in Carrie Bradshaw's glamorous New York City life, leaving my own behind.

MAGGIE

Olivia was waiting for me at our usual table when I walked into Burt's later that evening. For the past three years, Burt's had been our Opening Day routine. It was a run-down diner that had the best food in Chicago, but it was a well-kept secret. Every year at some point during the last few days leading up to Opening Day, we ordered the greasiest items on the menu and shoved them in our faces before our lives weren't ours anymore. It was the second-best day of the year.

"Find it?"

"The guys picked it up for me," I told her as I slid into the sticky vinyl booth. The vinyl was cracking and it caught on my jeans.

I was sure that there were far better places in town to celebrate the beginning of the next baseball season, but Burt's would always be home to us. Diane, our favorite waitress, always saved the best slice of chocolate cake for Olivia and me on the days we frequented the restaurant. Our cups were never empty, and our stomachs often felt like they'd burst at the seams when we left.

Olivia slid my usual coffee across the table to me, followed by a plate of french toast piled so high that I was sure I wouldn't be eating for the rest of the day. Burt's had become one of the few places in town that didn't remind me of my old life. It was purely something new that Olivia and I had discovered. I didn't feel cold sweats when I walked through the door. I wasn't nervous to run into any of my old friends from college. It was a safe haven for me.

As I was halfway through the monstrosity in front of me, Olivia caught my eye over her cup of coffee. The look on her face told me I was not going to like what she was about to say. It was a look I'd come to know well whenever she was planning on pushing me out of my comfort zone.

"What if we went tonight?" My fork stilled halfway to my mouth. She wasn't asking what I thought she would be asking. Of all the things that I thought would come out of Olivia's mouth, that was at the bottom of the list.

"We always watch *Pretty Woman* after Burt's."

"What if we didn't?" Olivia looked at me with her signature puppy-dog eyes.

I started to shake my head, putting my foot down about this one tradition. Olivia probably thought this was the perfect opportunity to get me out of my apartment, but there were just some things I wouldn't give up, and watching Richard Gere fall in love with Julia Roberts was one of them. But Olivia continued to give me those stupid puppy-dog eyes, and I knew I was a goner.

———

Those puppy-dog eyes were the exact reason why I found myself in a dress at a nightclub and not on my couch with my favorite blanket while watching *Pretty Woman*. I wasn't the only one that wasn't comfortable with the club environment. Olivia's sister, Charlotte (or "Lottie"), joined us tonight. Olivia had gone on during the car ride about how Lottie needed a night away from her clinic. Lottie was the best sports physical therapist in the city of Chicago and worked at a private practice where she spent practically all of her time. She was ambitious, with the goal of joining the staff of one of the professional teams in Chicago, and worked exhaustingly to try to achieve that goal.

The three of us scanned the crowd, looking for the VIP section where Jamil had told us they'd be. The club was all of the things I hated: loud, crowded, and poorly lit. It was more packed than a stadium during the World Series, the music was reverberating through what felt like my very soul, and I had the urge to pull out my phone to use the flashlight just so I could make it through the dance floor without falling over some poor guy passed out on the ground. And all of those very reasons were why Olivia would be having the time of her life by the end of the night and I would be counting down the minutes until I was safely under the covers in my bed.

Olivia pulled her sister and me in between bodies and around couples displaying a little too much affection on the dance floor before we finally ended up at a roped-off section that was elevated from the rest of the club. I spotted Jamil holding court with some of the younger players. Most of the married guys were nowhere to be found, probably at home with their families. I found myself jealous of them as Olivia gave the bouncer our names and he unclipped the rope to let us in. Jamil noticed us a few seconds later and excitedly motioned for us to come over.

"Are my eyes fooling me, or is Canon bestowing us with her presence on a night out?"

I rolled my eyes at him before letting him wrap me up in one of his massive bear hugs.

"It's all Olivia's fault," I mumbled into his ear.

"Sounds like Olivia deserves a drink on me," Jamil exclaimed as he turned to embrace my best friend. Olivia loved Jamil as much as I did. The two were like twins, and I was sure there would be disastrous consequences from them partying together tonight.

Jamil set Olivia down. "And who is this?"

"This is my sister, Lottie." Olivia introduced her sister to the group.

"Your sister?" Jamil reached out to give the back of Lottie's hand a kiss. Lottie's eyebrows shot up toward her hairline, not yet used to Jamil's antics.

A chorus of hellos echoed around the rest of the group. Lottie gave them all a wave before finding an open spot on the couches. She immediately pulled her phone out and began typing away on yet another work email. She had been practically glued to her phone the entire car ride over.

Jamil and Olivia disappeared to the bar, leaving me standing by myself in the entrance of the VIP section with guys from the team I was not familiar with. At the stadium, I knew my place and felt confident in it. Outside the stadium, I felt like a foreigner. I glanced around the seating area, hoping to find somewhere I could sit and immediately blend into the couch.

"Hey."

My eyes snapped over to see Tommy sitting on one of the couches with an empty spot right next to him. *So much for trying to avoid him for my own sanity.*

If I thought he was gorgeous in his practice uniform, he was beyond sexy in a short-sleeve white button-down that had most of the buttons undone, revealing that the tattoos on his arms weren't the only ones he had, and a pair of black pants that were rolled up at the bottom. His dark hair was tousled in a way that only guys could pull off—perfectly imperfect. I stared at him for a few moments, trying to weigh my options before I decided that the open seat next to him was more appealing than fighting back through the crowd of people to find Olivia and Jamil.

"Hi," I finally replied as I sat down.

Tommy's arms were stretched out over the back of the couch, his body turned so he could keep an eye on the rest of the guys in the VIP section. His eyes danced over to them, watching as they talked with each other. There was a glass of whiskey sitting on the table in front of him, but it looked like it hadn't been touched.

"I thought Jamil said you don't normally come to these." Tommy looked over at me to assess the black dress I had had to pull from the back of my closet for tonight. The last time I had worn it was in college, which was probably also the last time I was any fun. Every place his eyes roamed over my body felt like they had been lit on fire. It felt like he was taking his time as he drank me in from head to toe. I wanted to preen from the attention, but then my brain remembered those pictures of Tommy leaving the club. A small part of me screamed to remember his reputation and to stop swooning.

"I don't."

"But you're here," he noted, his eyes returning to look at his teammates.

"I am."

Tommy didn't respond, thankfully, and it gave me the perfect opportunity to study my surroundings. But mostly him. I noted his glass of whiskey and saw that condensation had started on the outside, confirming my suspicions that it hadn't been drunk yet. My eyes drifted to the rest of the guys around us. Some of them were talking among themselves, but most of them had found a girl that they were in deep conversation with. If someone were to ask me what I thought this very scenario would look like tonight, Tommy Mikals being one of the few guys who wasn't drunk and wasn't talking to a girl would not have been on my bingo card.

"You said earlier that this isn't your scene."

I froze when I realized Tommy was talking to me again and had probably caught the fact that I was staring at him.

Smooth, I told myself.

"So what is?"

"What's my scene?" I asked, watching him dip his chin slightly in a nod of confirmation. "A night in with a bottle of wine, a good romantic comedy, maybe a pint of ice cream, and my skin care routine. This"—I waved my hands at the scene around us—"hasn't been my thing since college."

"So what got you here tonight?"

Everything about Tommy seemed put together. He paused before every time he spoke, like he actually *thought* about what he wanted to say. His words were sure, and his gaze was even as he looked at me. It was utterly intimidating because I was anything but put together. My brain never felt like it could expertly navigate through a conversation with a new person. I also avoided making eye contact with people, mostly because I didn't want them to see the parts of me that weren't whole anymore. Everything about Tommy scared the hell out of me.

"Olivia." I motioned toward my best friend who was leaning against the bar, laughing with Jamil as they waited for drinks.

Tommy didn't follow my hand motion though. He just kept his eyes focused on mine. He was giving me his undivided attention. I could feel those damn butterflies soaring back around inside me. Desperate to take my mind off the way my heart felt like it was squeezing with emotion, I blurted out the first thing that came into my head. "She's the extrovert, and I'm most definitely the introvert of our friendship. She's like the yin to my yang or the splish to my splash."

Right after those words escaped my lips, I wanted to stuff them back in. I wasn't sure what it was about me making a fool of myself in front of Tommy today, but I was officially two-for-two. I guess if there were any place to die from embarrassment, a club I never wanted to be in wearing a dress I didn't want to wear would be perfect. Tommy just continued to stare at me for another few painful seconds before a smile broke out across his face.

"You're funny, you know that?"

The smile stayed on Tommy's face, which gave him a boyish look that softened his hard edges.

Dammit. Why does he have to be so goddamn attractive?

My mind flashed back to those articles about him leaving clubs with models on his arm. I knew that I would be the last girl that he would pick out in a club like this to leave with him in front of all the paparazzi waiting to get the perfect picture to smack across every news outlet the next day.

"People don't normally call me funny," I told him, torn between wanting to stare at him and admire the lines of his face or avoid making eye contact with him because it seemed like he had the same thought about studying me.

"Maybe you don't hang around the right people."

It took everything in me not to let my mouth drop open in surprise at Tommy's response. Was he actually voicing that he thought I was interesting? Earlier today, it felt like that was all in my head. But I was sitting next to him on this couch in a bar full of women who were much more attractive than I was, and still he was choosing to give me all of his focus.

I thought about the photos of Tommy stumbling out of bars looking bleary-eyed and greasy like he had consumed way too much alcohol, and tried to reconcile that with the sober guy who was talking with me like I was the most important person in the room. The guy who didn't know who he was when he left bars at three in the morning was the type of guy I'd never be caught dead with. I finally braved the idea of making eye contact with him again, only to see him staring directly at my lips. I cursed the way my mouth went instantly dry and the way my legs felt like they would give out beneath me if I tried to escape.

Luckily, I was saved by Jamil and Olivia coming back into the VIP section with their arms loaded down with beverages. Both of their personalities seemed like they could fill up the entire space from the way they laughed with each other, and that energy was a thankful distraction from Tommy's intense stare. Jamil collapsed back into his seat and pulled Olivia down next to him as they continued their conversation. Lottie had finally gotten off her phone and was busy describing different routines some of the rookies should implement in their pregame warmups to help with their arm health.

Great. There go my lifelines in this club.

Whenever we went out, I relied on Olivia to introduce me to the other people she so easily befriended. She always made sure to insert me into the conversation to help me feel included because she knew that if I was left to my own devices, I would slink back to a dark corner of the room and avoid conversing with any humans the entire time. And on nights like tonight when Olivia decided it was her time, my inability to socialize was forgotten.

It felt like the walls of the club were closing in on me the second I realized that I was on my own. The dress I was wearing began to feel too tight, and the music started to feel like it was pressing on every part of my head. My eyes searched for an exit that didn't include me shoving my way back through the dance floor, but I struck out.

"Need to leave?" I jumped when I realized that Tommy's mouth was inches from my ear.

He must have shifted closer to me during my mental breakdown. His breath tickled the inside of my ear and sent shivers down my spine. A traitorous thought of his lips brushing against the skin behind my ear flashed in my mind. Goose bumps spread across my skin as I imagined what it would be like to be kissed by him. Judging by the way that

Tommy did everything else in life, I was sure kissing him would be all-consuming. My skin burned hot enough to finally make me realize that I was dreaming in a room full of people with the main character of my dream sitting right next to me. I blinked a few times, trying to clear that image away before it became obvious that I was thinking about something I shouldn't be.

"Uh . . ." I shifted between glancing at Tommy and back toward the club's entrance, debating if I could fight my way through the horde of people on my own. Part of me knew that if he was offering to help me get out of here and I took it, I would then be *that* girl that left the bar with Tommy Mikals.

"Come on." The next thing I knew, his hand was wrapped around mine and he was pulling me toward the dance floor. Olivia didn't even bother to look in my direction as I tried desperately to grab her attention. She was too wrapped up in the conversation she was having with Jamil. Tommy put himself firmly in front of me as he carved a path through the sea of bodies. It was like watching Moses part the Red Sea. I was sure that no one could actually tell who he was, but the way he carried himself demanded that people move out of his way. Before I knew it, we had emerged from the mosh pit unscathed and out into the cool spring Chicago air.

"Thank you," I told him as I pulled my phone out of my pocket to call for an Uber. Olivia had driven me to the club, and there was no way I was getting on the L this late at night. A homeless man kept trying to touch my hair the last time I found myself on the train after midnight.

"Need a ride?" I glanced up to see Tommy still standing next to me, his hands shoved deep in his pockets. His shoulders were bunched up near his ears to help fight off the slight chill in the air. He had definitely dressed for the heat of the nightclub and not spring Chicago weather.

"You didn't bring a coat?" I asked him, Uber forgotten, as I pulled on my own jacket.

"I never wear a coat when I go out."

"You never wear a coat when you go out?" I repeated, my voice climbing a couple of octaves. "You do know you moved to Chicago, right?"

"Oh, I hadn't realized." Tommy turned around in a circle. "The hot dog stands on every other corner and the fact that anytime anyone runs into me they say 'ope' definitely didn't give that one away."

I stood there, my mouth hanging open at his sharp comeback. There was a playful glint to his eyes as he watched me struggle to figure out a response. Playful banter was definitely not on the list of things I imagined him to be good at. I would have placed my money on him firing off a rude response. It took me so much by surprise that I remained there in front of him opening and closing my mouth like a fish out of water. Tommy, thankfully, saved me from the further embarrassment of being dumbstruck by him.

"Do you want a ride?" he repeated.

It was telling enough that I was seriously debating risking having some homeless man try to braid my hair versus getting in a car with Tommy Mikals. But I realized that my capacity for public spaces had been met for the day, so I found myself nodding at Tommy's offer.

"I'm just around the corner." Tommy's hand went to my lower back as he steered me around the side of the building toward the parking lot behind the club. I hated myself for actually liking the feel of his hand pressed into the back of my jacket. It felt strong, secure. Like if someone were to jump us in the alleyway right now, I'd probably live to tell the tale.

"Tommy!" Maybe I had thought too soon about someone jumping us in the alleyway. A flash went off, and I barely had time to cover my face before I was blinded.

Oh shit.

I heard Tommy curse a much worse word under his breath before that hand on my back started to apply a little more pressure to quicken our pace. The lights on a car ahead of us started to flash as he hit the unlock button on his key fob about a hundred times. I glanced over my shoulder to see a man with a camera coming after us. A part of me wanted to tell him that there were so many better ways to use his photography skills than taking photos of celebrities, but then reality hit me.

That photo.

If it hit the news outlets tomorrow, the optics would probably look less than stellar. An innocent situation would look more like any other picture of Tommy leaving a nightclub than what was really going on. I would be lumped in with the rest of Tommy Mikals's one-night stands, and I'd probably find myself in May's office with my job on the line as soon as I stepped into the stadium. There was a strict no-fraternization clause in my contract that, if broken, would be grounds for immediate termination.

Wonderful.

Tommy pulled my door open, keeping his body between me and the paparazzo before he hurried around the car to the driver's side. I kept my hand firmly in front of my face as the guy continued to take pictures of us through the front window of Tommy's car. Luckily, he gave us enough room to leave the parking lot without hitting him.

"That was . . ."

"I'm sorry you had to experience that," Tommy interrupted me. "I didn't think there'd be any paparazzi out tonight."

I just nodded, because honestly, what was I supposed to say to that? Never before in my life did I have to worry about whether or not someone would be waiting to take my picture while I was out having a good time. Tommy's hands were gripping the steering wheel tightly as he pulled out onto Lake Shore Drive, his knuckles going white. We drove in silence for a moment before he let out a breath.

"Where to?" he asked me after the tension slowly dissipated from the car. I rattled off the directions to get to my apartment before letting the car go quiet again. Tommy's eyes were fixed on the road in front of us. The way he drove the car was exactly like how he moved on the baseball field—confident. After a moment, his eyes slowly looked back over toward me.

"So how'd you get to be a photographer for the Cougars?" He was clearly trying to make an effort at conversation, but the last thing I wanted to do was fight through a normal conversation with the guy I had imagined making out with. Especially while I was wondering if I'd have a job in the morning.

"That's a long story," I told him, watching as Lake Michigan went by in a blur of streetlamps and black water outside my window.

"I'd like to hear it."

My eyebrows shot up in surprise at his comment, but I kept my gaze firmly out the window as Tommy pulled into the parking lot of my apartment building. My entire experience with Tommy was the opposite of what I'd pictured him to be. He had barely drunk anything, had no women falling over him, and he seemed genuinely interested in me. A nobody. All of those things were dangerous. They canceled out every reason I had firmly placed him in the *no* pile. If none of those reasons were true, then I was in serious trouble. There was no practical reason to deny the way my body seemed to react around him.

"I don't want to tell it." I opened the door and stepped out. "Thanks for the ride."

I didn't bother to see Tommy's reaction. My mind was firmly worried about the fact that I might be out of a job by tomorrow morning thanks to a guy with a camera. Kind of poetic.

MAGGIE

"It's not that bad," Olivia told me as I hid under a blanket on her couch. When I had woken up the next morning to multiple text messages from her saying that photos of Tommy and me were all over social media, I immediately took the first bus I could grab over to her apartment. This felt like a massive disaster, and one that I knew I couldn't face by myself.

I was kicking myself from the moment I got on the bus. I had known what Tommy's reputation was and had warned myself not to become one of the girls that left clubs with him. Even if all Tommy did was offer me a ride home, it was becoming painfully obvious that the media loved to twist the reality into something that would draw in traffic for them. If anything, I deserved the consequences for getting distracted by the attention of an attractive man. I knew better than to put myself in any kind of position that could be questioned by anyone. The entire bus ride to Olivia's apartment I had opened and closed each one of my social media accounts with the intention of looking at the photos myself, but chickened out before I could actually scroll to them.

"I don't care if it's not that bad. My face is out there for everyone to see!" I groaned.

"Well, it could've been a really ugly picture for people to see. At least it's not that." Lottie peered over Olivia's shoulder from the opposite side of the couch. She tilted her head, her honey-blond hair falling over her shoulder as she studied the screen. Her blue eyes squinted as she analyzed the photo with a critical look that was Charlotte Thompson's signature look. "You look beautiful in it, Maggie."

Olivia's eyes were also glued to her phone as she thumbed through a thread talking about the paparazzi photos. She had been giving me a play-by-play of Tommy's fans freaking out over the new photos. He had developed a fanbase much like if he were an attractive actor or performer, and from what Olivia was reading off social media, they were ruthless.

Many of them were trying to figure out who I was. Those girls were practically intelligence officers. Within hours, they had found my head-shot from the Cougars' staff page and my name. Luckily, no other infor-mation had been leaked so far. The unhinged posts from random strangers that were fans of Tommy's were enough to remind me that he was far from the kind of guy I normally dated. Being anywhere near him would put me in the public eye, and that was the last place I wanted to be.

"So what even happened with you two last night?" Olivia asked.

"When you started having your fun, I decided I wanted to go home. Tommy offered to take me so I didn't have to get on the L." Olivia would be the hardest person for me to sell this to. She could sniff out a lie better than a bloodhound on hunting days. "There was a guy waiting to snap a picture by the parking lot."

"Unlucky," Olivia mumbled. It was Olivia's typical catchphrase for my life. She started using it after one thing after another went wrong in my life as a way to lighten the mood. I don't think I had it in me to tell her it never really lightened the mood.

"None of this would have happened if we'd stayed home and watched *Pretty Woman* like we always do," I whined, still hidden under the blanket.

"If we had stayed at home, you would have missed getting to talk with him." Olivia pulled back the blanket that I had been using to shield myself from the world. She was wiggling her eyebrows suggestively like I was not on the brink of potentially falling apart. For all I knew, those groupies that fawn over Tommy after games would show up at my apartment and throw their foam fingers at me. I shuddered as I imagined that scene unfolding.

"And how does that make up for missing *Pretty Woman* and having the hashtag 'Mommy' trending on social media?"

Olivia grimaced at the hashtag.

"At least you had a good night last night from the sounds of it," I directed toward Lottie. Olivia had sent multiple photos in our group chat last night of her sister actually letting loose on the dance floor with her and Jamil.

"You act like I'm attached to my email inbox," Lottie murmured as she scrolled through her email inbox.

"Lottie, you are the very definition of a workaholic. Your face would be stamped in the dictionary next to the word," Olivia replied as she switched to a different social media app.

There was a reason that Charlotte Thompson was the most sought-after sports physical therapist in Chicago. Charlotte Thompson didn't do fun, and last night was a definite exception to her very strict rules.

Lottie rolled her eyes at her sister before she looked at me with sympathy. "'Mommy' is a terrible couple's name."

It was definitely not the most glamorous couple name the public could have come up with. I groaned inwardly at the fact that my brain was already using the word "couple" for me and Tommy. But I couldn't deny the flutter of my heart that I felt at the idea of being associated in any way with him.

I blamed my hopeless romantic tendencies. When I met Luke, I swooned the first time that he looked at me like I was the sun and he was a planet in orbit. At that moment, I knew what people meant when they said it was love at first sight. It was amazing to me that out of all the people in the world, someone like Luke had decided to give me a chance. After Luke, I was sure I would never have something like that again. I was sure that Luke was my once-in-a-lifetime kind of love, and I was either doomed to live my life alone or never feel fulfilled romantically.

Another piece of me felt guilty to even find another person attractive or have daydreams of tracing every tattoo on a certain person's arms and running my hands through his long hair. It felt traitorous. But what was even scarier was that the piece of me that had felt called to Luke the first time he had looked at me like I was the most important thing in the world felt like it was stirring, knocking the dust off itself the moment that Tommy had caught my eye there with Jamil and Adam.

It would be a lie that he didn't pique my curiosity. Everything I had read about him made me think that he was a self-centered asshole who only cared about having the prettiest woman in the room on his arm. The man that I had sat with at the club was the exact opposite of the person I had painted in my head. He hadn't bothered with any woman that had been hanging around the VIP section waiting to pounce on the first player that paid them any attention. He also hadn't even sipped one drink. It was a complete one-eighty from the person I had read about in articles that had been posted when he was in San Diego.

When I considered the way he had protected me against the paparazzo and actually seemed genuinely interested in my life, it had me questioning everything I knew about him. I was becoming increasingly curious in a dangerous way, like a door opening, calling me to try to peel back more layers of Tommy Mikals to figure out the truth.

"Okay, yes. The current situation is less than stellar. I get it," Olivia continued. "But my Spidey senses are tingling, and I feel like this could be something."

"What do you mean?" I asked.

"Just hear me out," Olivia started as she threw her arms wide and situated herself on the couch. Lottie and I shared a look, because we knew whatever was coming next was going to be the kind of far-fetched idea that Olivia was known for coming up with. "Judging from how the only interest that Tommy showed that night was directed toward you tells me that he must find you fascinating. That's something we can work with."

Lottie let out a loud sigh from the far side of the couch. "Maggie is not you, Olivia. She doesn't pursue men like a game."

"Excuse you." Olivia shot daggers at her sister before she turned back to me. "What I'm trying to say is, what if he's actually interested in you? What if you flirt a little bit with *the* Tommy Mikals and see what happens?"

"There is no reality in which Tommy would ever want to date me," I tell her.

"Maggie, you need to stop this self-doubt train that you are constantly on. I'm tired of watching you think of yourself as a second fiddle when you are the star of the show. You always have been." Olivia finally put her phone down so she could take my hands in hers.

"I can't risk dating a player, Olivia," I told her. "I love my job too much. And I have so many ideas to help our media department that I haven't been able to implement yet."

"You are such an asset to the Cougars, Mags." Lottie reached across her sister to wrap me in a hug. "If you feel like Tommy would jeopardize that, then don't pursue it."

"I'm afraid that photo is going to jeopardize my job without my even trying to flirt with Tommy." My chest felt heavy at the thought of losing the job that had saved me from one of the darkest moments in my life.

"It'll be okay, Mags." Olivia joined in on the hug. "I promise."

Everything in me sincerely hoped that Olivia was right. That everything was going to be okay and my job wasn't on the line because of some guy with a camera and Tommy's reputation. I was hoping that maybe for once the world would skip me on this deliverance of luck or lack thereof. But if I had learned anything over the past year, it was to not hold my breath for the tide to turn.

MAGGIE

The afternoon of Opening Day, I found myself exactly where I didn't want to be. In May's office, feeling like I was waiting to be told I had detention from the school principal. I was cursing Olivia with everything inside me. Of course the one night I finally agreed to go out, something like this would happen.

If there was some lesson to be learned from all of this, it was that I should have stayed home with my ice cream, romantic comedies, and face masks. There were no paparazzi lurking around corners, waiting to ruin my life on rom-com night. There was only Peter Kavinsky, Edward Lewis, Graham Simpkins, and Jake Perry.

May entered a few moments later, interrupting my mental break-down. She looked less than pleased, sending my hopes and dreams crashing down into the cold, deep depths of unemployment.

"You're going to want to follow me." May motioned for me to come with her back out of her office and toward the C-suite.

Oh shit.

I wasn't going to get fired by my boss. I was going to be berated by the owner of the team for helping add to the bad-boy image that Tommy Mikals had created for himself. The exact image the PR team had been working to fix. My mind thought through all of my back-up plans as we drew closer to the main conference room. Maybe JCPenney would hire me to take those eighties headshot photos that were trending on social media.

We rounded the corner, and I was greeted by the entire PR team seated around the long table with Tommy sitting in the middle. He looked as surprised as I was to see him. So not only was I about to lose my job, but I was going to have to do it in front of him? Could this day get any worse?

"Have a seat." The head of the PR department, Monica, motioned for me to sit down at the head of the table facing everyone else. I slowly sank down in the chair, wanting nothing more than to be anywhere else. If I could wish for something bad enough, it would be to disappear from that conference room at that exact moment.

"So I'm sure you two have already seen it," Monica started.

I knew what "it" was, but a small part of me hoped that maybe this meeting was for something else entirely. But with a click of a button, there it was up on the large flatscreen in the conference room in high definition. A picture of me and Tommy in his car, my hand doing a poor job of covering my face. The looks on our faces made it seem like we had been caught doing something we shouldn't have been.

Which I guess was true.

It was probably the best picture the paparazzo had gotten that night. On the bright side, I didn't look half bad. My normally wild curls looked perfectly unkempt. There was a flush on my cheeks from the cool air, and for once, I didn't hate how my body looked in a photo. I looked pretty. At least there was one win on this day.

"This photo has been plastered across practically every news outlet and all over social media." Monica sat back in her chair, lacing her hands together in front of her on the table. Her body language screamed *don't mess with me*, and I didn't really feel like testing that. "And you've been trending on social media. So we've come up with a plan."

A what?

My head snapped over to Monica, my eyes tearing from the picture on the screen. Did she say a plan? That was not how I imagined I would be fired.

"Tommy, you knew the terms of your contract when the Cougars signed you." Monica's attention changed to look at the man sitting across from her. The confident aura that Tommy had radiated the day before, both at practice and at the club, was long gone. He was slumped in his chair, looking like someone who had been told off by his mother. "The owner was less than happy to see these photos this morning, because as you know, your reputation from previous years drove ticket sales down at San Diego. That's the last thing we need here. But the PR team and I see it as an opportunity."

My heart was pounding. Could Monica get to the point already? This long, drawn-out talk seemed like a torture tactic, and if they didn't cut me free in the next five minutes, I was considering turning in my resignation to put myself out of my own misery.

"Part of the terms of your contract were that you had to help us clean up your image, and that included no girls." Monica gave me a pointed look, and I was back to wishing I could melt through the floors. I was being lumped into the same category as the ditsy blondes that Tommy had been photographed with one too many times. "However, Maggie isn't just any girl."

I'm not?

"She's not outside the boundaries of the club. She's a controllable factor." The words now coming out of Monica's mouth sounded like a foreign language. I had no idea what she was talking about.

"Maggie is the perfect answer to help us rehabilitate your image," Monica continued. "Social media is loving that picture. So, we thought this would be the perfect opportunity for the club to capitalize on. We had our team do a quick audit on Maggie's social media pages. Her online presence is innocent and much more appealing to the wider audience of our fanbase than any of your previous"—Monica paused—"relationships. She's more relatable to the everyday fan than any of the actresses or models you've been attached to in the past. She's the perfect person to showcase stability."

"What are you saying?" I asked, seeing the same confusion I was feeling mirrored on Tommy's face. Monica looked like she had won the lottery the way she was glancing between me and Tommy.

"Maggie, you and Tommy will pretend to be a couple." And there was the point I had been so desperately wanting, and now that I had it, part of me wished they'd fired me. "We haven't nailed down the details yet. All you two would need to do is show up at the events we tell you to be at and be seen around Chicago a few times. That's it. Strictly business."

"I'm a professional athlete." Tommy's voice was deadly quiet. There was a venom there that sent chills down my spine. "I don't need to be in some fake relationship."

"Unfortunately, Tommy, you do. If you get caught in another compromising photo, no matter how innocent, the club has grounds to terminate your contract. And from what I understand, the Cougars were your last option of staying in the pros." Monica leveled Tommy with a stare that would have frozen over a river in the middle of the Sahara Desert.

Tommy's jaw clenched, but he didn't deny Monica's point. Then everyone's eyes in the conference room moved to me. My own darted around the room, trying not to land on anyone for too long. I was sure everyone in the room was in on some joke that I had been conveniently left out of. Like at any moment, Ashton Kutcher would jump out of his hiding spot and tell me I'd been punked.

"Maggie, we know that we can't ask you to do something like this," Monica continued. "So we compiled a package for you. We feel like this would be a great option compared to the alternative of what could happen."

I didn't need a magnifying glass to read between the lines of what Monica was saying. Either I agreed to this contract or I'd be fired from my dream job. One of Monica's assistants slid a manila folder over to me. I stared down at it, feeling like this was all some cruel trick and when I opened that file, it would be contracts terminating my employment with the Cougars.

Monica motioned for me to open it. Inside was indeed a contract. But there was no letter of termination. Instead, it was my amended contract with a staggering bonus attached at the bottom. My eyes felt like they were going to pop out of my head. It was more money than I had ever seen in my entire life. I glanced up from the contract to find Tommy staring at me. His nostrils flared as he stared down at the folder in front of me, and there was a grim twist to his mouth.

"What do you say?" I tore my eyes away from Tommy's to look back at Monica, who was like a shark that smelled blood in the water. She had trapped both of her prey with exactly what they needed and she knew it. "The only condition before either of you accept is that the only people who know about this relationship are in this room."

Silence stretched on. Tommy still hadn't stopped staring at the folder. It was like he was waiting to see what I would say before he would share his thoughts. I glanced back down at the contract, trying to decide if this was prostitution and if I was going to be okay with that. My mind flashed to my run-down apartment and the dreams I had of investing in myself and my career to take my skills to another level, and the ways this money could help me further my media skills.

Did I really want to sign a contract to be Tommy Mikals's girl-friend? Not particularly, but I wasn't sure I'd have another opportunity like this. Part of me also thought about what would happen if I said no. Would I lose my job then? I spun the ring on my middle finger that I never removed as my mind rushed through the thousands of questions I had, calculating my options.

After a few more silent moments, I finally nodded my head. Monica studied me and then Tommy, and he gave one curt nod, his mouth pressed into a firm line. Monica clapped her hands together excitedly, like this was the best news she had heard all year. Tommy and I stayed quiet because we knew the truth.

Our fate was sealed.

———

I tried to escape the conference room as quickly as I could. There was absolutely no way that I could look Tommy in the eyes after that meeting. Monica had practically been my madam selling me out to him to help solve his problems. But apparently the universe had every intention of making my day as terrible as possible, because before I had the chance to escape into the elevators and away from the mess that had ensued in the C-suite, Tommy slipped in right after me.

The two of us stood next to each other, staring straight ahead. Neither of us spoke a word until the elevator doors opened onto the main concourse. We stepped out together like we were emerging back into the normal world, still not a single word spoken between us. The silence that was stretching out felt like a weighted blanket over my face, and I worried that if I didn't push it off, I'd suffocate.

"Listen, Maggie . . ." Tommy turned to me, one hand pushing through his hair and the other waving around in the air. He looked like he wanted to unload all of his apologies on me, and honestly, I didn't want to hear whatever he had to say. If he apologized to me for getting us in this mess, I would have to acknowledge the guilt I had for feeling like this could have been the best thing that had happened to me in the past four years. It was like my luck was finally turning around. So I cut him off with the first thought that came to mind to stop him from being able to speak those words.

"What do you want to do on our first date?"

The look in Tommy's eyes said that he wanted to give me some sort of out, and quite frankly, I actually didn't think I wanted it. My mind flashed back to the contract and the amount of money written on it. There was no way in hell I was walking away from this deal. Tommy blinked at me like I had grown three heads.

"You're telling me you really want to do this?"

"Is Tommy Mikals dismissing the opportunity to have a girl on his arm any time he wants?" I didn't want to let him see how terrified I was of doing this, and in that moment, the only way to distance myself from the very real situation happening was to try to diminish the seriousness. He studied me like he was trying to figure out the answer to some complicated equation before he gave up.

"How about after the game?" he asked.

As if this day hadn't been eventful enough, I still had a game to shoot.

"You know where to find me," I told him before heading toward the tunnel where I knew Olivia would be waiting for me. I pushed open the door to the break room to see her with her feet propped up on the table I had left my gear on. She turned when she heard the door open.

"Did you lose your job?" she asked. I had texted her the moment I started following May toward the C-suite that I was probably going to lose my job but had left it at that. I'm sure she was practically bursting for an update at this point.

"Surprisingly no," I told her as I started to unpack my gear. I hesitated telling her anything more after remembering Monica's warning. No one was allowed to know, not even Olivia. But could I keep a secret like this from her?

"Just a slap on the wrist," I added after a moment.

"Good." Olivia stood up from her seat and wrapped her arms around my shoulders. "Because I couldn't stand coming to work and not having you here."

"You couldn't get rid of me even if you tried." I snaked an arm around her waist and started to steer her back out toward the tunnel.

The closer we got, the more I could feel the energy bouncing off my chest from the stadium. It was still a little over an hour before the start of the game, but it was already almost a full house. Music was blasting through the speakers, and the opposing team was taking practice swings on the field. It was like Christmas morning, but better. Everything felt right in the world again. It was almost enough to make me forget about the last twenty-four hours.

Olivia and I worked together to snap the photos that the social media team always requested and the photos that the league would also use for their publicity releases. I passed fans who looked like they had been coming to games for decades, fans that looked like it was their very first game, fans that were on their first date, and diehard fans with their entire bodies painted in the team's colors. I made sure to take a few pictures; May would love them for the social media pages.

An announcer's voice came over the speakers to get the crowd riled up as the Cougars ran onto the field for warmups . Olivia and I edged closer to the dugout to grab some shots. The outfielders ran past us first, and Jamil flashed a goofy smile. Then the infielders were next. Tommy was the very last one out of the dugout, and his eyes immediately found my camera as he exited. I wasn't even making direct eye contact with him as I watched him through my viewfinder, but I still felt like his eyes had seen right to the very depths of me. The heat rushing to my cheeks had me wondering if I honestly could fool everyone into believing that I was dating him. Or maybe the better question was if I could remember that I was supposed to be faking it.

"Maggie!" May was hurrying down the stairs of the stadium toward the two of us. "You're stationed in the dugout today. Olivia, you're over on the visitors' side."

I narrowed my eyes at May.

Every game one of us would be stationed in the home dugout and the other would be stationed outside the visitors' dugout. Surely it was a coincidence that I was placed in the home dugout tonight after just signing a contract with the club's biggest player to save his image and his career. The moment that May looked at me, I knew that my thoughts weren't far from the truth. The powers that be were pulling the strings to help further the narrative that I just agreed to. Olivia hurried off to her side of the field for the night, throwing me unknowingly to the wolves. Or, in particular, to one wolf.

"Don't tell me we'll get you the first game of the season, Canon!" Jamil exclaimed from the dugout. The guys had shuffled back in, getting ready for the announcement of lineups and the national anthem. I ducked under his attempt for a hug and turned around to snap a picture of him.

"Unfortunately, yes, you do."

"I don't think there's anything unfortunate about having you around." Adam smiled at me as he leaned against the fence. I could always count on Adam to say something sweet. He was the dad of the group, after all.

Jamil sidled up next to me with a mischievous smile on his face that was my second least-favorite look, right next to the smile Olivia got whenever she developed a plan that would surely go terribly.

"Can I help you?" I asked him, already dreading what would come out of his mouth next.

"You have fun after the club?" Jamil's eyebrows danced up and down. I froze the second I realized what he was insinuating. My mouth started trying to form words to explain to him what he saw, but then I remembered the ink that had barely dried on a contract up in the C-suite.

I hoped that the blush spreading across my cheeks made me look like a girl who had been caught red-handed in a new relationship and not a girl who was completely mortified to be in this situation.

"I guess." I shrugged with the hope that I looked nonchalant and not like I had a nervous twitch.

Jamil's smile widened as he watched me for a beat. He reached out to squeeze my arm before he turned to head back into the dugout. I pushed a long breath out between my lips and started to bring my camera up to my face when I noticed Adam watching me with interest. He gave me a soft smile before he turned his attention back to the field.

I tried my best to blend into the background. Most of the coaches tolerated the media presence, but they only put up with it as long as it wasn't a distraction. Soon, the announcer came over the loudspeakers to give the starting lineups. I took my place outside the stairs on the field so I could get a shot of each player as he emerged onto the field after his name was called. Each player came out one at a time, completely locked in for the first game of the season. The sound of my shutter going off was lost to the cheers of the crowd. It had grown to a loud roar.

Then Tommy's name was announced. The crowd went wild for him. At least his reputation didn't hurt his fanfare. He bounded up the stairs, the gold chain he wore while playing bouncing off his chest. He stopped at the top of the stairs to give a wave to the crowd before he turned back toward his awaiting teammates.

Goddammit. Why does he have to look so attractive in his uniform?

I was beginning to worry that I was going to have to remind myself this relationship was fake. Because if Tommy ever caught me staring at him the way I was in that moment, he'd probably think I thought otherwise.

MAGGIE

The first time I ever picked up a camera, I was twelve. My mother had given it to me as a birthday present. She was the first person to notice my eye for photography. I had this obsession with postcards and the way they captured a place perfectly, making it look almost like a fantasy. I pinned them all over my room, but instead of talking about going to the places in those postcards, I would tell everyone about how I would have taken the picture differently.

I still had that camera. It was an old Polaroid that broke when I turned twenty, and it now sat proudly on one of the bookshelves in my apartment. That camera stood as a reminder to me of my dream, which was to show the beauty of the world to others, even in the places where people didn't think there was any. The world was full of it, if you knew how to look for it.

And right then, I was looking at the beauty that was Tommy Mikals through my camera lens. It was the bottom of the ninth, we were down by one run, and we had a runner on second. All Tommy needed to do was punch something through the infield so our runner could score.

My camera followed the pitcher's windup and the pitch, and then I watched through it as Tommy squared the ball up with his bat and sent it deep into center field. I pulled my eyes from my viewfinder as I watched the ball go deeper and deeper before the crowd went wild as it landed on the other side of the fence. A roar erupted around the field and every part of me wanted to join in as one of the fans, but I pulled my camera back up to watch Tommy take his home run trot.

As he rounded second base, I watched through my camera lens as he pulled the gold chain around his neck up to his lips before pointing both of his pointer fingers up to the sky, his eyes looking up toward the clouds. I knew the moment I captured the shot, it would be the image of the night. The new trade resulted in an Opening Day win. A sports-writer couldn't have written it any better.

The guys doused him with a Gatorade bath as he crossed home plate, celebrating their first win of the season. The stadium was electric with fans going wild: popcorn being thrown in the air, beer cans flying, and people bouncing into each other's arms. It was the perfect start to a season. The team jumped up and down, celebrating their comeback win with Tommy at the center, the biggest smile on his face.

I continued to snap photos of the team as they started to make their way to the dugout. They filed slowly down the stairs, picking up their bags as they made their way into the clubhouse. Jamil came up behind me and wrapped his arms around my waist. He picked me up off the ground and spun me around as he yelled in excitement. I laughed, unable to not join in on the energy. Jamil set me back on the ground to go run into the clubhouse, probably to go bug one of his teammates, and left me facing Tommy. He was still looking out at the field as the stadium slowly emptied and the grounds crew came out. I brought the camera to my eye to capture the moment.

"Nice game," I called out after a few seconds. He turned to take me in. I couldn't be sure, but it appeared that his eyes were a little wet, but it very well could have been the reflection from the stadium lights.

"Thanks," Tommy replied, the tears that looked like they had been there moments before nowhere to be found. He took a few more beats to glance around the stadium before he turned his attention back toward me. "I have a press conference and then I have to go get changed. Wait here?"

"Sure."

Tommy left me alone on the field to watch as the cleaning crew started to work their way through the aisles of the stadium and the grounds crew pulled their rakes off the field. It was like the calm after the storm and even better than the anticipation before the first pitch. The game was over, the war fought, the warriors gone to mend their wounds or to celebrate their victory. The game had transported all of them to another world for those three hours, and these quiet moments afterward were the return to reality.

I wandered toward the edge of the field, not daring to step on the dirt after the grounds crew had worked so hard to get it back in shape after the game. The lights were still on, and the sky was almost pitch black at this point. It made me wonder what it would be like to play in a stadium this large, under the lights, with the entire crowd cheering for or against you.

"Amazing, isn't it?" I turned to see that Tommy had reemerged from the clubhouse, freshly showered and wearing a pair of jeans and a light blue crewneck that made his eyes shine even brighter. A shiver raked down my body as I watched him get closer.

Part of me wanted to curse that damn contract. I had to remind myself why we were in this mess in the first place: Tommy's reputation. Even though he looked incredible in his uniform and my body responded to him in traitorous ways, he was off-limits and would be nothing but bad news for me.

"What's it like?" It was a chore to rip my mind away from Tommy and turn it back toward the stadium.

"Like I'm in a dream." Tommy walked up next to me, his hands deep in his pockets. "Every day."

I watched as Tommy took in the stadium, from the lights to the screen and everything in between. The way he looked at the field was like it could be his last time and he wanted to memorize every detail. The two of us stood in silence together as we stared out at the field, a mutual appreciation passing between us.

As the lights began to turn off, Tommy extended his elbow toward me. At that moment, I was at a crossroads. The second I put my arm through his, this was really happening. I would be Tommy Mikals's fake girlfriend.

I thought about the person I had been for the past four years, and to be honest, it wasn't a version of myself I was proud of. The me who had always been excited for a new adventure had died on that fateful night years ago. But it was time that someone new took her place. So I found myself sliding my hand through his arm and letting him lead me back toward the tunnel.

We dropped my camera off in the small office that Olivia and I shared, Tommy's eyes roaming over the shots that we had captured over the past three years. Many of them had turned out to be the perfect shot and had become well-known photos that memorialized different points in time for the Cougars. I followed his eyes as he studied each picture, remembering the game each still had come from.

"You're very talented," Tommy said after a few moments. That simple comment sent my heart soaring.

Growing up, I had never thought I could do anything with my camera besides take beautiful pictures for myself. If someone had told me that I could share pictures with the world taken from my point of view, I never would have believed them. When I first started with the Cougars, I would avoid all forms of feedback on social media. I didn't want some fan telling me I wasn't good enough to do this. It was a leap of faith, pursuing a job with the Cougars, and I didn't want someone to confirm my fears that I wasn't up to par.

However, those thoughts slowly faded away as the excitement around my pictures grew and the Cougars began to feature more of them on their accounts. Even now, my heart beat even harder with each small piece of praise I received. It was like a tiny confirmation that I was on the right track.

"Thanks," I replied as I plugged all of my cameras in so they'd be ready for the next practice. "Okay, all ready. Where are we going?"

"That's a surprise."

"You know this isn't like a real date, right?" I asked as I followed Tommy out to the player parking lot. "Surprises are typically what real boyfriends do for their real girlfriends."

"Just because this isn't real doesn't mean I can't still treat you right." Tommy looked at me over the top of his car as the two of us got in. "I owe you."

I stayed quiet, thinking about what Tommy had said. Did he really owe me if I was getting paid to do this? He took off down the interstate, heading east. My curiosity spiked as we crossed the state line into Indiana. I looked over at him questioningly. There definitely weren't paparazzi expecting us to be out and about in a different state.

He pulled off on a quiet road lined with houses that backed up to Lake Michigan, before parking the car in a parking lot that looked right over the lake. The waves crashed against large rocks that were on the other side of the chain. Tommy popped his trunk and grabbed a blanket before coming around to open my door. He lifted the chain, giving me room to dive underneath it and walk out onto the large rocks with Lake Michigan meters below. Tommy unraveled the blanket with a flourish and laid it out on the rocks before taking a seat.

"Coming?" he asked as I stood staring down at him. When Monica had talked through what would be expected of us, I thought I could handle public appearances where we acted in love, no feelings involved. But Tommy was asking me to sit next to him, and it wasn't like we could just stare out at Lake Michigan in silence. The moment felt more intimate than just two people who were both in a terrible predicament that were trying to get to know each other better.

This felt like a first date. But that couldn't be what this *actually* was. The only reason that he was giving someone like me the time of day was because we had both signed on the dotted line.

"I don't think this is what Monica had in mind when she told us we had to be seen in public." I motioned to the emptiness around us. "There's nobody here to see us."

"I thought that if we were really going to do this, we might as well get to know each other. It would help us sell that we really do like each other." Well, I guess that made *some* sense, but this was definitely not what I had mentally prepared myself for. But I guess it would be easier for me if I were to get to know the man behind the image. So I sat down next to him.

"What do you want to know?" I asked as I watched the water crash into the rocks below. Tommy looked over at me, like he was studying me, before he actually said anything. He was always doing that. Staring at me like I was some puzzle to unravel or solve. It set me on edge, making me feel like I was something foreign he'd never encountered before. Or something intriguing enough to want to understand.

"How'd you get your job with the Cougars? I feel like that's something I should know . . . since we are supposed to be dating and all." Tommy flinched. It was a quick flash of emotion that marred his face before he schooled his features back into normalcy. It was only there for a split second, but I still caught it.

My mind flashed back to the main catalyst behind me ending up with the Chicago Cougars.

I heard the screech of tires.

The lights blinded me.

"Maggie!"

Then everything went black.

But I wouldn't tell him any of that, so instead, I told him only part of the truth.

"I had just finished college," I started, leaning back on my hands as I looked out toward the horizon where the water met the sky. "I didn't have a job lined up like everyone else, but I knew I wanted to take photos of the world. To help me take my mind off job hunting, my dad took me to a Cougars game." I smiled over at Tommy and noticed him watching me intently like he truly cared about what I had to say. "I brought my camera with me and just so happened to get the picture of Adam Steel when he threw his perfect game that year. I had posted it on my social media and tagged the Cougars. They reached out the next day and hired me."

"You're the one that took that picture of Adam?" Tommy asked me. I wasn't surprised that he had seen it. It was used on the cover of *ESPN The Magazine* that year. It had been like a dream to see my name printed below that picture. My mom had it framed and hung it up on one of the living room walls. I pulled my knees up to my chest and nodded at him in affirmation. "You definitely have a special eye."

"What about you?" I asked, leaning my head against my knees as I watched him. Every experience I'd had with Tommy Mikals defied the image I had had of him in my head. "How did it all start with baseball?"

Tommy let out a long breath and lay back on his elbows, as he looked up at the sky and the stars that were twinkling down on us. His face looked conflicted as he rolled his lower lip between his teeth and he thought about my question. I watched him wrestle with whatever was going on inside him before he finally spoke.

"My dad put a bat in my hand at two years old. When it first started, it was something we bonded over. He taught me how to throw and field and took me to my first game back home in California. But by the time I was fourteen, I was on a baseball field more than I was in school. I thought it was something I wanted up until recently."

"What do you mean?"

"Baseball's brought me more terrible things in the past few years of my life than good. It makes me wonder if any of it was worth it."

I had no idea how to respond to that. Everything about Tommy was confident young hotshot who had the entire world at his feet. The man sitting next to me right then looked like he was ready to hang everything up and never touch a baseball again. He looked like he really did believe that baseball had basically ruined his life. There were layers of pain etched in every hard line of his body and the way he held tightly onto his knees.

The strained look on his face made me want nothing more than to pull the megawatt Tommy Mikals smile back onto his face. I wanted to erase all of the pain that he was feeling. It was an odd feeling to want to make someone else happy other than myself, but it felt like heavy pressure weighing on my chest that was begging to be released.

"Have you dived into the Chicago pizza debate yet?"

And there was the smile that I missed, mixed with a sense of relief to be changing the subject.

"I've only tried Lou's so far."

I leaned my head back and groaned. "Lou's? You haven't even gotten to Southside yet?"

Tommy's smile grew as he watched me. "Maybe you'll just have to take me sometime."

"*Me* take *you* on a date? I didn't think that's how this worked." And there was that conflicted look back on his face. Pain flickered across his eyes, and I filed that moment away to dissect later. It was clear that he was struggling with the fact that we were in this situation at all. "How about tomorrow? You guys are off, right?"

The strained look vanished like it had never been there. That smile that I couldn't seem to get enough of replaced it, bringing back the happiness and confidence that normally lived on his face. It made me wonder if this version of Tommy was the real one and the version the media knew was the image they'd created of him.

As I sat next to him, waiting to see if he'd want to widen his pizza tastebuds, I found myself forgetting about the fear I'd felt the day before from how Tommy had made me feel. Instead, all I could think about was the puzzle of this man. He seemed to be more than the professional athlete who liked to party too much and enjoyed his time with women. That was beginning to seem far from the actual truth of who he really was. I wasn't sure if it was supposed to be alarming that the folder with all of my feelings had slowly been pulled forward toward the front of my mind without me even noticing.

"Can I pick you up at six?" Tommy asked me, and I nodded, excited to have the opportunity to spend more time with him and unravel who he really was.

Tommy

I woke up to another text from my dad the morning after our win on Opening Day. He hadn't even told me congratulations. Instead, he critiqued the ball I had missed up the middle in the bottom of the fifth that had put the other team up. Apparently, he thought my first step hadn't been hard enough and that was the reason why I hadn't wrangled in a missile of a hit. I didn't bother giving him a response, but the anger that had begun stirring inside me the moment I rolled over in bed to read that seemed like it was going to come to a head if I didn't do something about it.

Between that and my date with Maggie, I had too many feelings floating around inside me to sit still today. If I did, one of them would consume me, and I wasn't sure which one would be worse. So I sent Jamil a text and asked him to meet me at the clubhouse for some swings. He responded right away that he'd be there in thirty minutes. His willingness to be down for any practice session I wanted was quickly becoming one of my favorite things about him.

When I pulled into the player parking lot, his car was already there and he was nowhere in sight. I punched the code into the door of the entrance to the clubhouse and pulled it open. Jamil was setting up inside the batting cage for us when I walked in.

"Hey, man!" he called, the biggest smile on his face. "How are things with Maggie?"

I groaned. Jamil was the last person to be polite and not bring up all of the circus that was happening in the media. The talk around me and Maggie hadn't slowed down since that first photo had been posted from the club. We hadn't even had any public appearances to add fuel to the fire. It seemed like people liked the idea of the two of us together and were clinging on to it with all their might. Two new articles had been pushed out into the news cycle this morning with close "sources" talking about how Maggie and I had clicked during our first week together and couldn't deny the attraction between us. It smelled of Monica's doing. At this rate, it would be a full-time job trying to keep up with the narrative the PR team was pushing out.

"You guys must have really hit it off at the club that night. I was pretty buzzed, but I do remember how you couldn't take your eyes off her." Jamil tossed me my bat from my locker. "But it seems like the media is really running with this whole thing."

I started to tell him that photo was completely innocent when I remembered Monica's warning about not telling anyone. Part of me understood why she was requesting that. She didn't want the truth getting out, but I trusted Jamil and I was honestly at a place in my career where if a fake relationship was what was keeping my career from ending, I probably didn't deserve to have my career anyway. Most important, I didn't want to lie to Jamil like that at the beginning of our friendship.

It killed me that my mistakes had dragged Maggie into a position where she was practically forced into signing a contract to help me. If she hadn't been sure about it, I would have willingly packed up my stuff that day. I remembered the rage that had settled within me as I watched her read the contract. If I had the chance, I would have ripped that contract up and excused myself from the situation to save her any trouble this could cause her.

Maggie didn't deserve any of the negative attention that could come with being associated with me. But I also couldn't deny the way she made me feel. Everything about her seemed to be intoxicating to me. I had never had someone listen so intently to me before and truly care about me as a person rather than me as a player.

I also couldn't get out of my head how much Maggie physically affected me. I had dated some of the most conventionally beautiful women in the world during my time in San Diego. But something about Maggie seemed to drive me wild. That black dress she wore at the club flashed in and out of my mind. When I went to bed that night after I had dropped her off, I turned over and over how guarded she was when I asked her simple questions to get to know her.

Last night wasn't any different. After our first date, I replayed every detail like it was a movie to be dissected. She was impossible to figure out. There was the look in her eyes when I had cornered her about accepting Monica's contract. It seemed like she had been terrified by the decision she had made. But when I gave her an out, it was like a mask replaced her fear and a façade of confidence was there instead. During our date, she seemed hesitant at first, but her exterior started to melt as she got more comfortable with me. She had been constantly on my mind as I tried to decipher her, and I was at the point where I needed to tell a friend. I needed to tell Jamil.

"That photo at the club was innocent," I told him as I went to feed the machine for Jamil. "I offered to take her home when she got overwhelmed by being there. The guy was waiting for a photo outside. Problem is that Monica didn't like the photo. It was almost a breach of my contract with the Cougars."

"You're telling me your contract says 'no girls'?" Jamil asked.

"Yeah. But she thinks Maggie is controllable since she works for the Cougars. So she proposed a contract for the two of us to fake date to help rehabilitate my image." Jamil swung, launching a ball to the back of the cage.

"And she said yes?" Jamil's mouth was practically hanging on the ground. His surprise showed that this was completely uncharacteristic of Maggie. He had known her for the past three years.

"Monica offered her money," I told him as an explanation.

"Still. That girl avoids anything romantic with the opposite sex like the plague."

I had spent the past few days wondering what had motivated

Maggie to say yes to Monica's proposal, but the truth was that I didn't know her well enough to know her true intentions. Maggie also wasn't the only person with their own reasons for agreeing to the contract.

"I wouldn't say I'm upset about being in a fake relationship with her," I admitted as Jamil smacked another ball into the screen that was protecting me. A slow smile spread across his face at what I said.

"You like her."

"I'm not saying I like her," I amended. "But I will say that she's been on my mind nonstop since the first practice where I saw her."

Last night had firmly solidified Maggie in my thoughts. My mind flashed back to Lake Michigan. I had suggested the excursion as a way for the two of us to get more comfortable with each other, and I found myself hanging on her every word, desperate for any piece of information she was willing to give me. Everything about her was so different than any other girl I had ever known. She had an easy confidence about her, but it was plagued with moments of hesitation. Almost as if she didn't fully trust herself. There was clearly something that had happened in her life that had impacted her greatly. She carried the weight of it like armor, but she wore it with pride. She made whoever she was talking to feel so important by giving them her entire attention. She listened intently and asked questions that made you feel like she cared. Her energy made me feel at ease, like I had known her for years rather than a few days.

"This fake dating thing is just making it complicated," I told Jamil after he finished his round and we were picking up balls.

"How?" he asked.

"It's forcing us to fake something that could have happened naturally," I told him. I remembered sitting at the conference table, so angry that the contract was even being suggested. But then I remembered looking across the table at Maggie, and how I just found myself agreeing to it despite my better judgment. There was this small voice inside me telling me to take the opportunity to be near her because it would be worth it once it was all over.

"I don't see it that way. Maggie never in a million years would have given you the time of day if this hadn't forced you two together. Sure, it may be fake right now. But why not use it as an opportunity to get to know her? You never know what could happen."

I stared dumbfounded at my friend. How could he make an impossible situation sound so easy? I mulled over what Jamil said. It was a worthy plan, but there was something still holding me up—like the nerves inside my body that felt like they would swallow me whole whenever I was near Maggie. She was out of my comfort zone, completely unlike anyone I'd been with before.

"I'm going to need help. I've never dated someone like Maggie, and you know her. I just don't want to mess anything up with her or do something that I would have done for the girls I previously dated. She deserves better than that."

Jamil studied me for a minute. "You like her."

"I told you—"

He shook his head and walked toward the pitching machine. As I walked to the plate for my turn, I thought about what he said. The way that she had been a constant fixture in my mind for the past couple days made me rethink whether I had been lying to myself about only wanting to get to know her because I found her interesting. That alone made me realize that maybe Jamil was right, and I did like Maggie Redford. I didn't feel the need to pretend with her. All of the outside noise ceased when we were together, and I was finally able to think about something other than what others expected me to be. It honestly terrified me that this was happening during a fairly controversial season for my career. But I was over letting baseball ruin relationships for me. My relationship with my dad was a victim of the game, and I wasn't going to let something that could be very real with Maggie be the next one in line.

After hitting with Jamil, I still had pent-up energy to burn. Once I pulled back into my garage, I immediately took off down the street after dropping some of my stuff off inside the house. A run seemed like the only thing that would quiet the thoughts racing through my mind. The repetitive pounding of my feet on the concrete took up my focus, replacing the image of Maggie's smile, which had felt like it might be permanently ingrained there.

I pushed myself harder, wanting to feel my lungs strain to bring oxygen into them. The struggle kept my mind occupied and away from the mess that I had gotten myself into. I wanted nothing more than for my career to be just about baseball. But my decisions had effectively erased any potential of that happening. My lungs squeezed as I pushed my legs to go faster. I weaved in and around people walking on the sidewalk, letting the hum of the Chicago traffic be my music. At the next intersection, I didn't hesitate before turning left, not caring if I was about to be lost in a city I didn't know very well yet. At this point, if I ended up in an unsafe area, I would say I probably deserved it.

A large, fenced-in basketball court came into view next to me. Kids were laughing and yelling while playing a pickup game. My legs started to slow down as I remembered a similar scene of me and my friends going to the local park baseball field like a scene out of *The Sandlot*. A large sign on the building read Chicago Boys & Girls Club. I took in the court with new eyes, seeing the asphalt that was starting to tear up, making it unsafe to play. I saw the hoops that were missing nets and basketballs that looked to be decades old. My chest was aching for a very different reason than the run I had finished.

My entire career had felt like it had been handed to me. I had been put in the most prestigious travel clubs, setting me up for more success than the next player. My parents had never hesitated to throw more money at lessons or strength and conditioning coaches to give me the best chance to achieve my dreams. As I watched the boys playing a game of basketball in front of me, bile swelled in my throat. These kids would kill to have the opportunities I had in my life, and here I had almost thrown my entire career away.

I turned and took off running back where I came from, thoughts of *needing* to be a better person this year racing through my head. It didn't matter how fast I pushed my legs on the way home, those boys making the most of what they had were stuck in my head. No amount of running could make that go away.

When I got back home, I pulled open social media to try to find the Boys & Girls Clubs' page only to come face-to-face with my profile photos once again. I had avoided posting anything on social media since moving to Chicago besides the obligatory *I've been traded* photo. The sole reason for that being Sutton. Our photos were still on my page, even though she had erased any trace of us almost instantly after we had broken up. I had struggled to take them down, not wanting to part with the relationship I had thought we had.

As soon as everything hit the fan in San Diego, I realized that the relationship I *thought* we had was fake. She wasn't any better than any of the other women that had dated me for my money. But as I stared at those photos, I still couldn't bear to delete them. Not because I was still pining after a failed relationship with a girl that didn't deserve me. I wanted to remind myself that I was worth finding someone that truly loved me for all that I was. Even for my stupid mistakes. I knew I was more than those actions, but I desperately wanted someone else to see that too. So instead of deleting them, I tapped into the Boys & Girls Clubs' page and sent them a message asking to meet with their director.

I still had so much to work on when it came to bettering myself, and I wanted nothing more than to take steps toward being the man the younger version of myself would have dreamed of.

MAGGIE

Tommy pulled up outside my apartment at exactly six o'clock. His timeliness was yet another annoyingly perfect thing about him that blatantly juxtaposed with my inability to show up anywhere on time. Which was exactly the reason why I had planned to be ready thirty minutes early and was still barely on time.

The sun still shone high in the sky at this time of the summer as we drove through the city toward the South Side. Tommy's car ate up the road as he slid in and out of traffic. Typically, any sort of aggressive driving made me uncomfortable, but Tommy's driving wasn't necessarily aggressive. It was another piece of who he was: confident. My mind was trying to ignore the fact that I hadn't felt uncomfortable once in the passenger seat with him. Instead, I felt at peace.

Monica had asked if we would go out publicly tonight doing something casual, even though making a planned public appearance for show didn't feel casual at all. She was thrilled to hear that we had already planned something. She agreed to our plan and told us that she'd make sure a couple of paparazzi were there to grab a few photos of us.

To say I was only a little disappointed that I would now be expected to play a role and it wasn't going to be just me and Tommy again would be an understatement. The paparazzi part of this entire thing was what I was least looking forward to. It felt like I was walking into an ambush that I knew was going to be there but couldn't avoid. My parents had been suspiciously silent about the photos of the two of us in his car after the club. I could only assume they hadn't seen them yet, but once we were spotted together again, it was sure to be even bigger news than the first time.

Tommy pulled up across the street from the pizza parlor, and the two of us immediately noted the three guys with cameras hanging on the corner of the street, waiting for their big payday.

I sucked in a breath as I watched them, feeling like I was willingly walking into a lion's den. A hand wrapped around mine, trying to reassure me with a squeeze. My breath started to come in quicker bursts as I imagined that group of men with cameras surrounding us, pressing in on us, a panic attack coming over me, and—

"What if we let them get their picture of us ordering the pizza and we just take it back to my place? Then we don't have to go through the feeling of being in a fishbowl as they take pictures of us through the front glass of the store."

Immediate relief flushed through my body at Tommy's words, but part of me didn't want him to realize how close to a panic attack I was. So I raised an eyebrow in surprise. I definitely didn't think that Tommy would be concerned about me at all during this process. This whole thing was for him, and so far he'd shown nothing but distaste about the idea of us being forced to be together.

"I'd actually really like that," I told him, feeling every bit of anxiety I previously had leave my body. Tommy's hand slid into mine and gave it another squeeze to show his support. That hand squeeze was him telling me he had my back. It was enough to give me the courage to put my hand on the car door.

"Ready?" It was time. We couldn't avoid this any longer.

The next few minutes were an out-of-body experience. Tommy ran around the car to open my door, but it was like I was watching in slow motion. As soon as he was outside the safety of the car, the paparazzi perked up, pulling their cameras up to their faces.

Flash.

I felt myself jump at the light, something I had never done before in

my life. The door was pulled open and there was Tommy, holding his
hand out for me. The look on my face was probably one of pure panic,
but there was no way out.

Only forward.

To the pizza parlor.

Tommy gripped my hand tightly, keeping me close to him. His hand
was like an anchor as I pulled myself out of the car and turned to cross
the street with him. I kept my chin tucked down into my coat, trying my
best to hide my face.

Flash.

Flash.

Flash.

My breath was coming in fast as we looked both ways before
walking across the street. Every part of me wanted to run the rest of the
way and into the safety of the pizza parlor, but Monica would probably
string me up the flagpole at the stadium if I ruined this for the club. And
then the shouts started.

"Tommy! Tommy! Who's the girl?" The paparazzi closed in on us,
their cameras like weapons.

"Tommy! How are you liking Chicago?"

"Is she your girlfriend?"

It was like all of the oxygen had been sucked out of the air. I was a
fish out of water, my mouth opening and closing as I tried to gulp air
into my lungs. But nothing seemed to help as we shoved our way past
the three men. Tommy's arm wrapped even tighter around my waist,
pulling me into his side. My body melded perfectly, giving me something to focus on besides the fact that three grown men were staring at
me like I was a gazelle with a broken leg and they were the lions looking
at their next meal.

The air didn't change until we walked through the doors of that
parlor. As soon as the bells rang overhead and the door closed behind us,
I could breathe again. Tommy's arm loosened around my waist, but I
felt his hand stay firmly on the small of my back. I didn't want to admit
that I appreciated the presence of his hand. Even though I knew the
paparazzi wouldn't come inside with us, it still felt like we were in enemy
territory and his hand was the only armor I had.

The pizza parlor was practically full, and every head turned toward us as we walked up to the counter to order. I could see a few people pull their phones out to take pictures, most of them probably not knowing who we were, but the fact that paparazzi chased us inside gave them the impression that we were someone important. The girl behind the counter took our orders, her eyes glancing between our faces, trying to figure out what celebrities were standing in front of her.

It was in those few moments as Tommy and I did something as normal as placing an order at a pizza shop, with people staring at us like we were zoo animals, that I realized my life was no longer mine and I wondered if it ever would be again.

I caught myself wondering if I should have agreed to this the entire way back through the city. Tommy chatted away, like nothing that had happened was out of the ordinary for him. He asked me about the city, pointing at different landmarks as we passed them. My brain was on autopilot as I replied to every one of his questions as my mind became consumed with regret.

It wasn't until Tommy pulled up to the curb of a brownstone on the south side of Lincoln Park that I felt normal again. My mouth dropped open at the sight in front of me. I wasn't surprised by how lavish the brownstone looked. It was easily worth a couple million dollars. No, it wasn't that. It was that I had not picked Tommy Mikals to be in a brownstone in Lincoln Park. I had imagined him up in some penthouse in one of the high-rises downtown looking down on the world like it was his kingdom and he was holding court.

Neither of us said anything as we walked up the steps leading to his front door. Tommy balanced the pizza in his hands as he fumbled for his keys. I found myself thinking back through the last few days and wondered how in the hell I ended up here.

The inside of the brownstone was beautiful. It was a newer construction, but it kept the integrity of what a stereotypical brownstone looked like. Had Tommy hired an interior decorator before coming to Chicago? Because everything was beautiful. Nothing felt like it didn't have a purpose or was there simply for looks. It was a reflection of who he was living out loud. It was industrial and dark, with straight lines and clean angles.

It was the exact opposite of what my small apartment looked like. There were multiple blankets crumpled on the couch on any given day. Dishes were stacked high in the sink from my lack of time to do them. My apartment was best described as messy and eclectic.

"I'm ready to see if this pizza is as good as you say it is," Tommy called from the kitchen as he hunted through a cabinet for a couple of plates.

"If you don't like it, I'm not sure this friendship can continue," I told him as I slowly took in a couple of bookshelves he had in the living room. There were pictures of him with his parents from when he was a kid, pictures of him with his college teammates, and baseballs in cases that were from monumental times in his career. I stopped to appreciate each moment of his life, finding myself wanting to hear the story behind each item.

"I'll be sure to lie then if I don't like it." I turned around to find him holding two plates of pizza. He was giving me a cheeky smile that warmed my body. Part of me wondered if that meant he wanted to be friends with me no matter what. Because if that was the case, I found it kind of scary that I was beginning to think the same thing.

Tommy handed me a plate with a couple of slices on it and the two of us took our pizza over to his couch. He made a show of bringing the pizza up to eye level and inspecting it from all angles, making me laugh, before he took a bite with his eyes closed. He continued to chew in silence next to me, savoring the bite he took.

"Verdict?" I asked him, watching as he swallowed.

"Definitely better than Lou's," he told me, a smile spreading across his face.

"You"—I pointed the end of my pizza in his direction—"can stay."

The two of us ate in silence for a few more minutes before I finally got the courage to ask the question that had been plaguing my brain since May had pulled me into that conference room.

"So how did you even get yourself in this position in the first place?"

Tommy knew exactly what I was asking. I watched him grimace at my delivery before he grabbed a napkin to wipe his hands with.

"I was young and stupid," Tommy started. "I had just hit the big leagues and had my first real taste of life as a professional athlete. Girls had never really thrown themselves at me before."

I couldn't possibly imagine how girls hadn't been throwing themselves at Tommy his entire life.

"I fell into the typical rookie trap of spending my money on expensive things I didn't need and letting the distractions take all of my attention. The paparazzi started to take notice, and I was in the tabloids every other weekend. The Kings wanted me to get an agent to help manage some of it. So I did. I thought the agent was helping me, but what I didn't realize was that he was being paid off by different tabloids to supply me with a new girl every time I went out and make sure someone was there to capture it. The Kings released me last year, and no other team wanted to touch me until the Cougars."

Silence stretched out between us as I imagined a young Tommy being taken advantage of by someone he trusted, someone who continued to destroy his image and the career he had worked so hard for. The pain from that time in his life was still etched across his face, baggage he still had to shoulder. My hand itched to reach out and give his hand a squeeze of reassurance like he had done to me in the car earlier, but something stopped me.

"I'm sorry, Tommy."

"It was a life lesson," Tommy replied, his eyes on the bookshelves full of pictures and memorabilia. It was the same look that had been on his face at the stadium after the game, like he was trying to remember everything in case it all disappeared in the blink of an eye. "Look, I've been meaning to thank you for doing this. You really didn't have to."

"It's not like I'm not getting anything out of it," I reminded him. Tommy screwed his mouth to the side as he nodded, remembering the money I was offered. I couldn't be sure, but it almost seemed like disappointment flashed across his face at the reminder.

"Right. Well, I've been thinking that we should talk about what we're okay doing together." This man kept surprising me with his thoughtfulness. It was completely unexpected. "What do you feel comfortable doing in public?"

"Well," I started. "I hadn't really thought about it. Obviously, holding hands doesn't bother me; we've already done that."

"Of course," Tommy agreed. "Hugging?"

"That can be on the table."

"Hand placement?"

"Above the butt."

"Kissing?"

That one made me pause. The thought of kissing him sent those stupid butterflies fluttering around inside me like someone had trapped them in a jar and they were buzzing with an intense energy to find a way out. I couldn't deny that part of me wouldn't mind being kissed by Tommy Mikals. Maybe that could be a perk to this whole thing. I knew that in a normal situation, Tommy would probably never want to kiss me.

"Potentially on the table. Cheek and head are acceptable right now."

Tommy nodded seriously at my requests, like discussing the parameters of fake dating were normal conversations to be had on any given day.

"Do we need to write this down?" he asked me. I instantly laughed at the thought, but stopped when I realized that Tommy wasn't laughing with me.

"Wait, are you being serious?"

"I just want you to be comfortable. You're only doing this because of my mess." I didn't want to remind him again of the significant amount of money I was getting to do this. He was acting like I was a saint doing this out of the kindness of my heart.

"I think we're okay to not write it down right now," I told him as I grabbed another piece of pizza. This time I folded the piece longwise and went to bite off the end.

"You're a folder?" Tommy asked.

"Are you judging me?"

"Absolutely," he told me as he grabbed the remote off the coffee table.

Tommy flipped through different movies before he extended the remote to me. "Why don't you pick something?"

"Why? So you can make fun of my movie selection too?" I asked him, my eyes narrowing playfully.

"I'm a gentleman," Tommy told me, holding up three fingers like a Scout.

"That's a Scout's Honor." I pointed at his hand. Tommy blushed before dropping his hand back down. That rosy color made my insides squeeze. I flipped through a couple of movies before I found one of my favorite romantic comedies.

"A romantic comedy?"

I flashed Tommy a warning look, daring him to make fun of my favorite movie genre. He held his hands up in mock surrender. "I love watching love," I mumbled, busying myself with grabbing another slice of pizza to avoid seeing any judgment in Tommy's eyes. I wasn't sure I could handle it if I saw a look of pity for the poor girl that had fucked up with love so badly in her life that she had to resort to watching it on a television screen.

"I like that there's always a happy ending," Tommy added, settling into the couch next to me. He grabbed a blanket that was draped over the back and slung it over both of our legs. My cheeks warmed at such an intimate act. I was sure Tommy had shared a blanket with plenty of girls and that it meant nothing to him. But for me, I had only ever done it with the person that had meant the world to me.

"Sometimes it's nice to live in a world where that happens," Tommy whispered, the reflection of the opening scene in his eyes. I watched him for a moment longer, wondering what demons plagued his mind. It was starting to seem like we had more in common than I had originally thought.

I secretly studied Tommy, admiring his jawline and how long his eyelashes were. If this sincere side of Tommy was how he really was, *God save me*, I was going to have to pray that I made it out the other side of this without falling in love with him.

MAGGIE

"So now you casually get pizza with Tommy Mikals?" I switched the phone to my other ear as Olivia yelled through the receiver. "While holding hands?"

"I was going to tell you . . . ," I started, grimacing as Olivia went off again about how we told each other everything and how she hated finding out about me dating one of the hottest guys we'd ever seen on social media.

She stopped suddenly, a thought occurring to her. "Are you getting fired?"

I had to think fast on my feet and cursed my inability to lie. Olivia knew me well enough that if I blatantly lied to her even over the phone, she would know. I was going to have to settle for something close to the truth. "HR cleared it."

"You already brought it up to HR?" I was crossing my fingers, hoping that Olivia would believe it. If she pressed any more, I was sure to crack and spill my guts to her. I was not made for this stupid plan. The last thing I wanted was to put *her* job in jeopardy.

"Olivia, I'm sorry," I told her again for the hundredth time. Olivia sighed on the other end of the line. It was the telltale sign that she was giving in to me. I was thankful for the fact that neither of us had ever stayed mad at the other for very long.

"You can make it up to me by telling me if Tommy is as good of a kisser as he looks." I could practically picture Olivia waiting eagerly on the other end to hear all of the dirty details.

"We haven't kissed yet, but I'll keep you updated. I promise." Part of me felt horrible lying to Olivia like this, but what was I supposed to do? I was sure that if she knew the whole story, she would understand.

"Is he nice?" she asked. "He has to be nice if you're willing to go out with him. He can't be some massive dick, right? You're not into that, are you?"

In the almost three years that I had known Olivia, I had not gone on a single date. She knew the reason why, which was probably why she found this such a big deal that I had gone out with Tommy Mikals. If this whole charade were real, *I* would know how big of a deal this was. Which was exactly why I couldn't even bring myself to tell her that I was attracted to him in the first place. I didn't want to get anyone's hopes up, thinking I was healed or that I was finally moving on. That would never happen.

"Have you seen the new photos?" Olivia continued before I could respond. I hadn't seen the photos yet this morning, and part of me didn't want to go looking for them. The first time I laid my eyes on the paparazzi photo that Monica used in that fateful meeting, I had looked at a stranger. The girl in that photo had been unrecognizable to my eyes, and I wasn't sure that I was ready to see what version of myself was in the news this time.

"Listen, I'm walking up to my parents' house. How about I fill you in on the plane tomorrow? We have the entire flight to California to catch up."

Olivia sighed but agreed.

Thankfully.

I was quickly approaching my lying threshold for the day.

My parents lived in a suburb of Chicago, still in the home I grew up in as a child. All of the neighbors that had raised me still lived on the same street. A couple of them waved at me as I walked up the driveway. The house looked the exact same, even though my dad had done countless updates to the exterior. Gnomey, my mom's garden gnome, still sat in the same spot in the front garden. Our next-door neighbor's tabby cat was perched on their fence, looking over into our yard like a permanent fixture. Nothing had changed.

An immediate sense of safety washed over me. No matter what was happening in life, this place would always be home to me and allow me to escape the chaos of life. I walked up the cobblestone pathway that led up to the big wraparound porch that still had the old porch swing I had spent many nights on. The front door was open, leaving only the screen door to let in the fresh air.

The moment I walked into the foyer, I could tell my mom was in the kitchen by the smell of oatmeal cookies drifting through the house. My favorite. The sound of the mower came from the backyard, and I knew it would be me and Mom for a little bit as my dad finished up with the outdoor chores.

"Maggie?" my mom called.

"I'm coming," I told her as I navigated from the front door to the kitchen. My mom was pulling out a sheet of cookies from the oven when I walked in. My mouth watered at the sight of them. The recipe had been passed down through our family for generations and was a cornerstone of my childhood. They were so famous that my mother had to start baking big enough batches so I could take some for my friends at school. I swore those cookies were so magical they could cause world peace.

"Hi, sweetie." She peeled her oven mitts off and came around the corner to wrap me in her arms. "Have you eaten anything?" She held me at arm's length as she looked me over from head to toe.

"I just did right before I came over." My mom pulled me over to the couch so we could catch up as we waited for the cookies to cool off.

"You know better than that," she scolded me.

"You told me we were eating dinner, so I had lunch." We always did the same runaround every time I came over. She missed getting to take care of me, so any chance she had, she was going to do it.

My mom was the best person I knew. She had grown up with the aspirations of being an artist. Many of the paintings in our home were her original pieces. When she met my father, he had championed her

dreams like the amazing partner that he was, but when a positive preg-
nancy test had surprised them both, my mom's dreams were put on the
back burner. She had sacrificed her career to raise me, only painting
when she had time, but still trying to help contribute to the family.
Every aspect of her was what I aspired to be: poised, selfless, and beyond
cool. I didn't know a single other person that loved to use squirt guns
full of paint as their tool of choice.

She was my best and longest friend and always had my back during
the hardest part of my life. When I had nowhere to go after graduation,
she was supportive of having me move back in until I could get on my
feet. The photo of Adam Steel sat proudly framed next to her most prestigious painting. There wasn't another person in this world that wanted
my success and happiness more than my mom.

"All right, fill me in on what's new." My mom sat back against the
couch with a look on her face that made me hesitate. It was the same
look I gave others when I was trying to hide that I knew something.

"What're you digging for?"

"I'm not digging." She started to shake her head, but I cut her off.

"Yes, you are. Let's not beat around the bush here."

"You didn't tell me you were seeing someone."

I froze. Since when did my mom go on social media? My brain
kicked into hyperdrive as I tried to figure out some explanation for what
was going on that my mother wouldn't catch me in a lie about. "It's
nothing serious."

"You used to tell me about guys even when you had a crush on
them," she reminded me. "What happened to that?"

"And with Tommy Mikals," my dad's voice boomed through the
room as he came in from the backyard. I wanted the couch cushions to
eat me alive.

"We're just friends."

"Who hold hands?" my mother continued to press. "I knew something was up when you called me the other day."

"Mom." I decided the *please don't embarrass me* tactic would be the
best option for this situation. My mother could read me like a book and
knew the second I tried to lie to her. If my parents were now keeping up
with my very public, very *fake* dating life, I was in more over my head

than I thought.

"All I wanted to say is that it's nice seeing you put yourself out there again." She held her hands up in mock surrender.

I looked over toward one of the framed photos on my parents' mantel. It was me in the arms of a guy with sandy-blond, curly hair. Our smiles lit up our entire faces. His arms were around my waist, his face buried in my neck, as I smiled at the camera and showed off the new ring on my left hand. That same ring now rested on my middle finger on my right hand. My mom still hadn't taken it down, and I still hadn't taken the ring off. She had asked me if I wanted her to, but I told her no. They had loved Luke as much as I did. We couldn't just erase him from our lives like he hadn't existed. That wasn't fair to him or the love we had.

My mom had tears in her eyes when I looked at her again. So the only thing I could do that wouldn't put me in a pile of tears was reach over to grab her hand and tell her, "I know."

Both of my parents had watched me turn into a shell of myself over the last few years. I stopped reaching out to my old friends because the reminder of my old life hurt too much. I couldn't go out because the entire city had become one giant reminder of Luke. The only thing I could do was throw myself into my photos and perfect my craft.

When Olivia came into my life, she managed to break down some of those walls I had erected and immediately became my mom's new favorite person. Olivia would force me out of my apartment and help me recreate some semblance of a social life.

"He would want you to be happy, you know." My mother squeezed both of my hands, the emotion of the last three years evident on her face.

"I know."

"You have so much life ahead of you, Maggie." My father joined our conversation, which made my insides twist. He was not a man of many words, and he avoided any situation that involved feelings, which made this conversation that much more uncomfortable for me. When I had been at the lowest point in my life, I watched him struggle with what to say to make me feel better. Instead, he showed up every other weekend to help clean my apartment, showing he cared in other ways. "You shouldn't have to stop living just because Luke isn't here anymore."

We never had conversations like this after Luke died. I was too distraught to have allowed it, and my parents respected my wishes. But eventually, a conversation like this was bound to happen. I never thought it would be propelled by fake dating Tommy *fucking* Mikals.

"I know, Dad."

"We just want you to be happy, sweetheart."

And honestly, I wanted nothing more than that too.

MAGGIE

The next day, I was walking out onto the tarmac of a private airport toward the team's jet. Traveling with the team was one of my favorite perks of being a professional sports photographer. It was never a guarantee that the other team's media crew would cover the visiting team, so the club sent me and Olivia to every away game.

Chicago was still on the chillier side in April, so I was excited to trade the Midwest weather in for the California sun. The team had a week-long trip up and down the coast of California and I was hoping that we would have some free time for the beach. My body turned as pasty as a sheet of paper in the winter, and I was afraid if I didn't get any sun, I'd turn translucent.

But those hopes of free time were quickly crushed when I sat down in my seat and checked my phone, only to find an email from Monica waiting for me. She went into extensive detail about a formal event that was happening this week that she expected me and Tommy to attend together. It would be our unofficial "announcement" to the world if we showed up together.

Her words, not mine.

I grabbed a seat toward the back of the plane, away from the players.

So I had the perfect view of Tommy as I watched him read the same email. He glanced around once he was done, clearly looking for me. When he glanced over his shoulder toward me, I gave him a small wave. He pointed at his phone discreetly, giving me a look like *did you read this?* I gave him a small nod. Tommy looked at me for a moment longer before he turned back around in his seat. I could tell from the set of his shoulders that he was less than thrilled about Monica's demand, but he knew that this was what the two of us had signed up for.

Olivia came sauntering down the aisle a few moments later, her eyes zeroed in on Tommy's face as she passed him. Part of me was sure that he was ducking his head to avoid looking my best friend in the eyes. He probably wasn't certain if I had even talked with her yet and was afraid she was going to toss him out of the plane once we reached cruising altitude. She slid into the seat next to me, immediately skewering me with a look. One did not have to be a psychic to know exactly what she was about to say.

"Just because your boyfriend is on this trip doesn't give you the opportunity to ditch girl time." She pointed her finger at me, her eyes accusing.

"First of all, he's not my boyfriend," came out of my mouth before I could stop it. Technically, Tommy Mikals wasn't officially my boyfriend publicly until Monica deemed it so. So what I said to Olivia wasn't a complete lie.

"Whatever he is," Olivia interrupted, "doesn't mean you can ditch me the whole week."

"Like I told you before, you're never getting rid of me."

Olivia wrapped an arm around my shoulder to give me a hug as the flight attendants announced that it was time to prepare for takeoff.

"One more thing . . ." Olivia turned back to me. "We all have to hang out. If you start dating someone, it's the best friend's job to deliver the speech."

"What speech?"

"About not breaking your heart." My eyes drifted to the back of Tommy's head. I wanted to tell myself that I was safe from any heart-breaking potential. But I was beginning to become unsure due to the way my heart leaped at the sight of him.

As soon as the plane leveled off, I unbuckled myself from my seat to head toward the bathrooms in the back, leaving Olivia snoring with her face pressed up against the window. The room in the back of the plane was more spacious than a normal lavatory area and had a private sitting area that was unoccupied.

When I emerged from the bathroom, I came face-to-face with Tommy sitting in one of the empty chairs, the door to the back of the plane now closed. His arms rested on his knees as he leaned forward, staring at his feet. He looked up when I came out as he wrung his hands together. The concern I saw on his face right after that HR meeting was back.

"Everything okay?" I asked as I hesitated in the doorway of the bathroom.

"Yeah." Tommy stood quickly. "Yeah, everything's fine. I was thinking about Monica's email, and I wanted to make sure you were okay."

I wished I could be mad at Tommy's sincerity. It wasn't like there were real feelings involved in this. But all I felt was touched at his thoughtfulness, once again.

"All's good here." I started to walk back out toward my seat when Tommy's hand wrapped around my wrist. My eyes stared down at it, hating the way that one simple touch sent my emotions haywire. His eyes seemed to plead with me to tell him something more than that. It was almost like this entire situation was eating him up more than it was me. I had to remind myself we were on the team plane and anyone could walk back here at any time. The last thing I wanted was for Olivia or someone else to come back here and hear us talking about this event we were expected to show up at to confirm we were—fake—dating.

"Let's talk somewhere else."

"People are already talking, Maggie."

"Let's talk later," I repeated. Tommy's face dropped as I walked away from him and back toward my seat. I hated that I was the one that had made him feel that way. It was odd that some part of me didn't want to disappoint him.

Olivia was still asleep when I returned. I watched her for a second, thinking about how my life had taken the turn that it did. It wasn't that

I was afraid of getting caught with Tommy. If I was afraid, I never would have agreed to any of this in the first place. I was more afraid of being a girlfriend again, even if it was a fake one.

It had been four years since I had been one, and I wasn't sure if I would be any good at it anymore. At one time, I had excelled at being Luke's girlfriend. I knew that he liked candy but hated chocolate. He thought *Ocean's Thirteen* was the best one in the movie series, and he loved the Chicago Cougars. I knew how to be Luke's girlfriend, but I didn't know how to be Tommy's.

But what was even scarier to me was that I didn't have an answer as to why I cared.

————

By midmorning I found myself lying on my hotel bed, staring at the ceiling and trying not to make eye contact with the dress that had been hanging in the foyer when I walked in. I wasn't sure what superpower Monica had, but that woman deserved to be working as a publicist for a famous celebrity rather than a professional baseball team.

It was a classic, black, floor-length dress that had two slits up either side and a low neckline in the front. It was designed to show off as much skin as possible and was the exact opposite of what I would have picked out for myself to wear to a red carpet event. Luckily, I wouldn't be expected to wear it for a couple of days. The team would play tomorrow in San Diego before we started north up the coast. Our event wasn't until we made it to Los Angeles the day after tomorrow. Monica had arranged for me and Tommy to go to a Red Cross event while we were in the city. So for now, I planned on shoving it in the hotel room closet and forgetting that it existed before Olivia and I rode with the team to the field for their practice.

But it didn't seem like I was going to escape my problems anytime soon. As the practice started to draw to an end, Tommy ran over to me in front of everyone. Trust me when I say that I noticed the suggestive smile Jamil was giving me and the way all the other players watched us with interest, as if they were watching something unfold in front of them. I was thankful that everyone was being respectful enough to not ask us any questions directly for our privacy, but that still didn't stop them from stealing a few glances at the two of us like they would catch us in sharing a private look.

"Hi."

"Hi?"

"Listen, before I ask you, I want you to know that you can say no," he started. "But we're in my hometown, and my mom called. She wanted to have me come over for dinner tonight. I thought I could bring you."

Bring me home? That was not in the contract that Monica had given us. Public events—that was what we had agreed on. Meeting Tommy's parents? That definitely was not something I was prepared for. Tommy must have read everything I was thinking on my face because he hurried to continue.

"My mom has started asking about you, and I figured that it would help sell the relationship." His reasoning seemed perfectly plausible, and as I stared into Tommy's bright-blue eyes that looked at me with urgency, I knew there was no way I was going to say no.

I was beginning to realize that I enjoyed hanging out with Tommy. He was the first person I'd been willing to leave my apartment for besides Olivia in a long time. I didn't dread not being able to watch movies on my couch or in my hotel room because I had to do something else. What I still couldn't reconcile was that Tommy acted like he really wanted to hang out with me too.

So that was how I ended up walking into Tommy's childhood home, holding his hand as he led me through a gate to the backyard where an older couple sat at a table laughing with each other. I instantly saw Tommy in each of them. He had his mother's eyes and mouth, and the shape of his face was all his father's. The second his mother noticed us, she jumped up from her seat with a cry and ran across the yard toward Tommy. He dropped my hand so he could wrap his mother up in a hug, and I watched as Tommy lifted her off the ground to swing her around in a circle. It was a completely different perspective of Tommy than I had seen. He looked lighter, happier. When he set her down, she turned her warmth on me.

"And you must be Maggie." Her arms wrapped around me, and it felt like I was standing in the sun for the first time. I watched the way Tommy looked at his mom as she hugged me. It was like she was one of the few people in the world he would do anything for. She was obviously very important to him.

"I am. It's wonderful to meet you, Mrs. Mikals." I squeezed her back, immediately comforted by this woman's hospitality.

"Those photos on the internet did not do you justice, honey." Tommy's mom led me over toward the table on their patio. "You are gorgeous, and please, call me Linda."

"Oh, thank you." I laughed awkwardly, feeling like I was drowning in a lake of my lies.

"Hi, Maggie. I'm Scott." Tommy's dad reached his hand out for me to shake, and I did my best to make sure my grip was firm enough. My dad always told me that people would judge me by the grip of my handshake. It was nothing I cared about except for when I was meeting people that I wanted to impress. I had no idea why that was floating through my brain now.

"You two sit." Linda pushed me and Tommy into the two open chairs. "Scott is finishing up the food. In the meantime, you two just *have* to tell me how you met."

All of the blood drained from my face at her request. Tommy and I hadn't talked about what we would say when we were asked this question. We hadn't gotten our stories straight. Tommy glanced over at me and a smile spread across his face, clearly trying to cover for my obvious panic.

"I think I'll take this one. It was the last practice before Opening Day, and Maggie was taking pictures of the team during batting practice. She was too busy taking pictures of me to notice a foul ball coming her way and nearly gave herself a concussion."

A heat spread across my cheeks, and I ducked my head slightly to try to hide the blush that I knew was there. I definitely didn't think that Tommy had noticed me taking pictures of him that day, much less found it memorable. It was my job, after all. But apparently, Tommy had filed that memory away like it had some worth to him.

"Ah!" Linda exclaimed. "So this is relatively new, how exciting."

"And you went out to a club that night," Scott mumbled from the grill. If I wasn't embarrassed already, I definitely was now. Scott's tone implied that he didn't approve of Tommy's pastimes. Tommy cleared his throat.

"The team celebrates the start of the season. I thought it would be best if I went to bond with the guys." Tommy shifted in his seat as he offered an explanation he didn't need to give to his dad. "Maggie and her friend were there. Jamil Edman invited them. Maggie was having less than a stellar time, so I offered to take her home."

Tommy looked at me the entire time he told his parents of the first day we had known each other. His eyes crinkled at the corners as we both thought back on that day. I had been under the impression that Tommy was nothing more than a ladies' man. But after getting to know him so far, he was much more than that.

"You'd think by this point that you'd learn to avoid the tabloids," Scott said.

"How's Chicago?" Linda butted in. I could practically see the years of practice with this dynamic. Scott said something backhanded to Tommy, and Linda would jump in to redirect the conversation, smoothing out the rough edges.

"Colder than California." Tommy gave me a shy smile. "But the pizza's good."

I ducked my head again. He was only doing this to help sell our relationship. There was nothing else to the way he shared a conspiratorial smile with me. When I glanced back over at Tommy, I noticed he was still looking at me. The look in his eyes made a warmth grow within me. It was like I actually meant something to him. Linda and Scott went to grab the condiments and toppings for the burgers, leaving the two of us alone.

"Your parents are nice."

"My mom definitely is," Tommy agreed as he leaned back in his chair. "My dad not as much."

"I'm sure he loves you."

"He doesn't know how to have a relationship with me outside of baseball." Tommy's hands rubbed at the arms of his chair as he stared out toward the ocean.

His childhood home backed up to the beach, and they had a private walkway that led right to the ocean. It was the complete opposite of my apartment that sat on an alleyway of some office building that had been built after developers came through and bought up a bunch of older properties to tear down. I could imagine a young Tommy running on the beach as he worked to sharpen his body for college. I remembered the pictures on his social media page of him surfing and wondered if some of those pictures had been captured here.

It was an odd feeling to suddenly have someone come into your life and to find yourself wanting to know everything about them. Tommy continued to stare out at the ocean, a far-off look on his face. He was still deep in thought and nowhere near our current conversation.

"Are you excited to play against your old team tomorrow?" I was starting to pick up on Tommy's signs, and right now, his body language was telling me he'd rather not continue talking about his dad.

"Honestly, I'm not." Tommy turned his whole attention toward me then, and I could see a tortured look in his eyes. "It feels like a reminder of how badly I fucked up."

I could imagine the battle that was waging within him. He was having to play against his old team with teammates that knew him as someone he previously was and for the mistakes he had made. Even if he had changed, his previous indiscretions were still on the minds of the fans there. It was eating Tommy up, that much could be seen in the lack of a smile on his face. He looked sad.

"Everybody messes up, Tommy. That part doesn't matter because you can't change it." I reached over and took his hand in mine, watching his eyes drift down to stare at them. "The only thing that matters is if you let it define you."

Tommy turned his hand upward so his fingers laced with mine. My own eyes dropped to our joined hands. An energy that only he and I could feel seemed to electrify the air around us. It was magnetic as the two of us looked up from our hands to stare at each other, both of us seeming to acknowledge whatever was happening between us. The air grew heavier as Tommy's eyes slipped to my lips and the warmth that had grown within me from the moment that we had shared that conspiratorial smile morphed into a bonfire. I glanced at Tommy's lips and wondered what they would feel like pressed against mine.

"Dinner's ready!" Linda came through the back door with plates of burgers and toppings in her hands. I dropped Tommy's hand like it had burned me and sat back in my chair, trying to put as much space between us as possible. Tommy stared at where our hands were for a second longer before he stood up to help his mother with the food.

My hand drifted up to press against my lips as I realized I hadn't thought about Luke that entire time. There wasn't an ounce of guilt within me from thinking about someone else. Instead, that warmth from before felt like glowing coals as I watched Tommy help his mom plate the food.

TOMMY

"Don't forget that McDaniels probably has a scout on you." My dad had yet to go five minutes over dinner without mentioning yet another thing that I already knew about the game tomorrow.

Dinner had been going relatively smoothly. Maggie and my mom seemed to be getting along really well. My mom asked Maggie about her family, and Maggie asked my mom for stories about me when I was younger. I groaned when my mom decided to tell her about the time I was learning to slide at a baseball camp when I was a kid. We were indoors, and they had us sliding into mats that were a couple of inches off the ground. My mom's face lit up as she recalled my very first attempt at sliding. My foot caught on the lip of the mat, sending me flying face-first into the pile of mats in front of me. I remember feeling so embarrassed as I looked up to see the college players trying to hold back their smiles. I could laugh about it now, but at the time, I refused to go back to any camps at that college. I had been thoroughly mortified.

Maggie laughed at the image of me as a little kid, gangly and uncoordinated. I watched as she threw her head back, letting out a throaty laugh that made a bubble of heat grow in the bottom of my stomach. I couldn't take my eyes off her all dinner. It excited me how easily she fit in with my family. However, my time admiring the amazing girl across from me was tainted by a short comment my dad felt like he needed to make. Every one of them revolved around baseball. He hadn't even bothered to ask me about how I liked Chicago. Or even if I had made any friends with my teammates. Every comment was centered around me and the game. It took everything in me to stay civil at the dinner table. I knew I needed to—not only for my mom's sake, but for Maggie's. I didn't want her to see how ugly my relationship with my dad really was.

"Thanks, Dad," I told him after finishing off the rest of my water. My dad was nursing a beer and a small part of me ached to grab one from the fridge and down it, but I had promised myself I would do better. That included taking a break from alcohol. So I was out of luck and liquid courage for this conversation.

"Have you gone over the spray charts I emailed you last week on their lineup? Those will help with positioning on the field." Anger began to boil inside me. I could feel both my mom's and Maggie's eyes on me as they waited for me to respond.

"How do you like your new place?" my mom cut in. I could drop to my knees in thankfulness for having her as my mom. She knew exactly when to switch the conversation before a nuclear explosion went off.

"I love it," I told her. "I'm in Lincoln Park. It's perfect. I love seeing all of the families on walks or people out jogging. It feels like somewhere I can grow into later. Maybe even start a family there."

Maggie coughed, her hand flying up to her mouth. I raised an eyebrow at her in concern. She waved me off, trying to tell me that she was fine. If I knew any better, I would have guessed that I had caught her by surprise with that comment.

"I can't wait to see it." My mom reached across the table and squeezed my hand. "I am so proud of you. You've been doing so well."

"If he'd been doing well, he wouldn't be in Chicago right now," my dad grumbled from his seat.

"Scott," my mom hissed at him. My dad chugged the rest of his beer in response.

"Maggie, why don't you help me clean up dinner?" My mom reached over and squeezed Maggie's hand before standing up from the table. Maggie's eyes remained glued to mine, concern etched across her face. It killed me that she had to see this part of my life. I didn't want her to see the remnants of chaos my past life had caused. I had hoped my dad could get through one dinner without opening his mouth, but I guess that was too much to ask. I wanted Maggie to see the man I was trying to become, not the mistakes the former version of myself had made.

I had no idea why I had wanted her to come tonight. My mind had tried to convince me that it would be a great way to practice our relationship for when we were in public, but I knew that was a lie. I wanted to see her here, with my family, and imagine what it would be like if all of this was real.

Maggie left with my mom, leaving me alone with my dad. I was beginning to wish that my mom had asked me to help her clean instead.

"Do you really think it's smart getting in a relationship right now? You've never had much luck before with picking them," my dad asked, wasting no time hounding me with questions again.

This one made my blood boil.

Who did he think he was, judging Maggie? She should never have been dragged into any of the mess I had made. But instead, she willingly signed a contract that she never should have been involved with in the first place. Of course her contract benefited her, but part of me constantly worried that the permanent effects this would have on her life would never be worth the money she was being paid.

"Maggie is not like any other girl I've ever dated." Having my dad lump Maggie in with the models I had dated previously set something off in me. I leveled a stare at him that would melt diamonds. "If you don't have anything nice to say about her, don't say anything at all."

"Someone has to have some common sense for you." My dad didn't even seem deterred by my threat.

"I am an adult. I can handle my own life."

"Are you sure? Because it doesn't seem like you've done a tip-top job of that so far."

My fists clenched under the table, and without a second thought, I pushed my chair back and began to storm away from the deck.

"That's right. Back down from the fight, just like you always have."

My dad's words rang in my ears all the way to the shed, where I grabbed a golf club and a bucket of balls that he always kept stored there.

Part of me couldn't help but think his accusation wasn't far from the truth. I had wondered if letting Maggie agree to this whole charade in the first place was the easy way out instead of letting the inevitable happen. But I refused to let my dad win. I would prove to him that I was still capable of being the son he could be proud of.

MAGGIE

Linda and I worked side by side as we cleaned the plates after dinner. She asked me questions about my job and my family, interjecting to comment when I told her that my mom was an artist. She asked me to pull up some of her work and gushed at how talented she was. When she looked at some of the shots I had taken, she told me that she wanted the shot I had gotten of Tommy after his homer on Opening Day to be framed and hung in their home. I could tell why Tommy loved his mom so fiercely. She was full of so much love and sincerity that it was impossible not to like her.

But after a while, the two of us grew quiet as we worked together in silence.

"He's a good man."

"I'm sorry?" I paused with the dish towel in my hand as I was drying one of the plates.

"Tommy." Linda dropped the sponge into the sink and turned to face me. "He means well. I know he made some poor decisions in his past, but that boy doesn't have a mean or disrespectful bone in his body. He was lost." The look Linda gave me made me want to crawl into myself because it was one that I didn't deserve. "I see the way he looks at you."

I averted my eyes, wanting to forget the way Linda talked to me, like there was hope for her son yet and I was exactly what he needed. His parents were good people, and we were stringing them along all because of a contract and our own selfish reasons. Tommy must have been really selling this fake relationship over dinner because I hadn't noticed a single thing different about how he looked at me.

"You do have a nice son," I told her after a minute before going back to drying the dishes. It was true and felt like something safe to say. Linda nodded, reading my distant response and not pushing the topic any further. I was extremely grateful for that woman. The two of us continued to clean and dry the dishes in silence.

After a few moments, Linda sighed as she watched out the window. Tommy stood out there, hitting golf balls into the ocean from his parents' walkway to the beach. His swing was violent as he sent golf balls sailing away.

"Scott must have said something to him," Linda said after a moment. My eyebrows drew together in concern at the tenseness in his shoulders. I glanced between Linda and Tommy before setting the dish towel down.

"I'll go talk to him." She gave me a grateful look before taking the dish towel from me.

I closed the door to the house quietly behind me as I watched Tommy send another golf ball into the ocean with a *thwack*. The muscles on his arms flexed as he pulled the club back and sent it flying down toward the ball again. *Thwack.*

"You've got a good swing," I told him. He stopped, club at the top of his swing. He dropped his arms and pushed away the golf ball he was about to hit.

"They disintegrate when they hit the water," he told me, like I had yelled at him for littering in the ocean instead.

"Okay," I replied, taking a few steps closer to him. "I'll add that you love the environment to the list."

A smile actually broke across his face then, and my knees felt weak at the sight. It was like a little part of me was proud that I could cheer him up.

"Want to talk about it?"

"It was the same old argument with my dad. Nothing new." Tommy threw the golf club aside and started off down the walkway to the beach. He didn't look over his shoulder to see if I'd follow, but I did anyway.

"About what?" I asked softly after I had caught up to him. He had stopped a few feet from where the waves were and had taken a seat in the sand.

He patted the sand next to him, and I let him take my hand to help me sit. "About my career. He thinks I'm throwing it away."

"What do you think?"

"I think I've screwed up enough that what he said isn't that far from the truth." Tommy stared off toward the ocean, lost in thought.

"You're one of the highest-paid players in the league. How could your career be done?"

"You heard Monica. The Cougars are my last chance." He didn't have to say it, but I could read between the lines that *I* was the reason his last chance was at risk right now.

"Then we'll sell this relationship so hard, every woman will fall in love with you and nobody will think you're a ladies' man. They'll just think you're one lady's man."

"I'm not really sure that's how this is supposed to work . . ." Tommy raised a brow at me skeptically.

"Don't worry, Mikals. You're in the right hands." I knocked my knees into his as I gave him a cheeky smile. "But seriously, Tommy. You haven't screwed anything up. You're still doing what you dreamed of as a little kid. When that's taken away from you, come talk to me."

I could feel Tommy's eyes on my face, studying me again. "Where'd you learn to do that?"

"Do what?" I asked.

"Be so optimistic."

The waves filled the silence that stretched out between us as I thought about what he said. I knew exactly where my optimism had come from. Four years ago, I had learned quite intimately what people meant when they said not to take something for granted. In the blink of an eye, the thing you never thought could happen does, and your life is forever changed. I knew I wasn't ready to tell him where exactly I had learned it, so instead I returned the focus on Tommy.

"No matter what happens, Tommy," I finally replied, "you are more than the player."

Tommy stared out at the waves as he thought about what I had said before he spoke again. This time, barely a whisper.

"I don't know how to be anything other than a baseball player." When he looked at me, his eyes seemed tortured. It was like he had spent many nights thinking about who he would be the last time he stepped off a baseball field, and he had yet to come up with an answer.

"You don't have to be anyone else, Tommy." My hand found his in the sand and covered it. "You just have to be you."

The look on Tommy's face after I spoke was one of curiosity and admiration. It was a look that made me want to run away as fast as I could. Only because it was the same look I remembered Luke giving me on our first date as I rambled on about why I loved photography. It was like a slice of reality had broken through this day to remind me that the last thing I needed was for my relationship with Tommy to get complicated with feelings. There was a contract that still legally bound the two of us together.

"You've got a game tomorrow," I announced to break up the tension within me. "We should probably get you back to the hotel so you can be well rested."

Tommy nodded, completely oblivious to the panic that was finding a home within my chest.

———

We were down by three runs going into the bottom of the seventh. Our bullpen was nearly exhausted and our hitting had stalled. Tommy had struck out twice and walked once so far in this game, and I watched as he sat at the end of the dugout by himself. Olivia was in the designated media section, leaving me to handle the dugout once again. I knew that Tommy's family was in the stands somewhere, watching him play for the Cougars for the first time in person. This game probably held a lot of weight in his mind, and he was clearly cracking under the pressure of it.

Without trying to draw any attention to myself, I slowly walked toward the opposite end of the dugout where he was sitting. He was due up to bat soon, and based on how he was holding himself, I doubted the outcome would be much different than the first few times. It was like I could practically see inside his mind and hear all of the horrible things he was saying to himself about his ability to achieve.

"Hey." I kept the camera up to my face as I snapped some photos, trying not to draw anyone's attention in the dugout toward me and Tommy. Tommy glanced up at me in surprise that I was talking to him during the game. I had made it known that we were to avoid each other until the last out was made. As I stayed silent for a few more seconds, he continued to stare at me expectantly.

"Remember what I said?" I took the camera away from my face long enough to take a good look at him. He was staring at me like I had said something in a different language. "You just have to be you, Tommy. You've got nothing to prove."

There was a determination that slowly leaked back into the set of his shoulders and the look in his eyes after he took in what I had to say. It was like my words had breathed a new life into him and released some of the worries he had been carrying on his shoulders. With his newfound confidence, Tommy grabbed his helmet and bat before walking out to home plate.

This time when he set up to wait for the pitch, it was like a completely different version of himself had appeared at the batter's box. Gone were the nervous twitches or the uneasiness in the way he moved his hands as he waited for the pitch. His confident demeanor, the one I had seen on that very first day of practice, had returned. The runner on second signaled to Tommy the side of the plate he thought the pitch would be delivered. The pitcher started his windup, and then it was like everything was in slow motion. The ball sailed slowly toward Tommy as he tracked it closer to the plate. His hands started moving as he lined his swing up with the pitch and then made contact. The ball was sent sailing out to right-center, deep toward the fence. The crowd's roar grew louder the closer it got to the fence before becoming deafening as it sailed over it.

Tommy threw his arms up as he rounded second and the ball landed outside the park, a home run. I captured the shot before pulling the camera down so I could watch the moment with my own eyes and not through the lens of a camera. He had cut San Diego's lead down to one and stirred up some new energy in his teammates and the fans. A piece of me couldn't help but soar at the idea that Tommy had used what I had said, giving him the confidence to be himself. My eyes tracked him as he stepped on home plate and pointed up toward the sky.

When he reentered the dugout to high fives and cheers from his teammates, Tommy's eyes found mine. His lips moved, mouthing the words *thank you* in my direction. I gave him a small nod in return, not wanting to take away from his moment and trying to ignore the way my heart had leaped when he looked at me coming down the dugout stairs. It was like my heart was *hoping*, and hope was a dangerous thing. It could make you do and say things you wouldn't normally. It could make someone foolish, and the last thing I wanted to be was a fool in all of this. The fool didn't come out on top. The fool was taken by surprise, used, and left in the trash after a person was done with them. I wouldn't be the fool.

MAGGIE

The day had come for the team to travel north up the coast toward Los Angeles. It was the Red Cross event, and to say I was nervous would be an understatement. I had stood staring at the dress hanging up in my closet in San Diego for fifteen minutes before I made a move to take it out and pack it with my other things. Part of me debated pretending to forget it at the hotel, but I knew that wouldn't keep me from my fate. Monica would magically have another dress appear in Los Angeles for me. There was nothing in the world that would stop her from making sure Tommy and I showed up at this event to announce our relationship publicly on that red carpet.

The ocean passed by out the window of the bus we were in. This trip had easily become my favorite trip we took each season, simply for the views. With the sun shining high in the sky, a breeze pushing the palm trees, and the ocean crashing onto the shore, it felt like nothing bad could happen in the world. Like such a beautiful place couldn't possibly allow for anything but goodness. But I couldn't afford to be so naive.

"How was your day off?" I asked Olivia.

"Magical. I went shopping before going down to the beach, where I saw some really hot military men running like it was straight out of a *Top Gun* scene."

I laughed as I imagined Olivia calculating what the best way would be to fake something terrible happening to her so one of them would run over to help.

"That does sound magical."

"How was yours?"

I debated telling her what exactly I had done, but part of me wanted to keep the visit with Tommy's parents to just the two of us. Our relationship was about to be public enough for everyone to see. It didn't feel like much to ask to keep a slice of us, the real us, to myself.

"It was relaxing," I told her. "Tommy and I are going to a Red Cross event tonight." I hesitated telling her about it, but I knew she would kill me if I had known I was going and she found out on social media again.

This entire fake relationship was so difficult for me. It was like I had thrown all of my normal tendencies out the window. If I had started dating some guy, I would have gone screaming to Olivia so the two of us could dissect everything I knew about him so far and spend a ridiculous amount of time searching social media to find out as much about him as we could. But with Tommy, it felt wrong doing any of that, like it was a slap to our relationship.

"You're *what*?" Olivia turned completely in her seat to face me. The look on her face told me that she was about to grill me for every piece of information she could glean.

"He asked me to go with him." Not technically a lie.

"Let me get this straight . . ." Olivia was still staring at me like I had told her I wanted to quit my job and move to the middle of the desert to sell tumbleweeds. "You are going to a black-tie event with *Tommy Mikals*? I thought you said it wasn't serious!"

"I never said it wasn't serious." Olivia's mouth dropped open.

"It's *serious*?"

I shrugged in response, not trusting myself to sell the lie. If I couldn't even lie to my best friend about this, how was I supposed to convince the entire world that I was in a relationship with Tommy?

Olivia leaned in closer to me and dropped her voice so no one around us could hear her. "Are you doing okay?"

I knew she wasn't asking if I'd lost my mind with this whole situation, even though I was seriously questioning it. She was only checking in with me to make sure I was truly happy because this was the first guy since Luke that I had gone on a date with, fake or not.

"I am." That was the truth.

Sure, I could be a nervous wreck at times around Tommy and wasn't sure how to navigate being his girlfriend. But over the past week I'd become more comfortable with him and didn't feel like I wanted to jump ship as quickly as possible. I'd call that progress.

"This all just seems like a lot." Olivia's eyes softened as she looked at me with concern. "Just over a week ago you were telling me that you didn't want to risk your job by dating a player, and now you're going to an event with him as his date?"

I cursed Monica as I tried to figure out how to navigate this conversation with my best friend. It was as if the Cougars' PR team had thrown me and Tommy into the deep end without any life vests. People were going to start looking more closely at the two of us, and I was certain there would be more people questioning the validity of our relationship. Olivia knew I was a terrible liar, so the only thing I could do was give her pieces of the truth.

"The Cougars asked Tommy to do this event, and he asked me to go with him. This is all new, and I realize I'm probably way over my head. I didn't expect the media to explode over all of this like it has and—"

"Maggie." Olivia reached for my hand to silence me. "Who gives a shit about the media? All I care about is if you like him and that you're happy."

I didn't deserve a friend like Olivia Thompson. No matter what I did—go through depressive episodes bad enough that I rarely left my apartment for weeks or threw her for a one-eighty and started dating the most eligible professional baseball player in the league—she continued to stand by my side with my best interests at heart.

"I do like him, Liv." Between the intense way Tommy listened to everything I said to file it away for later, his dry humor that felt refreshing, or the undeniable electric pull that existed between us, I knew that was the truth.

"What has your mom said?" I wasn't surprised that Olivia had asked about my mom. The two of them had bonded over their fierce protection of me, and she'd probably send her a text about me and Tommy after our conversation.

My mom had loved Olivia instantly when I brought her home after our game during our first season together. I hadn't told Olivia about Luke yet, and as soon as she had walked into my parents' home, her eyes had locked onto the photo of me and Luke on my parents' mantel. My mom had given me a panicked look, trying to convey her apology with her eyes for having not thought about that. But in that moment, I realized I wasn't terrified of telling Olivia the truth about what had happened to me. So I sat her down and told her the whole horrible story from start to finish. She held me when I cried, and since that day, she had been my bodyguard when it came to dating.

Dating Tommy had probably taken her by surprise because I hadn't needed her for a pep talk or to tell me that I wasn't selfish for moving on and being happy. The fact that I wasn't expressing any feelings about disgracing Luke by dating someone else was probably exactly why Olivia was concerned about me.

"She told me she was happy I was putting myself back out there again."

"I will second that statement." Olivia reached over and squeezed my arm. "Can I help you get ready?"

My heart melted at how lucky I was to be Olivia's friend. She was the most selfless person I knew, and at times I wondered if I deserved her. I often went radio silent, needing my alone time away from the world. But every time I would reemerge, Olivia was always there and understood why I hadn't responded to her texts or calls. I still worried that eventually she would reach her limit with me.

"I would really appreciate the help." I grabbed her hand in mine and brought it up to my lips for a kiss. "If I had to do my own hair and makeup, I'd surely be on the cover of every news outlet due to my lack of skill."

The two of us got up as the bus pulled to a stop in front of our hotel in Los Angeles. Olivia wrapped an arm around my shoulder as we waited to exit. "Don't worry, I've got you."

"I know you do."

———

Three hours later I was standing in front of the floor-length mirror in my hotel room, staring at a stranger. Part of me wondered if this was how Julia Roberts's character felt in *Pretty Woman*.

Olivia must have used some sort of magic on me because she had managed to tame the normal frizz that accompanied my curls. Each curl was defined and shiny, no frizz in sight. She had pulled most of it back away from my face in a simple updo at the nape of my neck, leaving a few strands for framing. My green eyes looked like gems with the gold eyeshadow she used. Olivia had wrangled a pair of fake eyelashes on me after nearly gluing my eyelids shut due to my lack of experience with the process. She finished the look with a simple clear lip gloss, understanding my comfort level with makeup. The finished product made me look like I could actually walk a red carpet and not feel like I was way out of my realm.

As I stared at myself in the mirror, I was beginning to understand what girls meant when they said that they wore their makeup as armor. I felt like a completely new person, someone who had confidence and wasn't terrified of being the center of attention.

The dress that Monica had picked out hugged every curve perfectly. Normally I would have felt extremely uncomfortable with the amount of skin that was showing, but for the first time in my life, I felt beautiful. The tomboy version of myself was gone, replaced by someone that was sexier and more feminine.

"Tommy is going to *lose* his mind when he sees you," Olivia announced as she looked at me, satisfied with her work.

"I'm sure he won't." I ducked my head at Olivia's comment as I ran my hands down my dress. "He's been with models."

"Maggie Redford." Olivia's voice had turned serious as she pulled on my hand to turn me around. "Tommy *will* lose his mind. Why? Because you have something those models don't: a fucking ass and a goddamn amazing personality. Now, you're going to march your amazing ass down to the lobby and have a great time on this date."

Olivia's words sang through me, lighting up every inch of my body. That was exactly why I loved her. I grabbed my clutch off the bed and gave myself one more look in the mirror. While I may not have fully believed every word Olivia said about being able to compete with a model, I did know I looked damn good for my usual self.

"I expect a full report in the morning." Olivia pointed a finger at me as she opened my hotel room door. "Full report, you hear me?"

I laughed as I followed her out into the hallway and toward the elevators. Olivia's room was on the opposite end of the hallway, and she walked me to the elevator bay like a chaperone.

"Have fun tonight, Maggie. You deserve that much." I gave Olivia a small smile before I stepped into the elevator and watched her disappear as the doors closed.

The ride down to the lobby was agony. All of the confidence I had been feeling in my hotel room left my body with each passing floor. I tried to remind myself that I didn't care what Tommy thought of me because none of this was real, but the bundle of nerves inside me didn't seem to listen. The doors parted, and I walked out toward the main entrance, thankful Tommy hadn't been waiting for me right by the elevators. I needed the short walk to breathe and clear my head.

As I rounded the corner, I saw Tommy standing near the entrance to the hotel, looking out the glass walls at the city beyond. He looked sharp in a black suit that would match my dress perfectly. I took a moment to admire him before he realized I was there. His suit showed off his broad shoulders and was tailored to his fit waist. His legs looked powerful in his dress pants, which accentuated his muscles. He looked like any girl's wet dream. After realizing that if I stood there any longer, I'd probably start getting weird looks, my heels clicked across the marble floors of the lobby. Tommy turned around at the sound. His eyes started at my feet and slowly traced their way up my body before landing on my face. He shook his head slowly from side to side as he took a few steps closer to me.

"Wow," he whispered softly. "You look stunning."

The way he looked at me made me feel like I was the only person in the lobby. It was like I filled up his entire vision with my radiance. A blush crept across my cheeks, and I ducked my head to try to recover. Tommy offered me his arm, and I gladly slipped mine through his. This simple routine of ours was beginning to feel comforting, the feel of his arm under my hand.

"Are you ready for this?" he asked me. "There's no running from the cameras this time."

"As ready as I'll ever be," I mumbled as Tommy led us out to an SUV that was waiting for us in front of the hotel.

Even though I was a photographer myself, nothing could ever prepare me for the way paparazzi converged on you like a pack of rabid dogs. But I knew that this was a part of the job now. There was no escaping it.

The event was being held at the civic center in downtown Los Angeles, which was only a few blocks from where we were staying. However, LA traffic was bound to make what should be a short drive longer than it needed to be. The car was quiet as the driver weaved in and around other cars while Tommy and I stared out our own windows. Tommy began to rap his fingers against his thigh as we drew closer to the venue. I wasn't sure what had his nerves on edge. He'd been in front of cameras countless times before. But whatever it was that was bothering him was clearly weighing heavily on his mind, and part of me was relieved that I wasn't the only one who was nervous.

A red carpet ascended the stairs toward the front doors out of view from my vantage point inside the vehicle as we pulled up in front of the venue. Even from inside the car, I could feel the shouts of the photographers trying to grab the attention of the guests walking the red carpet. The flashes from the cameras made my chest tighten. I remembered the paparazzi that had been waiting for us at the pizza parlor. There had only been a few then, and I had felt like I was going to pass out before we had even made it inside the restaurant. Tonight, there were hundreds of them lined down the red carpet, greedily calling out people's names like vultures. How was I supposed to make it up all of those stairs without fainting? At least that picture would surely make the front page of all the news outlets. But I wasn't sure that was what Monica had in mind for front-page coverage.

Tommy pulled open my door, taking up my entire field of view and blocking my ability to see any of the paparazzi waiting for us. He bowed slightly at the waist and extended his hand toward me. "My lady."

Just like that, my fear for what lay ahead evaporated. His strong presence provided me with all the reassurance I needed to step out of the car. My newfound confidence lasted for a whole minute before the shouting started. With the first jarring shout, the world began to slip further away from me. With the first flash, I stumbled forward. Tommy's arm wrapped around my waist to keep me upright.

Flash.

My hand shot up to cover my eyes.

Flash.

Someone stepped in front of me, and I thought I could hear them calling my name, but I wasn't sure.

Flash.

"Maggie." The voice came through stronger, and I blinked a few times like I was coming back up to the surface. Tommy stood in front of me, both of his hands on my shoulders.

"You can do this." His voice was fierce as his eyes bored into mine. He was giving me the kind of pep talk that I had given him the previous night before his at bat. The confidence in his voice seeped in to fill my entire body, banishing any trace of the anxiety I had been feeling before. I nodded my head after a few moments to let him know that I believed it too. That I could do this.

Tommy gently placed my hand in his and laced our fingers together. The way our fingers interlocked perfectly felt more intimate to walk down a red carpet than my hand on his arm. No matter what happened, I realized that he and I were in this together. I wouldn't have to face any of this without him by my side.

The voices began to shout Tommy's name as we started up the red carpet. A reporter waited for us at the top of the first set of stairs, a cameraman standing next to her. Tommy and I both knew what we had to do, but I could tell in the way that Tommy's body tensed and the way he hesitated walking toward the woman that he didn't want to do this either.

"Tommy!" the reporter exclaimed, ruining any chances we had of escaping. "How are you tonight?"

Tommy finished the few steps up toward the woman before giving her his megawatt smile. He may have been a professional athlete, but he knew how to turn it on for the public. "I'm doing well and so happy to be here."

It was a perfectly polite response and showed off Tommy's skills with navigating the press. I knew that if I opened my mouth, however, it would be less than polished. It was best for him to lead this conversation.

"And who is your beautiful date tonight?" The woman flashed me a smile, but it felt more like an obligation than something sincere. Tommy hesitated, like he knew the second he said my name there was no turning back for either of us. My name had been leaked from that very first picture, but Tommy had yet to introduce me in a way that would make us official.

"This is Maggie Redford."

"You two have been seen out with each other quite a bit, if I recall . . ." The woman trailed off, leaving an opening for an exclusive. I could feel that neither of us wanted to give it to her, but both of us knew we had to.

"We have," Tommy replied with one of his normal short responses.

"Are you two seeing each other?" the woman pressed, seeing this as an opportunity and not wanting it to slip away. She wasn't going to let Tommy's lack of elaboration stop her. Again, Tommy hesitated.

"Yes."

There it was, the moment that my name would forever be associated with Tommy's. There really was no going back now. That one word would lock our fate together in more ways than I would realize.

MAGGIE

Every eye at the event seemed to trail me and Tommy as we made our rounds before excusing ourselves to our own private table. We were obviously the talk of the night. The exclusive that Tommy had given that reporter probably wouldn't hit social media for another hour or so, but those inside the event could put two and two together.

Tommy stayed by my side the entire night. He didn't let me go anywhere alone. Even when I had to use the restroom, he waited for me outside. Any other night and any other person, I would have thought it was a little suffocating, but tonight I was grateful. He was only making sure that nobody had the opportunity to corner me while I was alone to interrogate me about my relationship with him.

I stayed on Tommy's arm as he greeted people he knew and introduced me to them. It was comforting to watch Tommy ignore the stares or the pointed questions about me. He navigated every question with the intention of protecting me, but gave out enough hints about our relationship to keep Monica happy. It was difficult to find someone that prioritized your needs the way that Tommy was doing so selflessly with mine.

Most of the individuals that Tommy introduced me to were well-known people within the Los Angeles and San Diego social circles. I was grateful that the most famous people at the event tonight were reality television personalities. If I had been rubbing elbows with A-listers, I was sure I wouldn't have been able to handle the night as well as I had.

It was interesting to watch Tommy take on the personality of someone completely different. He morphed into someone that blended well with the people around him, almost like a chameleon. He navigated conversations with people almost like a politician. It was as if he knew what he should say and when he needed to say it. I knew he had learned how to be among people like this from the years when he had been thrust into the public eye as a professional athlete, but it was still jarring to watch someone you had come to know be a completely different person.

As the night wore on, I watched Tommy's shoulders inch closer to his ears with every interaction he had. It was like he was taking on a bit of tension in his body with every conversation that he had to fake. I could only imagine how exhausting it was. I wasn't sure how he survived being in San Diego for as long as he did.

When the event finally came to a close, Tommy led me back out the front door and down the red carpet toward the SUV that was waiting for us. Most of the paparazzi had left already, but a few lingered hoping to get a shot of some celebrity leaving the event wasted.

"Tommy! Your girl is gorgeous."

"Tommy, give her a kiss for me."

"Tommy!"

I was sure that I would never get used to the shouts. Their words were like slime coating my body, and I wasn't sure any amount of showering would ever make me feel clean again. My phone buzzed in my clutch, and I fumbled with the clasp to open it. Tommy must have gotten a notification too, because he was pulling his phone out of his jacket pocket. The two of us stared down at our separate screens, reading the same email.

Monica: Kiss her. You're on a livestream.

Tommy's head snapped up, and he scanned our surroundings to find the camera that was broadcasting us. One of the paparazzi had a large video camera perched on his shoulder, the red light blinking at us like a taunt. Tommy slid his phone back into his jacket pocket before offering me his arm again. He led me down a few steps in quiet, the two of us thinking about the same thing. We were going to have to kiss eventually to make this relationship seem realistic, whether that was now or staged later on.

I yanked on Tommy's hand, pulling us to a stop. His eyes searched mine, finding the decision I had made. He sucked in a breath like he was preparing himself for what he needed to do. My heart sank a little at the sight. It was alarming that part of me wished our first kiss had been brought on by more romantic happenings.

I didn't have long to think about that thought before he stepped closer to me and his hand came up to cup my cheek. The calluses on his fingers rubbed against my skin as they traced up the side of my face. I watched Tommy's throat bob up and down as his thumb ran over my bottom lip. My lips parted at the touch, feeling like every nerve ending was on high alert from the feel of his skin on mine.

My feet hesitantly moved closer to him, as if they were being pulled closer by some invisible string. Tommy's hand slipped from my face to cup the back of my neck, tilting my head up toward his. His blue eyes looked dark as they drank in every inch of my face. My heart felt like it was going to burst right through my rib cage as Tommy leaned closer, his lips now a breath away from mine. My eyes drifted closed as I waited for the moment to happen, to feel his lips against mine. An eternity must have passed before his lips brushed against the corner of my mouth, almost like a question.

When I didn't pull back, they enveloped mine. Tommy's hands drifted down to my waist as he pulled my body against his, pressing every inch of me against every inch of him. A moan escaped my lips as I felt my body melt into his, giving in to the feel of him everywhere on my body. Tommy's arms wrapped around me tighter in response, like he wanted to devour me where we stood.

Years must have passed by the time we had pulled away from each other. The night was quiet; not a single paparazzo yelled at us. Or maybe they did, but I couldn't hear any of them because my senses were still zeroed in on Tommy. His lips looked bruised as he stared at me with a look of bewilderment on his face. My chest was still rising and falling quickly as my brain tried to make sense of what had just happened.

Sure, Tommy had kissed me like Monica had asked, but that felt like more than a simple kiss. I had to shake that thought from my head. It was bad enough that I was having to pretend to date the hottest guy I'd ever seen. It was even worse that the hottest guy I'd ever seen had kissed me like I was water and he had been stranded in the desert for the past month. If Tommy was going to kiss me like that every time we had to in public, I was sure my feelings would forever be *fucked*.

My hand drifted up to touch my lips as Tommy continued to stare at me, his eyes dazed. All at once, the world came back to me as my senses snapped back to normal. First, it started with the sounds of the traffic and the distant throb of the music inside the party. Then, it was the intoxicating smell of Tommy's cologne, cedar wood. I managed to pull my eyes away from his face as I took in the lights of the city around us. Then I heard it.

Silence.

I glanced down the stairs toward the paparazzi to see them quietly staring at us. The guy with the video camera still recording while the others stood there, their cameras hanging around their necks as they watched us. It was as if they were as shocked by the intensity of that kiss as I was.

Tommy's arm slowly wound back around my waist, and the two of us finished descending the stairs. Neither of us looked at each other, even after we got in the car and started back toward the hotel.

Tommy walked me all the way back to my hotel room, still not a word shared between us. He kept a respectful distance away from me as I swiped my key card and opened the door. I turned to look at him, unsure of what to do or say. He looked exactly how I felt as he rubbed the back of his neck. Neither of us was sure if our kiss had crossed a line, and after I realized that Tommy wasn't going to break the awkward silence, I knew I needed to or I would explode from the anticipation.

"I'll see you tomorrow at the game." With that, Tommy turned and walked away. Leaving me standing alone in a hotel hallway in a dress far fancier than anything I'd ever worn before, with bruised lips and a pounding heart.

————

"I don't even have to ask you if your date was good. That kiss said *everything*." Olivia practically swooned next to me as we shot the game. The second I stepped on the bus the next morning she had swarmed me like a colony of wasps, stinging me with every question she had.

"Was it like straight out of a romance movie?" Olivia continued. I knew she meant well, and if my head still wasn't scrambled like eggs from the very kiss she was talking about, I was sure I would be playing along with her.

"Just like *Pretty Woman*," I replied absentmindedly as I took a few photos. My mind was too distracted for today's game, and I knew none of my pictures would be good enough to use. I was hoping I wouldn't hear about it from May.

Luckily, we were stationed outside the dugout for this game. I wasn't sure I would be able to keep myself from watching Tommy's every move if I were within five feet of him. I had waited anxiously by my phone all morning to hear from him after we had been congratulated for a job well done by Monica. But it was silent. That silence had been picking at a corner of my brain all morning. Luckily, Olivia didn't seem to read anything strange coming from me today and never pressured me for more information.

"Can we all hang out sometime?" she asked me after a few minutes of working. "I'd like to get to know him better."

The moment those words left Olivia's mouth, I knew I was stuck. There was no way I could tell her no without raising any suspicion from her. We'd already established that if we could sell this relationship to the ones closest to us, we could sell it to the world. So I reluctantly told her that I thought it would be a great idea for us all to hang out and that I would talk to Tommy after the game.

Which led to me cornering Tommy as he came out of the locker room. He was always the last one to leave, which was convenient for me to have this conversation with him. When the team started to trickle out of the locker room, they only looked at me for a few seconds before they moved on. Except Jamil. Jamil came out of the locker room, noticed me, and wiggled his eyebrows suggestively.

"Waiting on Loverboy?"

I rolled my eyes at the nickname he had given Tommy and tried to hide the smile that was spreading across my face.

"No." It came out of my mouth an octave too high, and Jamil let out a belly laugh so loud it brought heat to my cheeks, before turning and walking away. Thankfully, I didn't have to wallow in my embarrassment for long because the locker room door opened one more time and Tommy Mikals walked out.

His eyes widened in surprise when he noticed me. Honestly, I wasn't really sure why I had rushed to ask him about hanging out with Olivia. This question could have waited until we had all gone back to the hotel. Heat rushed to my cheeks at the thought of someone catching me knocking on Tommy's door like some lovesick girl.

"Maggie?"

My gaze refocused as I realized that Tommy had stopped right outside the locker room and was staring at me.

"Olivia wants to hang out." It was like I couldn't hold back the word vomit that had spewed from my mouth.

"Okay?" Tommy replied slowly, clearly not getting the situation I was trying to convey.

"With both of us." His eyebrows raised in surprise. "We have to convince her about us."

"Okay." Tommy let out a breath. "When?"

"On this trip, I think. I guess she really didn't say, but I'm assuming she wants to hang out sooner rather than later—" Tommy had taken a few steps closer to me and moved to cover my mouth, silencing me.

"Tell her we will tomorrow." Tommy had morphed into the man of action he had been last night. He took on the responsibility of the situation, easing some of the worry from my shoulders. "We'll be in San Francisco tomorrow. We can all go to the pier."

I stood there feeling like I had forced Tommy's hand, and guilt spread through my body. "Are you sure?"

But Tommy nodded and motioned for me to lead the way toward the bus. Silence stretched out between us as we walked out of the ballpark, but the tension that I thought had been there from the previous night seemed to have evaporated with the morning fog that had rolled off the ocean. Gone like a distant memory.

TOMMY

I had spent the entire night after the Red Cross event replaying that kiss in my mind. I hadn't wanted our first kiss to be such a spectacle. Maggie seemed to have painted a piece of herself over every inch of my mind. I couldn't stop thinking about how she had quickly become something like a safety blanket for me. Any time that I was under stress, my eyes would drift to find hers if she was in the room, like she could feel my anxiety and was the only pill to fix it.

In San Diego, I was drowning under the weight of wanting to prove myself not only to my dad, but to my former club. I wanted them to see that I was a different person, that I deserved success in my life. But every time I went up to the plate, it was as if I was watching a movie reel of every text and every news article that had detailed all of my wrongdoings. Only Maggie had noticed that I was practically underwater and at risk of drowning in that dugout from every opinion that said I was worthless. The moment that she had reminded me that I didn't owe anyone anything, that all I had to do was be me, I realized that she was more than someone special. She was someone that I needed to hold on to tightly.

From that point on, it was beginning to feel like I was almost becoming obsessive with how much I wanted this fake relationship to be something more. I had thought constantly about the Red Cross event and how I could slowly win Maggie over with subtle flirting. When Monica had told us that we needed to kiss, dread filled me. It was the exact opposite of what I wanted to happen. The kiss was forced and in no way would make Maggie think that I had real feelings for her. It was obvious when she was waiting for me outside the locker room. She was detached, like she wanted nothing to do with me but knew that we had an obligation to this fake relationship, and if her best friend wanted to hang out with me, it was something we were going to have to do.

I had felt so defeated when I watched her stumble through an explanation of why Olivia wanted to hang out. Gone was the girl that had acted so free and comfortable with me. If I was going to have any opportunity to make Maggie think about something more with me, today was important. I needed to flirt with her in a way that wasn't obvious and was vaguely under the guise of the contract. But at this point, I was losing confidence in my ability to win Maggie over, so I needed to call in reinforcements.

> Me: SOS
>
> Adam: What now?
>
> Jamil: On my way.
>
> Adam: Dammit. Fine. I'm coming.

A minute later, a knock sounded on my hotel room door. I pushed off my bed and went to open the door, revealing Jamil and a grumpy-looking Adam. Jamil slipped past me while Adam looked me up and down, his eyes narrowed.

"What'd you mess up now?" he asked as he followed me inside.

"I need help with Maggie," I told them as they found seats, giving me room to pace in front of them.

"What do you mean you need help?" Jamil asked. "You guys kissed last night! That's what I call progress."

"It was scripted," I told him. "And now I think she's regretting getting into this contract with me."

"What contract?" Adam asked, his brows drawing together. I was tired of keeping this charade up with my friends. It was tiring enough to remember that this whole thing was supposed to be fake. The lines were starting to blur between what was real and what it was I wanted.

"Monica forced us to have a PR relationship after that photo came out of the two of us."

"And you've fallen for her," Adam concluded, like an old sage. "So what? You need help wooing her again?"

"Who says the word *woo*?" Jamil looked over at Adam, concerned. "You sound like you're eighty."

Adam looked over at Jamil, unconcerned.

"So what do you guys think I should do?" I pressed, trying to bring them back to the problem at hand. "She asked me to hang out with her and Olivia tomorrow. Olivia wants to get to know me."

"Does Olivia not know?" Jamil asked.

"I don't think Maggie has told her."

"Treat her how you want to without any of the expectations of the two of you delivering a show," Adam interjected. "You've got to treat her tomorrow like she's your real girlfriend. There aren't going to be any paparazzi. Just other people. So, if you act like her boyfriend there, she may start to wonder why."

Jamil and I both looked over at Adam in wonder. It was so simple, yet so perfect. If I treated Maggie exactly like how I wanted to treat her without any cameras around, it had to catch her attention.

"How'd you come up with that?" Jamil asked, obviously thinking the same thing I was.

"I am the only one of us that's married, so I think I know a little bit about the art of dating a woman." Adam cocked an eyebrow at us, daring me or Jamil to say otherwise. "And if I'm being honest, you had me fooled that this whole thing is fake. And maybe Maggie is regretting being in the contract, but I don't think she regrets being around *you*. I've seen the way she looks at you."

I must have sat there with my mouth hanging open too long for Adam because he continued on. "I haven't seen Maggie's face light up with anyone like it does when she's with you. The circumstances surrounding you guys may not be normal or ideal, but I'm a firm believer that everything happens for a reason. There was a reason the two of you have been linked, and in my eyes, it's more than just a PR circus that has brought you two together."

Maggie and I had only known each other for just over a week, but it felt like a lifetime. I was finding myself changing my priorities, shifting my free time over the last week to spending time with Maggie. Everything around us had felt like it was happening at warp speed, but when it was just the two of us—those moments felt like they could stretch on forever. Adam might have been right—there was a reason the two of us had been twisted together. I might not have known what that reason was, but what I did know was that I felt myself wanting to *be* better and *do* better when I was around her. All my past mistakes—the drugs, the alcohol, the women—felt like a different person's. That moment in the office when Monica suggested this PR relationship was the worst day of my life and the best day of life crashing into one.

"Let us know how it goes," Adam added as he stood up, patting my shoulder as he walked toward the door. Jamil followed him, giving me a quick thumbs-up and an encouraging smile.

Never in my life had I felt this unsure of what to do with a woman. Most of my previous relationships were so easy. I didn't have to do anything because they wanted to be with me for the clout. Now I was faced with a woman that I actually wanted to be with, and I felt like I was treading in unknown waters, unsure of where the sharks were that would eat me the moment I made a wrong move. Every part of me wanted to stay afloat when it came to Maggie. After all of the shit I had done in my life, fate was finally giving me an opportunity at something good and testing to see if I was going to fuck this up too.

MAGGIE

The game against San Francisco had been postponed a day due to the gray clouds that blanketed the city, spewing raindrops on and off throughout the morning. Olivia had texted me asking if we were going to go to the pier earlier since we had planned to go that night after the game. She had continued by telling me that she wasn't scared of a little rain as long as "Pretty Boy" wasn't. So, despite having avoided him since our conversation the previous day, I sent Tommy a message.

> Me: Olivia wants to head to the pier earlier.
> You free?

I tried to ignore the way my heart pounded nervously as I waited for his response. Or the way my throat constricted at the thought of him taking back his earlier decision to go on this excursion with us. I knew that if I acknowledged the way I was feeling about a simple text message, I had bigger problems on my hands. My phone was a ticking time bomb that had a sensitive fuse, so I left it on my bed and started to pace my hotel room. I debated heading down to the lobby for an early lunch or walking to the coffee shop next door to grab something, anything to take my mind off the shortstop with blue eyes that had begun to stain every part of my thoughts like a spilled inkwell. The ding of my phone provided only a brief moment of distraction before the very person I was desperate to expel from my mind became the center of focus.

> Tommy: Meet you in the lobby in ten?

> Me: See you then!

The feeling that spread through my body when Tommy's name had appeared on my screen was almost euphoric. Everything tingled all the way down to my toes as I stared at our conversation a moment longer before I sent Olivia a message.

> Me: Meet you in the lobby in five. Be there or be square.

> Olivia: I could never be square.

A smile spread across my face at Olivia's response. To say that today would be interesting was putting it lightly. I was terrified that Olivia would sniff out the lie that was Tommy's and my relationship. But I was more terrified that Olivia would completely steamroll Tommy today as she grilled him, because I knew she was going to grill him.

Tommy was already down in the lobby when I walked in, much to my surprise. He was dressed down today in a pair of white shorts and a light blue button-down, an umbrella dangling from his wrist. I knew without even having to look that the blue of his shirt would complement his eyes because those eyes had been haunting my thoughts for days. He stood up from the chair he had been lounging in when he saw me. I couldn't help but notice the way his eyes lit up as he looked at me, and a small part of me wished that he could look at me like that for real.

"Olivia coming?" he asked me once I was standing in front of him.

"She should be down soon."

The energy that radiated off Tommy felt like something much more than a fake relationship, but I had to continue to remind myself that it could never be more than that. Because the moment I let myself believe that the energy between Tommy and me was something more, all of this would crumble around me. All of my fears would be confirmed that I wasn't meant to find happiness after Luke.

That he was my one and only.

My life's soulmate.

Before I could think anything more on the topic, Olivia came bounding into the lobby with the biggest smile on her face. "It's about damn time that this happened."

She slung her arms around Tommy's and my waists before she started walking us toward the door. Tommy looked down at me over the top of Olivia's head, his eyes widening in what I was sure was fear.

Oh yeah, Tommy. You should probably be very afraid.

We called an Uber to take us to the pier, and when it showed up it was already packed with people even as the sky dropped rain down on us. Neither Tommy nor I had planned for this to be a public appearance, but it seemed like that would be unavoidable if any fans took pictures of us. At the very least there wouldn't be any paparazzi.

Even though the sky was gray and the sun was nowhere in sight, the pier looked magical. Every building was a different color. They brought light to the otherwise dreary day. Olivia and I huddled close to Tommy as he held the umbrella high over our heads. As the rain came down harder, Olivia pulled the three of us into the first store she saw, a gift shop, to duck out of the rain. She disappeared around a display as soon as we crossed the threshold, leaving me and Tommy alone. After being her friend for a few years, I knew what she was doing. She was giving Tommy time to get comfortable around her before she pounced.

I walked over to a display full of shells and sand, allowing Tommy to trail after me. It was like we played a dance around the shop. One of us moved and the other moved closer from wherever they were in the store, like we were each one side of a rubber band. When one side stretched too far, the other would snap back within reasonable range.

The two of us were biding time until Olivia was ready to steer the day in the direction she wanted it to go. As Olivia went to wait in the checkout line, my eyes were drawn to a rack of postcards in the corner. My fingers reached out and brushed over the pictures as my eyes dissected each detail of the shot.

"Do you collect?" Tommy was hovering over my shoulder, inches behind me.

"I do."

"To keep track of the places you've been?" he asked. I shook my head, my eyes locked on the shot of the city I was looking at. The photographer had perfectly captured the way the sun bathed the buildings in a soft, golden glow. The shadows stretched long in the photos and were complemented by the way the sun hit the bay.

"For the picture." I flashed him a cheeky smile over my shoulder. It was probably the last thing that he had expected me to say. Tommy's arm reached around me as he grabbed the postcard I had been looking at from the rack before turning to head toward the counter.

"What are you doing?" I called after him.

"It's something you want," Tommy replied simply as he laid the postcard down on the counter for the cashier.

"I never said I wanted it." I watched as he handed over his credit card to pay for the postcard.

"I could tell by the way you were looking at it."

"What do you mean?"

"It was the same way you looked at that piece of pizza from Southside." The smile that broke across my face felt like it was going to split it in half.

"I'd say that is a fair comparison." The two of us went to exit the shop together to find Olivia. Tommy slipped his hand in mine as we weaved back through the displays and out into the rainy day once again. That simple gesture made a small avalanche erupt within my chest. It was one thing for Tommy to grab my hand when there were obviously paparazzi there to take our photos, but out on the pier there was no guarantee anyone even noticed us. It felt more intimate than any other time we'd ever held hands. Like this time was for the two of us and not for the cameras.

My mind flashed back to the previous night, and I remembered how Tommy had wanted to consume me with that kiss. The passion behind that kiss would have fooled me if I hadn't known it was for show, and now as we walked through this public place without a care in the world, it was hard to believe that Tommy's hand in mine meant nothing.

Olivia was waiting for us outside the gift shop, an ice cream cone in her hands.

"You already found ice cream?" I laughed at my best friend. Ice cream was her kryptonite. If I wanted anything from Olivia, all I had to do was bribe her with Moose Tracks and I knew she'd be there.

"Is that a serious question?" Olivia asked me as she licked her cone. I rolled my eyes before I linked my arm through hers. Tommy trailed along on the other side of Olivia, his eyes drifting lazily over the crowd.

"So, Tommy," Olivia drew out.

Here we go.

"What are your intentions with my best friend?" I tried to keep myself from staring at Tommy as I waited for his response, but Olivia had other ideas. She turned around to face him directly, walking backward through the crowd and blindly trusting that she wasn't going to hit anything. It was the most perfect depiction of Olivia as a person, barreling down a crowded pier while hoping she didn't crash into anything or anyone.

Tommy took Olivia's interrogation in stride. His eyes slid over to me before he began his response. "Well, Olivia, I want to date your friend."

"Why?" Olivia questioned. I gave my friend a look that said, *what the hell?* Because did I honestly want to hear Tommy tell her some lie to help sell this whole fake relationship? Part of me knew that as soon as I heard Tommy make something up that held no true meaning behind it, a crack would appear in my heart.

That alone should have scared me. I had sworn off dating after Luke and had believed that if I ever opened my heart up to someone again, I would only be disappointed. But something inside me was changing. I was beginning to care more about the way my heart felt when I was around Tommy than the possibility of him breaking it.

Tommy paused again before he answered, his eyes glancing back over at me. My palms began to sweat as I waited to hear what he would say.

"Have you ever met someone that is the complete opposite of everything you've ever looked for in a person?" My brow furrowed at Tommy's question. That was not the grand romantic response that I had been expecting him to give Olivia.

"Not particularly," Olivia replied.

"Well, for me, every person I've ever dated before was the same. They loved partying, found dating to be a status symbol, and really only wanted to be seen in pictures with me because of what I did for a living. They fit perfectly into the lifestyle I was living at the time." I was waiting on pins and needles to hear what Tommy was going to say next.

"None of those girls had ever shown any interest in who I was outside of the uniform. They wanted nothing from me but free tickets to games and expensive dinners. When I met Maggie, I saw a girl that wasn't impressed by expensive dinners or free tickets. She already has the best seat in the house and prefers getting a slice of pizza over caviar. She would rather have a glass of wine at home with a good romance movie than a night out. And every time I look in her eyes, I feel like I'm being transported somewhere magical where only Maggie Redford has been. She is everything I'm not used to looking for, but I realize she is exactly what I need."

My mouth grew drier the more he spoke. It wasn't that Tommy hadn't sold the bit. It was almost like he had sold the bit too well. He hadn't given Olivia some cheesy romantic speech about how when he first saw me he knew I was the one. Instead, Tommy had given my best friend a list of things he had come to know about me. Things he had taken the time to file away in a folder marked "Maggie." My heart was beating as fast as a prize racehorse coming around the final bend of the track. The small voice in my head was shouting at me about the reason that Tommy and I were even in this mess in the first place, but it was like my heart was slamming the door and silencing that voice as I watched him.

Tommy continued to hold eye contact with Olivia, but I couldn't pull my eyes away from his face. I was searching for something in his expression that would tell me he was observant and a very good actor and that none of those things he said had meant anything. All I saw was the same passionate look that he had on his face when he talked about the sport he loved, baseball. Olivia stopped walking.

"Are you going to break her heart?" My gaze shifted from Olivia's face to Tommy's. Olivia narrowed her eyes at him as if she were trying to find something off with Tommy's response.

"I never want to hurt Maggie." Tommy looked at Olivia first and then me, like he was trying to reassure not only Olivia but me about his intentions.

Olivia seemed to be satisfied with Tommy's answer because she flipped back around and started walking toward the edge of the pier. My mind was racing a million miles a minute as I tried to understand what Tommy had said. Did he really mean all of that? It was like a reel was set on a movie projector in my head, showing all of the moments we had spent together so far. The two of us had been forced into this precarious situation that normal people would never find themselves in, and it was like it had bonded us closer than we'd originally realized.

"Look!" Olivia shouted, pulling me out of my internal think session. She was pointing at the docks off the pier. They were covered in sea lions.

I fumbled for my purse, wanting to capture the moment. All I had was my phone, but it would have to do. My eyes scanned the scene, trying to determine the best angle before I lined up my phone for the shot.

When I pulled the phone down to study the picture, I could feel Tommy hovering over my shoulder. "Perfect."

I glanced up to see him staring down at me. My heart was in my throat. I was in serious trouble.

———

Later that afternoon, Tommy walked me back to my hotel room. Olivia had wandered back to her own, leaving the two of us alone. Neither of us wanted the day to end, which could be seen in the slow walk we took down the hallway toward my room.

"Can we talk about the other night?" Tommy asked me after a moment. The question took me by surprise. We had successfully avoided that conversation all day as we ran around in the rain and enjoyed ourselves. I thought we had both decided to move on.

"What about it?"

"The kiss."

My hand froze with my key card in it. I had come to realize that

Tommy wasn't the type to beat around the bush, but I was still caught off guard every time it happened. "What about it?"

Tommy stared at me in silence for a few moments, like he was trying to read what my thoughts were on the matter before he shared his own. After what he had said to Olivia earlier today, I was curious to see if he was bringing it up only to tell me that the passion I had imagined behind that kiss was real.

"I'm sorry that had to happen." That was the exact opposite of what I had been expecting. Each word was a knife to my chest. I felt embarrassment flush through me at the fact that I had thought that kiss had meant anything. How could I have forgotten about our contract? We had outlined what was allowed in this fake relationship at the start. Kissing had been a part of that on a to-be-determined level, and when we were pushed by the person behind the contract we had signed, it was suddenly on the table. I had been caught squarely in the category of the fool.

"It's part of all of this." I was trying my best to play nonchalance, but I wasn't sure it was working. Tommy stayed quiet as he studied my face with that same expression that felt like he could see past all my walls.

The two of us seemed to stare at each other for hours, something thick growing in the air between us, and the way that Tommy was looking at me had a little voice inside my head screaming, *Leave, leave! Before this gets complicated.*

But my feet felt like they had been encased in concrete and there was very little chance I would actually be escaping this situation. I wasn't sure who made the first move, but I blinked and then Tommy's hands were on my waist while mine were buried in his hair. A small moan passed my lips as he pressed me back against my hotel room door and then the thoughts started. The questions of what this meant for us moving forward.

Did this mean there was something happening between us?

I couldn't deny the connection we had. It felt like this invisible string that was pulling us toward each other was live with electricity, setting my nerves on edge.

All of the feelings that I had thought were dormant or doomed to never be felt again after Luke were exploding through my body as

Tommy's fingers pressed into my hips, his hands hungrily grabbing for more. His tongue parted my lips and the taste that I had experienced the night before, the taste I was now going to remember as purely Tommy, exploded in my mouth. The key card slipped from my hand, making a soft *thud* as it hit the carpet.

My hands danced down his shoulders and fisted themselves in his shirt, needing to feel rooted to something, anything, or I was sure that I would melt into a puddle at his feet. Tommy's lips pulled away from mine before leaving kisses along my neck, on my jaw, anywhere he could find purchase.

His hands brushed across my chest, sending pleasure down my spine, and I let my hands sweep down the hard planes of muscle on his stomach before slipping them past the hem of his shirt.

In one swift movement, Tommy's hands gripped the backs of my thighs as he lifted me up into his arms. He bent down while supporting me to pick up the forgotten key card before swiping it and pushing open my hotel room, taking whatever was happening inside, away from the possibility of someone walking up on us.

Tommy carried me farther into the room, stopping when he got to his destination. He slowly lowered me onto the bed but stayed standing when my back hit the soft down comforter. I was left staring up at him as he looked down at me, wondering what was happening.

"You okay?" I asked, my voice coming out in a squeak from the chain of events that had taken place. Tommy continued to stare at me before he shook his head like he was clearing his thoughts.

"Kissing you again has been on my mind every minute since last night." Tommy reached a hand out and let his fingers graze my thigh, causing a shiver to run through my body. Even though part of my brain was fully aware of what he was saying, my heart didn't want to believe it.

"What are you saying?"

"I'm saying that I haven't been able to stop thinking about you." Tommy's eyes looked like the brightest blue sky on a summer day as he stared down at me. I was beginning to understand what the movies meant when the main character said they could get lost looking into someone's eyes, because right then I could stare into Tommy's indefinitely.

When I didn't reply right away, Tommy took a step back, taking my silence as opposition to what he had said. I sat up quickly and reached for his hand to grab him before he got too far away.

"No," I told him. "Stay."

I didn't think I could string coherent words together to tell him he'd been on my mind since the first moment I'd met him, so I tugged on his hand instead to pull him back toward the bed.

"We don't have to do anything," I said softly. "Just stay."

Tommy climbed onto the bed next to me and the two of us scooted all the way until our heads were resting against the headboard. I grabbed the remote off the nightstand and thumbed through the channels until the perfect movie flashed across the screen: *When Harry Met Sally*. I tossed the remote to the side and snuggled farther into the bed, trying to ignore the giant elephant in the room that neither Tommy nor I were mentioning.

"Do you only watch romance movies?" Tommy asked as he settled down next to me. His hand brushed against mine, and it sent little sparks of excitement through me, making me feel like I was on my first date.

"They're my favorite," I told him as I lifted my pinkie to lay over the top of his.

"I think they're starting to become mine," he replied.

I turned my head to look over at him and he did the same, both of us ignoring the movie. Tommy stared at me with a goofy grin on his face before he slid his hand over the top of mine, encasing it with his.

MAGGIE

The air had grown warmer the week we arrived back in Chicago. It was like the weather was even reflecting what had happened between me and Tommy. We still hadn't addressed the kiss we shared when there were no cameras around, but that didn't stop the two of us from passing looks at each other or reaching out to give the other a fleeting touch during our travel day back. It felt as if the dynamic between us had changed completely and the rules that had been there before were now gone, leaving us to try to find the new outline for whatever we were becoming.

But the safety of our time away quickly faded the moment we walked back into the stadium. May was waiting for me inside the gate of the employee parking lot like she was ready to pounce the second I walked inside. And pounce was exactly what she did. She wrapped an arm around my shoulder and began to steer me toward the elevators that led to the C-suite.

My entire body deflated on the elevator ride up. The last time I had ridden this elevator, my life had been forever changed. I was beginning to like the path my life had started on, and I was really hoping this visit with Monica wouldn't change it again.

"Before we go in," May yanked me to a stop just outside the confer-ence room, "Monica wanted me to give this to you."

She handed me a white envelope. My name was scrawled across it. My fingers slipped underneath the seal to tear it open. Inside was a pay stub with a check attached. My eyebrows pulled together in confusion. I wasn't due for a check for another week.

"What is this?"

"Your advance for the agreement," May told me. My eyes snapped back down to the pay stub that detailed the payment for "team publicity."

My stomach dropped, and when I glanced back up, May's encour-aging smile felt like a joke. When I first agreed to this entire thing, the money had sounded like a nice perk. But now, with the check in my hands, all I wanted to do was rip it up.

"Come on," May gestured toward the conference room. "They're all waiting for us."

I pushed the guilt bubbling in my stomach down as I followed her. It was exactly like the first time I had walked into the conference room. Everyone was already there when May and I walked in. Tommy was sitting in the same spot, except this time he looked less defeated than before. His eyes tracked me as I walked in, a question in them like he was trying to make sure I was okay. Monica drew both of our attention away from each other before I could try to answer him.

"There are my two lovebirds!" My body tensed with fear at Monica knowing that something more was happening between us. But I pushed that thought aside as she continued, "You guys are doing such a wonderful job. The talk surrounding Tommy has been much better these past few weeks. It even seems like they're turning over a new leaf when it comes to what they think about Tommy."

I glanced away from Monica to look at Tommy. His eyes were already on mine.

"We want you two to attend the ESPYS together. Walk the red carpet, look truly in love. We think it will really seal the deal for the media on your relationship."

It wasn't the worst thing that Monica could have said. We had already done a red carpet event together. That wasn't anything new. But from the look on Tommy's face, it was something completely new for him. He looked like he had swallowed something sour, and as soon as Monica told us that was all she wanted to see us for, he left the room like a bat out of hell.

My chair screeched as I raced after him. He was jamming his finger into the button to close the elevator door when I slipped through, like someone had flipped the script from the first meeting. Tommy let out a sigh as soon as I stopped next to him.

"What?" I asked him, feeling like I was wading through uncharted waters with this new side of him that I hadn't seen.

"It's nothing," Tommy replied, his eyes firmly on his shoes.

"It's clearly not nothing."

When Tommy decided to stay silent, I reached out and pushed the emergency stop button on the wall in front of us. He startled as the elevator jerked to a stop. His hand thrust out to steady himself against the wall, but I didn't have the forethought to do such a thing, so I went flying straight into his chest.

"Ow!" I groaned as my nose bent at an awkward angle. Tommy's arm wrapped around my waist before I went bouncing away from him. The two of us froze as our eyes locked, almost exactly like one of the romance movies I liked to watch. Tommy cleared his throat before he let me go and took a small step away from me to give us room.

"What are you doing, Maggie?" Tommy asked, almost on a sigh.

"I don't know," I admitted, turning to pace toward the other side of the elevator. "You were running away and you wouldn't talk to me, so I had to do something."

"Like shutting down the elevator?"

"It felt like the right thing to do." I wrapped my arms around myself as my mind began to outpace me. "I want you to talk to me."

Tommy watched me from across the elevator, like he was weighing if he actually wanted to give in and tell me what he was wrestling with inside. After a moment, the tension in him seemed to release like a dam.

"I haven't been back to an event like that since before."

"Before what?" I pressed.

"Before I changed."

"Changed?"

I took a few steps closer to him, nervous that if I moved too fast I would spook him. He looked at me as I drew near and didn't speak again until I was back inches from him.

"Just over a year ago, I had a bit of a bender. I got behind the wheel of a car and drove myself home with absolutely no recollection of doing so the next day. I had never hated myself more. It was so unlike me that it made me rethink everything I had been doing. I stopped drinking more than a glass and only when I went out, and I stopped hanging around all the people that had been in my life at that time." Tommy looked away from me then, like he couldn't bear to see what I would think of him. "I could have killed someone that night."

———

"Do you think your mom made her oatmeal cookies?" Luke asked me from the passenger seat. We were on our way to my parents' house for dinner to celebrate the start of our senior year and our engagement. I didn't want to tell him that my mom had made about six dozen oatmeal cookies for Luke or she would kill me.

"We'll find out," I told him, glancing over.

"Are you still good to go to the party on Saturday?"

"Sure." This time, I turned my head all the way to look over at the beautiful man next to me. His smile set off fireworks inside me every time I saw it, and I would do anything in the world to keep seeing it, even if that meant going to a party I didn't really want to be at. I kept my gaze on him for a moment longer, thinking I'm so in love with this man.

Then I heard the screech of tires. I snapped my head back to the road only to be blinded by lights that I realized were coming right at us.

"Maggie!"

And then everything went black.

———

"Maggie?"

I blinked when I realized that someone had said my name. When the world came back into focus, I was staring up into Tommy's face.

"Where'd you go there?"

"What?" I asked as my body finally returned to normal. My heart had been racing and my breathing had gone shallow as I remembered the night that had changed everything for me.

"You went somewhere just now." Tommy's hands were moving up and down my arms, and I looked at them, realizing that they had probably been there for a minute or two.

"It was nothing." I reached out to push the button and the elevator jerked back into motion. Tommy started to argue with me, but the doors opened and I practically ran out of them to avoid whatever it was he was going to say.

He was hot on my heels as I started to head back toward the employee parking lot. My legs were no match for Tommy's long legs, however, and soon he was walking in pace next to me, his head swiveling around the parking lot.

"Which one is yours?"

"I don't have a car," I mumbled, trying to outrun the memory I had experienced.

"What do you mean you don't have a car?" Tommy wasn't going to let me shake him off.

"I don't have a car." I spoke a little firmer as I walked out of the parking lot to stop next to the bus stop. Tommy's eyes swiveled between me and the sign before he pulled his keys out of his pocket.

"Where are you going?"

My eyes drifted closed as I let out a slow breath. None of this was Tommy's fault. It wasn't like he was behind the wheel that night. He was on the other side of the country. The person who should feel at fault was me. I was the one who actually had killed someone.

"Maggie . . ." Tommy's voice had dropped to a whisper as he tried to keep me from drifting away again. My eyes slowly rose to meet his. If I wanted to avoid telling him what was going on in my head, I had one option.

"You want to take me where I'm going?" I asked.

"Yes. I don't want you to have to ride the bus."

"Then you're coming with me to see my parents." Without waiting for Tommy's response, I turned on my heel and walked toward the player parking lot where his car would be parked.

Tommy stayed quiet as we got inside his car, and I wanted to kiss him for it. I most definitely did not want to tell him about that part of my life yet. The only time we spoke was when he asked me for my parents' address, and then the rest of the ride was filled with the music from the speakers of his car.

The moment we turned down that familiar street, I felt all of the emotions I had been feeling slowly leave my body. It was like no matter what happened, home would always be a safe place. Tommy's eyes took in the wraparound porch and the old swing. I could see him imagining a younger version of myself walking up those very steps in front of us.

"Come on," I told him as I pushed out of his car.

He followed me up the stairs of my childhood home with his hands deep in his pockets as his eyes roamed everywhere, taking in every detail. My mom was in the kitchen, and my dad was nowhere to be found when we walked into the foyer.

It was as if I were looking at all of my mom's decorations for the first time as my eyes scanned for anything embarrassing that Tommy would see.

"Maggie?" my mom called from the kitchen. Whatever she was cooking smelled amazing.

"I'm coming," I yelled back, motioning for Tommy to follow me.

When I rounded the corner with Tommy in tow, my mom's eyes widened in surprise before she schooled her face like the sweet woman that she is. Her apron was covered in flour, and the smell coming from the oven was lasagna.

"Well, hello!" My mom smiled warmly at Tommy as she wiped her hands off and reached out to wrap him in a hug. "I'm Cindy."

"Tommy," he told her as he pulled away from the hug.

"I'm so happy you're joining us." The smile on my mom's face said everything. I was sure she felt that she'd never see the day when I brought someone home again, and quite honestly, I thought that day would never happen again as well. "Food will be ready in fifteen minutes. Can I get you two anything in the meantime?"

"I'm okay. Thank you, Mrs. Redford."

"Please, call me Cindy." My mom waved Tommy's formality off. "Mrs. Redford is Richard's mom. And speaking of your father, he's upstairs taking a shower. I'm sure he will be quite surprised when he comes down."

I held back a smile at my mom's subtle jab in my direction for springing Tommy Mikals on the two of them without any warning. She would be pestering me for days after this, I was sure.

"I have a few things to finish up in the kitchen. Why don't you two go ahead into the living room. I'll meet you there in a minute." I gestured for Tommy to follow me over toward the couches, wanting nothing more than to sink into the corner of my parents' sectional and close my eyes until the food was ready. Tommy had other ideas though.

Instead of taking a seat on the couch next to me, he slowly took a turn around the room. His eyes roamed the framed pictures on the walls and my mom's paintings. He stopped to look at a photo my dad had taken of me when I still played softball in high school. Tommy gave me a curious glance over his shoulder before he moved to the next one. It was a painting my mom had done, and her signature was in the bottom corner.

"Your mom paints?"

"Oh yes. She hasn't put anything in a gallery recently, but you'll see a ton of her paintings all over the house." Tommy started to move toward the shelves on the other side of the room before he stopped in midstep, his eyes zeroing in on something. His body blocked whatever it was he was looking at on the mantel, but I was waiting for him to make a comment on the picture of me in the Belle costume from the second grade.

"You have a fiancé?" My blood froze as I realized which picture Tommy was looking at. It seemed like all the events of today were leading up to this moment. The two of us stared at each other, Luke's face right over Tommy's shoulder in the picture behind him.

"I did," I replied. "I don't anymore, and I'm not sure there is much else to say."

It felt like we were in a standoff as Tommy weighed whether he should push the subject or not. He must have read something on my face that told him not to because he nodded and continued to move on to the next set of bookshelves. I let out a breath, full of pent-up energy I didn't know I had been holding inside me as soon as Tommy's back was turned.

If something between the two of us evolved into more than a fake relationship, I knew I would have to tell him about Luke. But today would not be the day. I was more confused about where Tommy and I stood today than I had been before the night we watched romance movies in the hotel in California. Before I shared with him one of the more intimate moments of my life, I was going to need some clarity on what we were.

Moments later, my father walked into the room to stir the metaphorical spoon on the awkward soup that was occurring in my parents' house.

"Tommy Mikals?" he shrieked, like a teenage girl seeing her favorite boy band member for the first time. My mouth dropped open at the sheer audacity he had to not control himself.

Bless Tommy, because he took it like a champ. "You must be Mr. Redford."

That was the last awkward-parent moment of the visit, thankfully. Tommy chatted with my parents and had them both won over by the end of the meal. I caught my mom giving me approving looks while my father had Tommy's ear.

As I stared across the table at Tommy, thinking about how the world brought the two of us together, a little piece of me dared to hope that this would last. Because sitting around the table with him and my parents felt normal, and I was craving a little normal.

MAGGIE

"And with that strikeout, folks," the announcer's voice boomed over the speakers in the stadium, "Adam Steel has sat down his eleventh batter of the night."

"He's unreal tonight." Tommy came up beside me to lean on the dugout fence.

Tonight's game was a chance for some of the rookies to prove themselves to the managers. We were playing a weaker team, and it hadn't been intended for Adam to throw this long, but after the seventh strikeout, the coaches decided to keep him in to let him have his moment. It was one of my favorite times to be a photographer capturing history.

"Unreal," I agreed.

"Want to go to another pier with me tonight?" I bit down on a smile, nodding in response. I felt like a teenage girl with her first crush around Tommy, like my emotions were going haywire.

"What's with you and piers?" I asked, trying my hand at being coy.

"The view." Tommy looked at me then like I was the only important thing happening in that moment.

"The view of what?"

"You'll see." The only thing keeping me from getting frustrated with another surprise was the look on Tommy's face. He looked happy.

It was lightyears away from the man I had seen in that conference room weeks ago.

Over the past week, Tommy and I had been wrapped up in the season. It was one of the busier weeks in the schedule this year, and our lives had been firmly attached to a ballpark across the country. Tommy had played in every single game, with tonight's game being the first time he'd been given time off.

Our interactions had been limited to conversations at the field and text messages, talking about different articles that had been posted about us. There were photos trending of us with Olivia at the pier in San Francisco and photos that fans had grabbed of us deep in conversation at various games. People had coined ship names for us and were calling the public storyline of our "love story" as one for the ages.

My personal favorite ship name was "Taggie," while Tommy continued to jokingly find a way to use "Mommy" in all our conversations.

It was overwhelming to watch. People I had never met in my life were passing judgment on the relationship that they could see publicly. I had debated deleting my social media accounts multiple times, and I would have if it weren't for another stipulation from Monica, asking us to post pictures we had taken on our dates. So I had to stay firmly plugged into the madness.

Because of our busy schedules between the game that we both loved and the other duties as assigned from the Cougars, neither of us had brought up what was happening with us. The chemistry that I had felt from the first day we met seemed like it was at its highest.

My emotions had never been more confused, but I would be lying if I said I didn't enjoy the casual flirting that happened in the dugout or the constant stream of texts full of funny videos, memes, and GIFs.

In the span of a month, Tommy had become one of the most important people in my life. My relationship with him was different from my relationship with Olivia. Olivia and I might be best friends, but there was a different level of intimacy to my relationship with Tommy.

The roar of the crowd brought me back to the present. Adam had struck out his twelfth batter of the night, solidifying his spot in the

Chicago Cougars' records book. Tommy cheered next to me, his hands lifted over his head in celebration.

"He did it!" Tommy screamed before he grabbed me by the shoulders to shake me. I laughed, feeling like his excitement was intoxicating.

"Go!" I motioned toward his teammates running out of the dugout to congratulate Adam on his walk off the mound. Tommy took off to celebrate with his teammates. The pictures I snapped were some of my favorite kind to take. When there was so much joy on everyone's face. It was the best emotion to capture in an image.

Jamil and Tommy had their arms wrapped around Adam as they tried to strangle him in a hug. Adam was laughing as he tried to swat them away. It warmed my heart to see Tommy finding some happiness with his teammates. I wanted nothing more than for him to have more moments like tonight where he was overwhelmed with so much joy; with the hope that moments like this would replace all of the bad ones that plagued his mind.

It was an odd feeling when someone who was once a stranger had become so important to you that you cared about their level of happiness. Maybe it was because the smile on Tommy's face whenever he was as happy as he was now did something funny to my heart. Maybe it was purely selfish, but all that I cared about in that moment was seeing more of that smile.

———

The view that Tommy had talked about at the game was of the city and Lake Michigan from the top of the Ferris wheel on Navy Pier. The last time I had ridden the Ferris wheel, I was in the fifth grade and we had come to Navy Pier for a field trip. I remember how the city looked so massive, so grand from the top at that age. Now, it was still breathtaking, but the world looked a little more manageable than before.

Tommy and I walked down the pier completely unnoticed. It felt nice, like it was a date just for the two of us. That feeling stayed with us as our carriage gave us the perfect few moments without any cameras or any expectations. With only Tommy and me in the carriage, it was like we were the only two people in the entire city. The silence stretched out between us like a comfortable blanket. Within the past few weeks, Tommy and I had grown from strangers into people that looked forward to talking to each other every day.

I leaned over toward him as the Ferris wheel began to descend and rested my head on his shoulder. Tommy's arm went to snake around me, and for a moment, I could pretend that maybe we were something more.

"I've been thinking we need to do this more," Tommy said, shaking me out of my daydream of the two of us coming back to ride this very Ferris wheel every year.

"Do what more?"

"Go out. Just the two of us." His hand squeezed my shoulder, pulling me even closer to him if it were possible. Then his free hand slipped under my chin and raised my lips to meet his. I was sure my heart would explode from all the emotions pumping through it. My words felt like they might fail me, so I nodded my head. That foreign feeling of hope was growing inside my chest, and it scared me that all of this could come crashing down around me.

Tommy hadn't said anything that blatantly confirmed what we were. He had simply stated that he wanted to go on more dates with just the two of us. I wasn't sure if he meant something more than what our contract stated our fake relationship was or only on dates that weren't planned by Monica. Sure, we were currently on a date as just the two of us. But there were plenty of people around that could take a picture of us and continue the narrative of our online relationship.

So I held on to that feeling of hope inside me a little tighter. I just didn't realize that it would come crashing down around me so soon. As Tommy and I started to make our way back down the pier toward the city, the shouts and flashes started.

"Tommy! Maggie!"

Flash.

"Want to give us another kiss?"

Flash.

"Maggie, what happened with Luke Greenberg?"

Flash.

My blood felt like it had frozen inside my body when my brain finally processed what had been yelled at me. Tommy wrapped his arm tightly around my waist to continue steering me away from the paparazzi. If he hadn't done that, I would have stopped in my tracks, sure to be surrounded by the vultures with cameras.

"Maggie! Does Tommy know about Luke?"

Flash.

I was sure those photographs would be everywhere tomorrow with my distressed face as the focus. The headlines were going to be horrible. I was only hoping that they wouldn't be complete monsters and that they'd leave Luke out of it.

But it seemed the world was only meant to laugh at me today because as Tommy and I entered the safety of his car, my phone rang and my mom's name flashed across the screen.

"Mom?" I asked.

"Oh, honey." My heart sank at the tone of her voice. I didn't even have to ask to know that whatever it was she was about to say wasn't going to be good. "Have you seen it?"

"Seen what?"

There was a pause on the other end that made me grip my phone tighter.

"I'll send it to you." Another pause. "Your dad and I love you, honey. Let us know if you need anything."

My phone buzzed, and I pulled it away from my ear when I heard the click of the line from my mom hanging up. Every part of me wanted to throw my phone out the window instead of opening whatever message was waiting for me. I was faintly aware of Tommy trying to ask me what was wrong as I clicked on the link in my mom's messages, but it was like he was speaking in a tunnel. The article loaded and my heart dropped, my worst fear being confirmed.

The picture must have been taken off my parents' or my social media accounts. It was the same picture that was framed on their mantel. I quickly scanned the article, feeling hotter with every second.

Maggie Redford, a photographer for the Chicago Cougars and recently attached to the Cougars' star shortstop, Tommy Mikals, was previously engaged to Luke Greenberg. The two met their freshman year and were engaged by the end of their junior year. Longtime college friends of the couple tell NewsWeekly *of their insatiable energy for each other. Where one half of the couple was spotted, the other would never be far away. Their love was undeniable, and they both knew they wanted to spend the rest of their lives together early on. However, tragedy struck when Luke passed away in a car accident that had Maggie Redford behind the wheel.*

"Maggie!" Tommy's hand gently laid over the screen, finally drawing my attention to him. "What's going on?"

My eyes danced across his face, taking in the sharp cut of his jawline with the slight stubble that had started to grow in. His blue eyes were a darker hue tonight than normal. The slight crease between his eyebrows showed me how worried he was about me. And the way his body was turned toward me, like if there wasn't a center console between us, he'd hold me forever to protect me from the world.

I started to shake my head, unable to speak the words. I didn't even know where to start. While keeping his eyes on me, he gently pried the phone from my hands and glanced down at the article so he could read it himself. It was ages before he lifted his eyes back to mine again. I was afraid that I would find disgust there when I finally looked into them again, but instead I saw understanding. He was putting the dots together between the picture in my parents' house, my reaction to his question, and this article.

"Maggie, I am so sorry."

The anguish that laced his voice made me realize that he wasn't necessarily apologizing for what had happened, which I was grateful for. Once you hear it about a hundred times, it begins to grate on you. He was apologizing for putting me in a position where the most private parts of my life would be shared with the world.

But I had to remind myself, none of this was only his fault. I had signed that contract willingly. I never thought it would come to this though. Tommy didn't say anything else. He sat with me in the silence of his car, giving me the space I needed to feel ready to speak. It was the most perfect thing he could have done, and I was so thankful for him.

"Can we go back to your place?" I asked once I was sure my voice wouldn't fail me. Tommy immediately put the car in drive and took off down the road. His presence was the only thing keeping me grounded as we drove through the streets of Chicago. The only bright part of that moment was the city lights out the window, slightly blurred in the tears that fell from my eyes.

MAGGIE

Neither of us spoke again until we were inside Tommy's house. He hovered near me as we walked to the couch. I knew he was probably scared I would drop right where I stood, but enough time had passed that I was strong enough to stand on my own two feet. Tommy draped a blanket over my legs after I had curled up in the corner of his couch. He took a seat on the opposite side. Part of me knew he was only giving me space, but the distance was an abyss.

Tommy watched me, his eyes soft. I was beginning to wonder how I had deserved someone like him to walk into my life. It was like life had known what was coming for me this summer and had gifted me someone who was patient and understanding. Someone I didn't deserve. But because of Tommy's patience with me, I knew I owed him an explanation.

The truth was ugly though, and I worried that once Tommy knew it, whatever was happening between us would come to a screeching halt.

"His name was Luke," I started, my fingers playing with the edge of the blanket for comfort. "We met on the first day of our freshman year of college."

Tommy stayed quiet as I finally gave him the part of me that I had been holding back this entire time. His gaze stayed steady and even on me, his patience unwavering. I held on to that steadiness like a life raft as I continued telling him about some of the best and worst moments of my life.

"I'd never dated anyone like him. Everything he did was like living out loud. He wore his emotions on his sleeve, he treated me like I was the most important thing in the world, and he *constantly* pushed me to be better." The tears started, like they always did when I remembered everything he was. "He never did get me to show up anywhere on time, though."

Tommy barked a laugh, and I gave him a grateful smile. He wasn't dumb. He knew something bad had happened between me and Luke; it was the *what* he was waiting for.

"He proposed to me the summer before our senior year. We'd never been happier. My parents invited us over to celebrate our engagement and the start of our senior year at the beginning of August almost four years ago now. We were three streets away—" I choked at the thought. We had been minutes away from walking into my parents' house together that night.

"I looked away from the road for two seconds to peer over at him. He'd been talking about my mom's oatmeal cookies. He loved those stupid cookies. When I looked back . . ." My voice broke off again as I remembered the car lights heading right at us, driving down the wrong side of the road. I squeezed the blanket in my hands as I worked up the courage to continue. "When I looked back at the road, there was a car driving down the wrong side. Right at us. I didn't even have time to react and save us."

I brought my hands up to cover my face as I took deep breaths, trying to stop the flood of tears. Part of me wondered how many more tears I had left to cry in my life. I was sure I'd spent them all already.

"Luke died on impact. I made it out with only a few scrapes." A few more tears fell down my cheeks as the familiar guilt roared to the surface. "How is that even fair?"

Tommy stood up and walked over to my side of the couch, closing the distance between us that had felt like miles moments before. He wrapped me in his arms, and I tried to bury the guilt back down as I huddled closer to him. The air was draping heavier around us as I waited for my tears to dry. Tommy's arms were like armor around me, giving me some of the strength I needed.

"The driver got life in prison. They were drunk." Pain flashed through Tommy's eyes, and I knew he was remembering when he told his story. He must have realized that it could have hit close to home for me because he began to open his mouth like he wanted to apologize.

"It's okay, Tommy." I pulled back so he could see my face to know that I meant it. Tommy's eyes danced between mine as he tried to decide what to do next. He must have come to the conclusion that he believed me and was going to allow me to continue as he stayed quiet. The next truth was the one that weighed the heaviest on my heart.

"I spoke at the visitation, but I couldn't bear to stay for the funeral and watch him be buried. I've never visited his gravestone."

Once the words passed my lips, it felt like a lock had been released off my heart. I had never told anyone that before. It felt wrong of me to still be here when he was buried six feet under dirt, his body being offered up to the worms like a sacrifice for my wrongdoing. I couldn't bear to see his gravestone; it would feel like a final confirmation of what had happened.

"I always wonder if I hadn't been looking at him, maybe I would have seen it coming."

Tommy held on to me. He didn't tell me it wasn't my fault like so many others had. That line always fell on closed ears. He hadn't been there that night and wasn't going to tell me something that could be false just to make me feel better about myself.

"He sounds like he was a great guy," Tommy whispered once my tears had dried.

"He was." That angry beast inside me reached its claws around my throat again, dragging my attention back to that article. "I never wanted this part of my life to be public. It was already so hard living through it the first time, and now the entire world gets to force me to live through it again."

"We'll face it together." My head snapped up, my eyes racing to meet his. It was like everything he was doing was exactly what I needed, and it was so unexpected. I'd rather he do exactly what I didn't need, like everyone else. It would make it so much easier to remind myself of the contract binding us together.

"You don't have to help me with my problems."

"But I want to." One of Tommy's hands came up to brush a piece of hair that had fallen in front of my eyes behind my ear. "Plus, you're not the only one who has a fucked-up past. You're in this mess because of me."

"I'm not sure it's the same thing," I whispered, my eyes dropping away from him.

"It may not be, but both are clearly heavy on each of us." Tommy glanced over the photos on his bookshelves, like he was rethinking every moment of his life. It was my turn to stay quiet as I watched him sort through where he wanted to start. When I imagined finally telling Tommy the truth about Luke, I had no idea it would turn into this.

"I stopped drinking after that night I told you about, but that wasn't the end of my rough patch. I was dating someone at the time that I thought was the love of my life."

I remembered the beautiful model, Sutton James, I had seen on his social media page. Tommy had looked at her like Luke had looked at me, like she was what his world spun around. I thought about how he had left all of those pictures of the two of them up on his page and she had erased him like he had never existed. It was hard to erase someone from your life that you cared that deeply about.

"When I started getting in trouble with San Diego and my contract was on the line, Sutton started to pull away. Later, I realized she was seeing someone else already as a safety net in case I was dumped from the team and couldn't provide her with the same lifestyle." I reached out to squeeze Tommy's arm.

Who would do something like that? Date someone for their money? My stomach dropped as the check May had given me flashed through my mind. Every night I walked through the door of my apartment, I saw that check lying on my kitchen counter. I had yet to do anything with it, the guilt of cashing it too strong. But that didn't stop me from thinking about all the ways that money would change my life for the better. But at what expense? Tommy's trust? Was I no better than Sutton?

A pained look crossed Tommy's face as he remembered one of the lowest moments in his life when all of his decisions had left him with almost nothing. I bottled my own guilt up and pushed it down to evaluate at another time. But a voice in the back of my mind still sang out, *You are no better than she is.*

"The part that still tears me up inside is that I used to think I would forgive all of that if she decided she'd choose me." Tommy dropped his head. "I was so used to her being with me that I was scared to let her go and lose a home we'd built together. Even after I realized that the home we'd built had been made of lies."

The two of us sat in silence again, letting our flaws and baggage sit out on the ground around us, too messy to ever be put away again. Tommy may have been right that our baggage was drastically different, but that still didn't change how heavily it weighed on us individually. We weren't here to compare whose life was the worst. We were two people who desperately needed to unload some of the weight for the first time in a long time and finally found someone who was trustworthy enough.

"So is that why you don't have a car?"

A laugh pushed through my body at Tommy's question. It was so innocent and broke the angry cloud that had been hanging over us. I snuggled back into him, feeling less like I was trying to hide from something and more like I wanted to appreciate the man whose arms were around me.

"It was obviously totaled, and I didn't have the money to replace it at the time, but I also didn't want to drive again after that."

"What about now?" he asked me. His chest vibrated against mine and sent shivers through my body all the way to my toes.

"I've thought about it," I admitted. It would definitely help my problem with being chronically late. I could leave the days of riding the bus behind me forever.

"Would you let me help you?"

I looked over at him like he had told me he wanted to marry me, completely confused and utterly surprised. Tommy's face was genuine as he waited for my answer.

"Like buy me a car?"

"No, just help you get comfortable with driving again," Tommy clarified.

Part of me wondered if I actually had it in me to get behind the wheel again. But a bigger part of me wanted to at least try if Tommy was offering. His presence made me feel the most relaxed I'd been in a while and made me believe that having him in the passenger seat would give me the extra push I'd needed.

"It's a date." I stuck my hand out for him to shake. The biggest smile broke out across his face as he wrapped his hand around mine.

"It's a date."

Tommy

That night after I dropped Maggie back off at her house, I stayed up staring at my profile page. The way Maggie had been so willing to try to move past her fears by letting me help her get comfortable with driving again stirred something inside me. If she could find the courage to push past one of the hardest moments of her life, I felt like I could do the same. We were starting to become a team, after all. If she was going to walk through hell to get out on the other side, I needed to as well.

My finger hovered over the three dots in the upper corner of the first photo I had of Sutton on my page. I hadn't kept them because I had hoped we would get back together. I knew now that I deserved better. I had kept them almost as a sick reminder of how fucked up I had let my life get before. But it was time to move on from that. To let myself fully heal and start fresh.

Without another moment of hesitation, I deleted the photo and all of the others I had of her as well. With each one that disappeared from my screen, I felt lighter, as though each photo had been a weight pressing down on me.

Everyone makes mistakes throughout their life and I was no different, but everyone also deserves a second chance. I never thought I would be deserving of a fresh start. I thought I had laid out the building blocks of what my life would be, but eventually I grew tired of keeping up the charade. With moving to a new city and away from the people that I had surrounded myself with in the past, it felt like I was finally breathing fresh air. Maggie seemed to be a piece of that. Being around her made me realize that I wanted something different for myself, and I was beginning to think it was in the shape of a curly-brown-haired woman.

But if I really wanted to pursue Maggie in the way I wanted, I needed to do this the right way. It was never that I needed to prove to Maggie that I was a different person. She had never looked at me in a way that made me feel broken. I needed to prove to myself that I could be a different person, that I *was* a different person.

I needed to prove to myself that I was worthy of a girl like her.

————

"All of the kids here come from homes below the poverty line in Chicago," the director of the Boys & Girls Clubs told me. "We try our best to provide an after-school meal for them daily, but we don't have enough funding to do it consistently. It's enough to keep the after-school events running."

The director was taking me on a tour of the building, showing me their amenities and what they had to offer the community. It warmed my heart how much they gave with how little they had to give. But what impressed me more was how grateful these kids were to have a proper pair of shoes without any holes or a dinner in their bellies.

It made me hate my old self even more because of how entitled I had acted. However, I was beginning to realize that I needed to let my past go. If I wanted to move toward the person I wanted to be, I had to stop beating myself up over something I could never change. What was done was done. There was nothing I could do to fix that. All I could do was be me and prove to myself that I could live up to the promises I had made to be better.

Chicago was quickly starting to feel like home, and I wanted to give back to a community that had welcomed me with open arms. The Cougar fans hadn't dismissed me when I first showed up in the city.

They had given me a chance, which was all I wanted. I could do something with a chance. Just like all these kids needed was a chance. They just needed someone to give it to them.

"How much funding do you feel like you lack to do the things you really wish to do for these kids?" I asked the director as we watched a group of boys throw a baseball back and forth. The gloves looked old, with rips in the leather. The baseball even looked like it had seen better days.

"Honestly, even ten thousand could do wonders. We would be able to guarantee meals for the next month after school and maybe even replace some of the gear the kids have now."

I watched one of the boys playing catch. When I was his age, I had dreams of playing in the MLB. For him, his biggest dream right now was making sure he was safe and could play catch with his friends. I wanted to give them all the same chances to reach their dreams that I had. Or maybe even dream something bigger for themselves.

"How does a million sound?"

The director sounded like he choked next to me.

"And I plan to make that same donation amount yearly. Will that be enough?"

"Enough? We could do so much with that. We could get new computers and help teach classes that they may lack at their schools. We could equip them enough to maybe even start a team that they could play on. We could guarantee meals for them and even for their families."

The director turned toward me with tears in his eyes. "You would change lives."

"I want to give them the same chances I had. Everyone deserves to have the same chance. Even a few second chances."

"Chicago is extremely lucky you chose to come here," the director continued. "You see, I was nervous having this meeting with you today. I wasn't sure how serious you were about all of this. But now I'm sure you're an angel in disguise."

"I'm no angel," I tell him. "I'm just someone trying to do better every day."

MAGGIE

The roar of the engine and the snores of Olivia provided the background noise for our flight to the East Coast. We had a three-day-long trip to New York City for a series, and the only thing that was on my mind was that with every minute that passed, the closer I was getting to Luke's childhood home. Every year the team traveled to the Big Apple, a quick thought about him would flutter across my brain before leaving like a moth once the light had gone out. I wasn't sure why this year was different, but the thought of being this close to where he grew up was emblazoned on my mind, never far from the surface.

I thought about it all the way from the airport to the hotel, unable to focus on anything else. Even during the game that night, I found myself wondering if his parents were at the game. They were big fans of the New York Reveres. With every picture I took, I scanned the crowd with my camera, like I was going to spot Luke's dad with his oval glasses and wiry hair or his mom with the same eyes as Luke and the warm smile she gave everyone she felt needed one. But none of the faces were familiar and I was left feeling like I was spiraling even more than I ever had been before.

By the end of the game, I was wondering if I was truly going crazy or if something bigger was happening. It was as if Luke had been standing over my shoulder yelling at me from the moment Tommy had kissed me at the Red Cross event. It didn't feel like he was angry because of the kiss, it felt like he was angry that I was letting my past get in the way of somebody that could be my future. I would have expected nothing less from Luke. He probably was tired of watching me put my life on hold for the past four years, locked away in my apartment with my movie collection and cheap wine.

It was strange that I was beginning to think of Tommy as someone that I could have a future with. I had shown him the ugliest parts of myself and he had stuck around, unfazed by my scars. I had expected we'd be closer, after that night we shared those pieces of ourselves with each other. But part of me knew that in order for me to be able to truly let Tommy into my life, I needed to make amends with my past.

"You okay?" Tommy sidled up next to me as we waited to board the bus that would take us back to the hotel. He must have noticed the emotions warring with each other on my face. I was glad he interrupted the mental argument happening within me or I was sure I would have jumped off the deep end.

"Yeah. Of course." It was like my brain went into autopilot and decided to give Tommy my normal response. I watched as Tommy looked at me like he knew better than to believe me.

"Got something on your mind?" he asked as he gestured for me to board the bus first.

"Yeah." I sighed as I claimed one of the seats. Tommy slipped down next to me. Jamil gave the two of us a wink as he walked by. If I hadn't felt weighed down by thoughts of Luke, I would have played along with him. Instead, I let him pass the two of us without a second thought.

"Want to talk about it?"

"Maybe. I think I want a distraction first." I knew in my heart that my mind needed to take a step away from the struggle happening within me to find any clarity or answers.

"Well, it seems you've come to the right place." Tommy gave me a sly smile. "I've got just the thing."

When we arrived back at the hotel, Tommy told me to meet him down in the lobby in fifteen minutes. It gave him enough time for a quick shower and for me to freshen up. Every time I walked out into the lobby to see Tommy waiting for me, it was like I was living some dream that shouldn't belong to me. He turned when he heard me coming, a smile lighting up his face when he saw me. I would never get over that smile. It lit up my insides and filled the parts of me with enough joy that wherever Tommy had planned on taking me felt bearable.

"Are you hungry?" When I was close enough, he offered me his elbow. My hand found its favorite place in the crook of it as the two of us walked toward the front doors.

"Always."

"Pizza okay?" The glint in Tommy's eye told me he knew what my answer was going to be. "I thought we could enter the great Chicago versus New York pizza debate."

"Chicago will win," I told him as we exited into the lively city streets on a mission to find the best New York City pizza. The energy was buzzing among the people out walking around. The air was warmer for the people in the city, and it was like everyone had emerged from hibernation on that very night. It was exactly what I needed to let the voices inside my head die down for a minute.

Tommy and I took turns pointing out different storefronts that looked interesting and guessing how much certain apartments were as we passed them. It was like the two of us had started to carve routines out with each other. When we crossed the street, Tommy always walked on the side of the road that the car was most likely to be coming from if someone were to miss seeing us in the crosswalk. I was physically incapable of walking in a straight line, and whenever I started to drift into Tommy, his arm would snake around my waist to pull me the rest of the way into his side. This easy give and take that we developed felt like the start of a song that I knew would become my favorite on the album.

"What about that one?" Tommy pointed toward a pizzeria with a line coming out the door. It was moving quickly and the place was clearly loved by many. I flashed him a quick smile before I looked both ways and dashed across the street. A holler sounded behind me, which I was sure had come from Tommy as I left him in the dust.

"Nobody said anything about racing!" he called after me as he bounded across the street.

"I like to live by the motto of never letting them know what you're going to do next." I shrugged before I took Tommy's arm again.

"Well, in that case, I feel like I should follow suit. After you, my lady." Tommy opened the door to the pizzeria, bowing as if I really were royalty. I laughed as I skipped through the door to the counter.

We ordered our pizza and took it outside to sit on the curb and people-watch everyone that was walking the streets of New York City. The pizza was completely different from Chicago style. The pie we got was thinner and was the perfect kind to fold over on itself. I grabbed my slice, folded it in half, and brought it up to my mouth to take a bite when I saw Tommy shaking his head at me, just like the first time he saw me do it.

"What?"

"It's sacrilegious to eat pizza like that," he told me as he took a bite of his own slice.

"Don't knock it until you try it."

We continued to pick through our pizza as taxis flew past us and people hurried by to an unknown destination. I knew what was on the other end of the silence that was sitting between us. Tommy waited until I had finished my first slice before he finally voiced the question I knew he was waiting to ask.

"So you want to tell me what was on your mind back at the field?"

I let out a sigh as I realized I couldn't keep these feelings to myself any longer. It wasn't fair to Tommy. I had already opened up to him and started to build that trust between us. If I denied him the opportunity to help me through this moment now, it would only crack the foundation we were building.

"Luke grew up here. Staten Island, to be exact." Tommy wiped his fingers off on a napkin as he gave me his full attention. "I'm not sure why, but the fact that I'm so close to his parents and his childhood home have been weighing heavily on my mind this visit to New York City."

Tommy stayed quiet for a minute, thinking deeply on what I had told him. After a moment, he turned to look at me with one of the most serious looks I had ever seen on his face. "You should go visit them."

"What?"

"You should go visit them." The way he said it was like it was final. The decision had been made and there was no way around it. My eyes danced around his face, trying to figure out if he was being serious about this.

"I don't know if I should."

"I think that . . ." Tommy spoke softly; his words felt carefully crafted as he delivered them. It warmed my heart that he was trying his best to be thoughtful. "In order to move on from this chapter of your life or get any closure, you need to visit them."

I stared at Tommy as I thought about what he had said. Maybe he was right. Maybe what I needed was to have a conversation with someone that knew Luke to fully move past this. There was a part of me that had always known I would need to talk with Luke's parents to overcome this guilt that was living inside me. I needed to share how I felt and offer them an apology.

It was time that I faced the demons that I had been avoiding. I had been running for the past four years, and I was growing tired from doing it for so long. The world had been pushing me toward this since that first practice when I had met Tommy, and it was time that I listened.

"Whatever happens, Mags, I meant what I said when I told you we'd face it together." Tommy reached out to squeeze my hand. "I've got your back."

MAGGIE

I glanced down at my phone for the tenth time, matching the address on it to the numbers on the house in front of me. It was surprisingly big for a house in New York. The red brick was bright and cheery against the white shutters. The large columns and half-circle driveway made the home feel stately. The window boxes had bright-pink flowers, and a sign propped next to the door told me I was welcome there. But part of me wondered if that would still be the truth when the owners opened the door to see who was standing on their porch.

After my conversation with Tommy, I had stayed up nearly all night wondering if all I really needed to do was forgive myself. But the only way to do that was to face my past. I hadn't been able to eat anything this morning. Olivia had asked multiple times if I was okay as I picked at my food during breakfast with her, but I dodged her questions. If I spoke out loud about what I was planning on doing, I was afraid that I'd realize how stupid it was and I'd chicken out. I knew that if I was going to do anything, it had to be this morning before the game tonight. The game would get over too late and I wouldn't have time tomorrow before the game and getting on the plane to do anything.

So it was now or never.

My lungs pushed the rest of the air inside of them out, trying to expel some of the anxious energy before I started up the stairs. I had never seen Luke's childhood home. He had planned to take me here for Christmas break our senior year, but he was gone before he ever had a chance. As I climbed the stairs, images of him walking down them on his way to school flashed through my head. I saw him as a little kid trick-or-treating down the street, dressed in the Darth Vader costume he had told me about proudly. The tie-dye chicken that he found his mom at a garage sale as a gag gift sat in the corner of the porch. Everywhere I looked there were memories of him, pieces of himself that he had laid out for all to see.

It took every ounce of bravery in me to push the doorbell and not run away as fast as I'd come. My heartbeat quickened at the sound of someone walking to the door, and one more doubt creeped into my head, wondering if I was doing the right thing, before the door was pulled open. Luke's mom stood on the other side. We had stayed in touch for a little bit after that horrible day, but communication slowly faded away. His parents had never blamed me for the accident. It was quite the opposite. They were so caring and attentive over me as I healed and tried to cope with the loss of my fiancé while they were grieving their youngest son. But I knew that in order for me to move on with my life, I needed to voice my guilt about that night and leave it out in the open for them to decide my fate.

It was a stupid idea, but I needed someone to forgive me and I couldn't ask Luke. Whether I needed to be forgiven or deserved it, I needed someone that understood to say the words and release me from this grief. If not, I was afraid I was reaching a point where I'd be lost forever under the weight of it all.

Luke had his mom's eyes and mouth, and it was jarring to see those traits in flesh again rather than in a photograph. I had to clear my throat to shove down the sudden onset of tears before I could speak.

"Hi, Mrs. Greenberg."

"Oh, Maggie," she exclaimed, full of warmth and sincerity. "What a surprise! Please come in."

Mrs. Greenberg ushered me inside and into a massive kitchen in the back of the house. It seemed that she was the only one home, but that was better than ringing the doorbell to find no one home and my plans foiled. She gestured to a stool at the kitchen island before she walked toward the fridge.

"Can I get you something to drink? Tea or lemonade?" I swallowed around the tightness growing in my throat.

"No. I'm okay. I actually came here to talk with you."

"Oh, honey. I saw that article." Mrs. Greenberg shut the refrigerator doors before she reached across the island to grab my hands. I hadn't thought about her reading the article. Embarrassment rushed through me, bringing heat to my cheeks at the thought that she knew I was dating someone that wasn't her son.

"That wasn't necessarily what I came here to talk to you about. But it did trigger something for me."

"What do you mean, dear?" The way that she was looking at me made me want to swallow myself whole and disappear. I wasn't sure if I could tell her about the big, ugly, black guilt that had been living inside me for almost four years. It would surely ruin the way she was looking at me right then, like I could do no harm. The black creature in my head felt like it was sneering at the thought of someone not recognizing what lived inside me.

"I need to talk about the night of the accident with you." There was nothing important about the accident that she hadn't already heard. It wasn't like there were details I had left out of the police report or something big had been missed. What I needed to tell Luke's mom was that night from my point of view. With all of the intimate details included. I needed someone to understand.

"The night of the accident," I started. "We were heading to my parents' house and Luke was asking about my mom's oatmeal cookies."

Mrs. Greenberg laughed. "He loved those cookies. He'd call me all the time to tell me how good they were. He wanted to mail us some, but he always ended up eating them before he could ever send them."

I found myself smiling at the image of Luke telling his mom sheepishly on the phone that the package wouldn't be coming because there was nothing to send. I had to school my expression back into something serious so I could continue.

"Well, the way he was so giddy about it, I couldn't help but look at him. He was so mesmerizing when he laughed."

Luke's mom smiled. She always thought Luke's and my love had been so special. She said our love had been one of those once-in-a-lifetime kind of loves, and I fully believed what she had said was the truth. "When I looked back at the road, the car was on us."

I choked on the tears that were rushing back to the surface and tore my eyes away from Mrs. Greenberg. I couldn't bear to watch the look of disgust that was sure to cross her face.

"What are you trying to say, Maggie?"

"I could have saved us! It's my fault he's dead." I could barely get the words out above a whisper.

"Maggie." Mrs. Greenberg walked around the kitchen island to sit next to me. She grabbed my hands in hers and tried to meet my gaze, but I kept my eyes on my feet. "Maggie, that car came around a curve. You know that. Even if you had been looking, you wouldn't have been able to do anything. It's a miracle that you didn't die too."

There had been plenty of nights that I had stayed up wondering why the world took Luke instead of me. He was full of so much more goodness than I was. If anyone deserved to die that night, it was me. But this woman was consoling me like I deserved to live.

"I like to think that Luke saved you. He loved you so much that he wanted to protect you until the very end." I finally looked up to meet Mrs. Greenberg's eyes. There wasn't a tear in them. I had expected her to be as much of a mess as I was talking about the night that her son died. "Honey, that night was not your fault. If I had known you've been carrying around this guilt inside you this entire time, I would have told you that sooner."

"How are you doing so well?" I asked her as I swiped at my tears.

"Because I had to learn that I will never lose my baby boy." She put a hand up to her heart. "He's in here, just like he's in yours. Honey, you have to let him go. You deserve to be happy."

"How can I find the kind of happiness I had with Luke again?" I asked her. "Even you said our love was once in a lifetime."

"Maggie . . ." Mrs. Greenberg's hands moved to cup my face as she made sure she had my full attention. "There are so many kinds of once-in-a-lifetime loves. You both were so fortunate to have found that in each other so young. But, Maggie, your heart is so full of love. You will find someone else. It won't be like Luke's and your love, and I know you would never want that anyway. The next kind of love you will find will be something completely different. Something you didn't know you needed.

"And, to me, it looks like you may have already found it."

"Oh, Mrs. Greenberg. No." I started to shake my head. There was no way that I would lie to this woman about my relationship with Tommy. I would surely end up in hell at the end of this if I did. "He and I aren't like that."

"Are you sure?" she asked as she pulled away from me. "Because from what I can see, the way you two look at each other is something quite special."

I wasn't sure what had happened, but it was like a dam had opened up inside me after I had finally unlocked the ugliness for Mrs. Greenberg. So after she insisted that Tommy and I were special, it was like my mouth had a mind of its own as it opened again to tell her the truth.

"We aren't really dating." I looked back up at her after the words passed my lips. Some part of me felt relieved to be able to unload the secret onto someone else. "It's for the media and to help his career. We aren't in love."

"Maggie, you have never been a good liar." Mrs. Greenberg gave me a wry smile. "Any time you've ever been around someone, your feelings for them are always written all over your face, good or bad. If you're trying to tell me that you don't like that boy right now, you're in denial."

A heat spread across my cheeks as she read my feelings plainly. I cursed myself for being so obviously enthralled with Tommy Mikals. I had told myself from the start that if I got feelings for him, I'd be made a fool.

"Even if that may be true," I replied softly, "he's only doing this to save his career."

"Are you that dense?"

My mouth dropped open at her candor. "I'm sorry?"

Mrs. Greenberg took out her phone and tapped away on the screen before flipping it around so I could see. She had pulled up a picture of me and Tommy getting pizza the night before. The two of us were laughing as we raced across the street toward the pizzeria. Pure joy was all over my face. It was the brightest I had seen my smile in a long time.

"Do you see the way that boy looks at you?" She pointed at the second picture on the screen. I was eating my folded pizza, and Tommy was watching me. His eyes had crinkled at the corners, and the way he looked at me made my breath catch in my chest. "Are you trying to tell me that a man that looks at a woman like *that* isn't in love with her?"

———

As I rode the ferry back to the city, I thought through what Luke's mom had said to me. She never said she forgave me because she didn't think there was anything to forgive me for. And did I really deserve happiness? A small part of me knew that I did, but a bigger part was scared to hope for happiness like that again.

I picked apart our conversation about Tommy. Mrs. Greenberg's perception was rarely off. But could she really be right about how she thought Tommy felt about me? It felt too good to be true.

Was Tommy my next once-in-a-lifetime kind of love? I was scared to hope that the happiness I had from Tommy would last. I didn't want to let myself hope for someone to make me happy again only to be disappointed in the end.

MAGGIE

The empty parking lot stretched before us. Tommy sat in the driver's seat, and I was still firmly sitting in the passenger seat. He had been trying to convince me to get out and switch places with him for about fifteen minutes now, but I refused to move.

The Chicago Cougars had a few days off from traveling, which meant neither of us had to go to the stadium, and apparently, off days were dangerous for Tommy because it was when he came up with terrible ideas. Today's terrible idea was finally helping me get back behind the wheel of a car. He had showed up at my house earlier than I would have liked and called me until I came out. When he didn't tell me where he was taking me once I got in, I knew I was in some serious trouble.

"Maggie, come on," Tommy said. "You've been wanting to do this for a while and now you have the opportunity to."

"I know."

"I'm not going to let you chicken out."

"I know."

Tommy got out of the car and walked over to the passenger side. He opened my door and stepped to the side, staring down at me with expectant eyes. After I realized he really wasn't going to walk back over to the driver's side this time, I sighed and pulled myself out of the car.

"There we go." Tommy slipped into my seat before I could even blink, forcing me to either sit in the back like a loser or face my fears and get behind the wheel again.

Every step I took felt like an eternity, and soon I was looking down at the wheel of Tommy's car, wondering how something I hadn't thought twice about at one time was now the most difficult thing in the world. Before I could talk myself out of it, I dropped down into the seat and stared out the windshield like it was the first time I was ever looking out this side of it.

"Okay, now put your hands on the wheel," Tommy coached. It felt like I was now the player on the baseball field and he was the coach. But instead of my hands doing what Tommy said to do, they stayed firmly in my lap.

"Okay, now put your hands on the wheel," Tommy repeated.

"I know."

Tommy paused as he watched me from the passenger seat. We'd at least made more progress in the last five minutes than we had in the last hour. "You don't even have to start the car yet."

"Okay."

What he said made sense, but it was like my body was fighting against what it should do. Tommy reached over and gently laced his fingers through mine before he raised my hands to the wheel. When he let go, he cheerfully looked at me and said, "See? That wasn't so bad."

As I sat there with my hands gripping the wheel, I half expected to have a flashback to that night. But nothing happened, nothing came. So instead, I gripped the wheel tighter as I felt some of the worry I had been feeling leak out of my body. With one more breath, I reached down and turned the key. It was different feeling a car start up when you were in control rather than sitting in the passenger seat. You were at the mercy of the engine under the hood and responsible for the safety of whoever was inside the car.

Tommy started to encourage me to take that small step, but he stopped when he watched me put my foot on the brake and the car in drive.

"Are you sure?" he asked as the car began to creep forward.

"We're already moving, Tommy," I told him as I edged the car around the empty parking lot. We were not zipping around the parking lot at a normal thirty miles per hour. It was a slow crawl around five, but I was driving a car for the first time in almost four years. The speed didn't matter, so long as the car was moving.

"You're doing it!" Tommy shouted. He was celebrating my accomplishment like the fans cheered for him when he made a game-saving play or hit a game-winning home run. It meant the world to me that he was celebrating something so small like the massive accomplishments people celebrated of his.

He didn't stop cheering for me as I moved his car around and around in circles in that parking lot. I knew I wasn't going to have the courage to take it out on the road today, but that moment in the parking lot was enough for me.

I was surprised when my chest didn't constrict and my palms didn't sweat as I drove. In fact, I didn't feel nervous at all. It was a little like riding a bike. Sure, I was a little rusty, but I hadn't forgotten how to do it. As I continued to drive in circles, I realized that it wasn't the act of driving I was afraid of. I had been a safe driver before the accident. Instead, I was afraid of the other people on the road and the unpredictability of what they would do. The accident had effectively given me trust issues with driving.

After a few more turns, I slowed the car to a stop and put it in park. Tommy stayed silent next to me as he waited to hear my thoughts. My eyes glanced between the dash and the road just beyond the parking lot we were in, my mind calculating the risks.

"How do you feel?" Tommy asked after I hadn't said anything for a few minutes.

"Like I need to actually go on the road."

"You don't have to," he replied quickly, trying to make me feel comfortable with what I had done so far.

"Driving isn't the problem, Tommy," I told him. "I trust myself. It's everyone else that I don't trust."

"Well, I'm sorry to tell you that will never go away." Tommy chuckled softly. When my eyes still remained firmly planted on the road in front of us, Tommy continued, "Okay, how about this? There's an ice cream shake place a couple miles away from my place. If you can get us there, I'll get us back to my house."

"Deal." This was a momentous occasion to reward with some ice cream.

MAGGIE

Tommy and I didn't get to enjoy the rest of the break the team had that week. After our day of conquering my fears with driving, he and I were on another flight to Los Angeles and the ESPYS. Monica had sent us both a detailed email about where we would be staying, the kinds of appearances she wanted us to do before the red carpet, and the designers that would be dressing us for the night.

It was overwhelming to say the least, and as we read the email, I found myself becoming disappointed that our relationship would be solidified by a grand orchestrated plan. Even though Tommy and I were not actually official, it felt like we were heading in that direction, and Monica's plans laid a layer of complication on top of all of this. Did Tommy consider this a confirmation of our relationship in real life? Or was it just me thinking along those lines?

"Can I ask you something?" Tommy said as the two of us sat in the back of a car on the way to the hotel we'd be staying at.

"Anything," I told him.

"How do you define yourself outside of your photography?" The words came out of his mouth like a prayer he was hoping would be answered.

"Why do you ask?"

"I've just been thinking about it a lot since we took off in Chicago." Tommy didn't have to go into any more detail for me to know that his mind was in a spiral, reflecting on his career and where it had taken him in life.

"Well, I guess it starts with what it is I want to leave behind in this world. It isn't necessarily *what* you do that defines you but *why* you do it. It's about what you want to be known for when you leave this place. I like to think of the old saying coaches always used to tell you as kids: leave the dugout better than when you found it. Leave the world a little better than when you first arrived. No matter how big or small."

Tommy's hand rested on the seat between us, and I reached out to slide mine underneath his. He gave me a grateful smile, and his hand curled around mine and squeezed.

"How do you want to make things better?" I asked.

"I want to make a difference." My heart swelled at the confidence in his voice.

"How do you think your career can help with that?"

Tommy thought for a moment in silence, weighing my words carefully. "I know my platform can bring attention to a cause that has gone relatively unknown. That could help with donations and opportunities."

"Exactly," I agreed, excited to see him happy about something for the first time in a while. "What kind of cause are you thinking you can do that for?"

"I want to help athletes of all ages, who will transition out of their sport, to find other hobbies that bring value to them. There are too many athletes out there that struggle once they stop playing because their sport was all they knew." Tommy's eyes were bright as he looked at me. "Like me."

"I think that's great. You should meet with Monica since you aren't represented by anyone anymore and see what you can do. She could probably help you get started with meeting the right people."

Tommy nodded seriously like he was making a mental checklist of the things he needed to do for this idea to be born. I laid my other hand down on his thigh to get his attention back.

"I've told you this before and I will keep telling you: you're more than a baseball player. You're a son. You're a friend. You have a big heart and a lot of love in there to spread around."

Tommy's thumb rubbed idle circles on the back of my hand as the conversation quieted down. It was crazy to me that every time I looked at him in moments like this, my chest could fill with so much emotion.

The city of Los Angeles slowly consumed us as we continued to drive farther into downtown where we'd be staying. Tommy and I stayed quiet the rest of the ride. I couldn't put my finger on it, but it felt like we were barreling toward impending doom with this event, like whatever fantasy world Tommy and I had been living in with whatever was going on between us was slowly slipping away from us.

I knew that shouldn't be the case. We were on our way to get ready for an event where we would proclaim our relationship for the world to know. But I was beginning to wonder if there were too many layers of complication that had accumulated throughout this entire charade.

Monica had reserved a hotel room for us at the closest hotel to the venue and had an entire team waiting for us when we arrived. There were hair and makeup crews, as well as employees for the designer label we'd be wearing tonight. As soon as Tommy and I walked through the door, they all sprang into action like they'd been waiting for us for hours. People swarmed around the two of us and pulled us in separate directions. I was sure the look of terror on Tommy's face was mirrored on my own.

The room was full of excited energy as a crew prepared to get me and Tommy ready for a red carpet walk. Through the sea of people, I caught Tommy looking at me with sadness written all over his face. Our eyes stayed locked on each other for a few minutes as people bustled around us. I couldn't be sure what was going through his head, but I was beginning to feel like all of this had been a mistake. I didn't want to date Tommy like this. The dates we were having to go on didn't feel like they allowed for the feelings that were growing between us to flourish.

Once the crew was done making Tommy and me look almost unrecognizable, they filed out of the room one by one. An employee of the designer took pictures of us and requested they be posted on our social media accounts before they exited the room, leaving us alone finally. As soon as we were alone, it felt like there was finally air to breathe again.

"That was a lot," Tommy said.

"I feel like I'm playing dress up." I walked in front of the mirror to catch a glimpse of the blood-red ballgown I was wearing. The skirt fell down in luxurious waves, and the bodice accentuated the little cleavage I had. It was the nicest dress I had ever seen, and while I should've felt like I was living out a dream, nothing felt like me.

"You look beautiful, Maggie." Tommy's eyes were dark as he took me in. My cheeks flushed as he shook his head in awe.

"You look amazing too." His suit jacket was an off-shade of red that complemented my dress and popped against the black pants and shirt he was wearing.

"You okay?" he asked me when he realized I was being more reserved than I normally was.

"This just feels like a lot." My hands nervously smoothed down my skirt as I stared at myself in the mirror of the room. "It doesn't feel like us."

Tommy's eyes scanned my face as he took in all of the emotion I'd been hiding from him. He took a step closer to me in response, his fingers coming up to trace down my jawline.

"I know."

"How did this happen?"

Tommy knew I wasn't talking about how we ended up at a red carpet event together. We both knew how that had happened. No, I was talking about how we ended up catching feelings for each other and were stuck living within the confines of someone else's idea of what they wanted our relationship to be.

Instead of telling me something to help make me feel better, he took another step closer to me and wrapped his arms around my waist. He pulled my body flush against his as he wrapped me in a hug that I desperately needed.

"What do you want, Maggie?" Tommy asked me as my face was tucked into his jacket. I was really hoping that the makeup artist's setting spray was expensive and not about to ruin the multi-thousand-dollar suit that Tommy was wearing.

His words bounced around inside my heart, only one answer ringing true inside me. I wasn't sure if it was the dress that was giving me the extra confidence, but I found my mouth opening and words coming out that I never thought I would admit to him.

"You, Tommy. I want you."

A growl escaped Tommy's throat at my words. One of his hands trailed up my back, making me shiver when his hand traced over my bare skin. It wrapped gently around the back of my neck and tilted my head, so I wasn't buried in his chest anymore. His eyes stared down at me intensely.

"Say that again." His voice was dangerously low as he waited to hear the words.

"I want you, Tommy Mikals."

Every part of me knew the words were true. They had been living inside me since the moment that he had kissed me the last time we were in Los Angeles. I knew the moment my pen had touched that contract Monica had put in front of me that I wasn't supposed to catch feelings. At the time, I had thought that would be an easy task. I had known Tommy Mikals to be a player that only cared about women, drinking, and money. But what I had learned over the little time I had known him was that that couldn't have been further from the truth.

I had fallen for a guy that was incredibly patient and kind, someone who saw me with all of my scars but still thought I was the most beautiful person in the room. The feelings I had for Tommy hadn't been there when I first met him. They had been watered through our time spent together and had slowly bloomed with every shared smile, fleeting glance, or hand held.

Both of Tommy's hands came up to cup my cheeks as he covered my lips with his. A hunger exploded from his mouth as it explored mine. His teeth skated across my lips, teasing me and sending shocks of pleasure down my body. Heavy want blazed through my body as Tommy pulled me even closer, trying to erase every nook and cranny of space that lived between us. I sighed into his mouth as he kissed me slower and with more passion than I had thought was possible. Tommy pulled back so he could study me.

"You have no idea how much I have wished to hear you say those words." I slid my hands down his chest, wanting desperately to fist my hand in his shirt, but I knew Monica would kill me if we appeared on the carpet a rumpled mess.

"I want you too." Tommy took a step back from me as he ran a hand through his hair. "God, Maggie. I want more for you than this."

"What do you mean?"

"I want to date you. Really date you. Without all of this." He waved a hand in the air to encompass the mess the two of us had gotten into. "I don't want to put our relationship out there publicly like this. I know what that can do to a couple. It can tear the relationship up from the inside out."

My mind flashed to the uncashed check that was sitting on my counter at home. I had stared at the zeroes on it for almost an hour, debating what to do before I decided I wasn't going to do anything and left the check on my counter where it had been since.

"We can't walk away now, Tommy," I reminded him. "You'd lose your contract."

"Part of me wonders if that's such a bad thing anymore," Tommy whispered softly.

"I would never let you give up baseball for me."

"I know that." Tommy's voice was still barely audible. "But I'm a wreck, Maggie. I've about fucked my way out of my career—literally. The girl I thought I was going to marry messed me up so badly, I don't know if I'll ever be able to trust anyone again. I'm constantly worried about screwing up and having all of this taken from me. But not because I'd lose the lifestyle—because I'd lose the only version of myself I know. I'm way too much to ask you to take on. These last few months have allowed me to have you without the risk of losing you because I've always known you could never be mine. I don't deserve you."

Tommy's hands continued to work through his hair, ruining the work that had been done to prepare him for the carpet we were about to walk down. The sadness dripped down his features like a steady rain as he looked at me.

"That doesn't mean I didn't mean what I just said. I want to be clear about that. I want you, Maggie Redford. So goddamn much. But you deserve to be with someone that can make you happy."

I had never seen so much raw emotion displayed on Tommy's face outside of the baseball field. He looked beautiful. Like a city with all the lights on at night. Warmth spread through my body, all the way to my fingers, because that emotion was there because of me. Because he cared about me too. My hands curled around his jaw.

"You make me happy, Tommy, and if you haven't realized it yet, I'm also a fucking wreck. So let's be one giant wreck together."

A small smile pulled the corners of Tommy's mouth upward. I pushed up on my tiptoes and brushed a gentle kiss across his mouth, sure that if I gave him the kind of passion he gave me earlier, he would crumble right in front of me.

"Are you sure?" he asked me when he pulled back.

"I could say something cheesy about standing here in my best dress, but I won't. So of course I'm serious, but how about this? For the past four years, I haven't even looked at guys in any sort of romantic way. Until I saw you. You changed everything for me, Tommy."

"Maggie . . ." My name passed his lips like a prayer as he leaned down to press one more kiss to my lips. "Let's do this."

The nerves I had felt from the moment we had walked into the hotel room left my body as Tommy slid his hand in mine. For the first time in four years, it finally felt like I had a little bit of luck.

MAGGIE

A car took us to the venue where SUVs were waiting to drop off their passengers at the red carpet. Police officers had the surrounding streets shut down, and fans stood on the sidewalks wearing their favorite athlete's jersey and holding signs as the cars passed them. I spotted a few Tommy Mikals signs as we edged closer to the carpet. He wasn't up for any categories tonight, but Monica had gotten him to present one of the awards.

"Are you doing okay?" I asked him as I watched his leg jiggle faster and faster the closer we got to the venue.

"Honestly . . ." His hand threaded through mine. "Not sure yet."

"Good or bad, we'll get through it together."

Tommy lifted my hand to his mouth and pressed his lips to it without looking over at me.

Our phones went off at the same time, tearing our attention away from each other. I tapped on my screen to see that I had been tagged in an article from *News Weekly*. The headline reported that Tommy and I were discussing moving in together. A headache that felt always present nowadays whenever it came to the media circus that Monica was orchestrating pressed against my skull.

"Unbelievable," Tommy muttered.

Our car pulled up next to the red carpet. There were even more reporters and paparazzi waiting down the carpet than at the Red Cross event. My anxiety built inside my chest, trying to grab hold and pull me under. I wasn't sure if I would ever be comfortable at events like this. Tommy's grip on my hand was firm and was the only thing keeping me grounded as one of the ushers pulled open his door. His hand left mine for a brief second, and it was like I was on a raft by myself floating in the middle of the ocean until I scooted out of the car and reemerged next to him. His hand immediately found mine again, and the two of us squared our shoulders like we were about to go into battle.

The cameras started immediately, and I could honestly say it was getting easier to try to avoid them. However, I was sure I would never get used to the shouts. Fans called out for Tommy. Reporters tried to grab our attention as we passed. Tommy stopped to answer a few questions for some of them about the season.

"Tommy! Maggie!" a reporter called out to us, waving us over excitedly. "You both look amazing."

"Thank you," I replied.

"Tommy, are you excited about presenting tonight?" she asked him.

"I am. I'm incredibly excited to be here around some of the greatest in sports right now. It's really an honor."

The reporter nodded enthusiastically. "Maggie, you're no stranger to professional athletes, but how are you feeling about tonight?"

I could sense Tommy tensing up next to me. His eyes danced around at the different athletes mingling on the red carpet around us. The purpose of this interview looked like it was getting further and further away from the front of his mind. It seemed like it might be up to me to deliver on what Monica wanted from us.

"I love watching the ESPYS, and I feel extremely honored to be able to watch it in person this year. Tommy knocked this date night out of the park." The reporter smiled like the Cheshire Cat with a bird trapped between its paws.

"Do you two have any comment on the article that came out this morning reporting that the two of you are discussing moving in together?" she asked. The two of us must have looked like a couple of deer caught in a pair of headlights. Neither of us had been prepped on the article or how the Cougars wanted us to respond.

I could feel Tommy square his shoulders. "The two of us have had discussions together about our future, but for the sake of our privacy we would like to keep those parts of our relationship private."

I fought to keep the gasp his response elicited from passing my lips. I knew that was Tommy's way of letting Monica know she had crossed a line.

The reporter deflated slightly when she realized she wouldn't be getting an exclusive scoop on the couple the entire world had been keeping under a microscope.

The reporter wished us a good night before directing her attention to the next guest walking the carpet. Tommy's arm swept around my waist as he began to lead us toward the entrance of the venue. The anger was radiating off Tommy, but the night wasn't over yet.

We walked into the theater to find our seats. Tommy moved us fast through the crowd and kept his head down so he didn't make eye contact with anyone he wasn't ready to speak to. Tommy had made strides in his life to turn over a new leaf and be someone better, someone he was proud of. Tonight was the ultimate temptation of his previous life. It would be easy for him to fall into conversation with people he used to share weekends with. They would catch up, chat about their new seasons, and then someone would throw out the idea of an after-party. I could tell from Tommy's face that was the last thing he wanted. He wanted to come out of tonight unscathed.

"Are you doing okay?" I asked him once we found our seats.

Tommy nodded. "So far."

I was hoping for his sake that the night would go quickly. Even though we were dressed up for a fancy event and out together, I knew this trip was the last thing he wanted. More people started to wander into the venue to find their seats for the show. Tommy stayed looking forward as he dissected the stage that he would present on later. I, however, looked at every person that came in. There were athletes that I had watched on television not even fifteen feet from me. It was odd seeing them in suits and dresses rather than in their uniforms. I had to stare at a few longer than was probably socially acceptable at events like this so I could figure out who they were.

A woman caught my eye as she drew closer. Her dress was practically nonexistent, and she hung from the arm of a well-known football player that played for San Diego. She looked oddly familiar, but I couldn't seem to put my finger on it. Then I heard Tommy suck in a breath next to me. I glanced over my shoulder at him to see his eyes locked on the woman I had been looking at. When I glanced back at her, something clicked. It was Sutton James.

Tommy grew tenser the closer she got. It was one of those moments that felt like it was happening in slow motion. We were close enough to the aisle to be noticeable. Sutton glanced over the people who were seated, and I watched as she looked at something over my shoulder, or someone. I was in the middle of something I shouldn't be as Sutton pulled her date to a stop in front of us.

"Tommy?" she exclaimed, her smile sickeningly sweet.

"Sutton," Tommy replied, his voice tight. "I didn't know you'd be here tonight."

Sutton didn't even bother to look down at me. Her gaze was planted firmly over my head on Tommy. I knew that she had probably seen all the photos over the past two months of me and Tommy. She made a living off social media, and the fact that she wouldn't even bother to look at me showed me exactly how she felt about those pictures.

"How are you?" Sutton asked Tommy. "You're in Chicago now, right?"

It was clear what she was doing. She was trying to distance herself from Tommy as much as she could to appear unbothered. She was playing the Breakup Code Book perfectly.

"Yeah." Tommy's reply was short, telling me everything I needed to know about how he was feeling. I wanted nothing more than to reach over and take his hand in mine for support, but now wasn't the time to do that.

"Let's find our seats," Sutton's date spoke into her ear. Her eyes stayed firmly planted on Tommy as she listened. Finally, she nodded and let him lead her away.

My hand finally felt free to reach over and take Tommy's into mine.

His fingers wrapped around mine and held on for dear life as the venue continued to fill. Neither of us said anything, but I knew our thoughts were drastically different. I doubted that Tommy was thinking about that time he told me he would forgive Sutton if she were to choose him.

He surely wasn't.

But I was.

———

The ESPYS went by in a blur. I wasn't able to focus much on the speeches from the winners and the videos being played up on the screens on either side of the stage. My eyes stayed locked on the back of Sutton James's head for much of the night. I barely even looked up when Tommy emerged on the stage to present the award he was assigned. Instead, I watched as Sutton's shoulders straightened and she sat up slightly in her seat.

I hated the sour feeling that was filling my stomach. That feeling felt oddly like jealousy. I was aware Sutton and Tommy didn't start a relationship because they had to. They got together because of pure attraction. Part of me wondered if Tommy would have chosen me if we weren't already stuck together. Or would he have found someone like Sutton?

Tommy's hand slipped into mine as the lights came on in the theater, signaling the end of the show. I blinked, realizing that I had missed a majority of the night while I was lost in my thoughts. The two of us walked out of the event together, completely ignoring the flashes from the cameras and anyone who may have wanted to talk to us. We'd both had our fill of the night. The car ride back to the hotel was relatively quiet aside from the music the driver was playing. I knew that Tommy was thinking about seeing Sutton again, and I would have given anything in that moment to have the ability to read minds.

The car dropped us off at the hotel, and neither of us spoke until we walked back into the hotel room we had been in hours before anything from tonight had happened. It wasn't until I was standing in front of the bed that I realized there wasn't a second place to sleep in the room. There was one single, massive bed.

"I can sleep on the floor." Tommy walked up next to me to join me staring at the bed.

"It's a tile floor."

"And your point is?" Tommy asked.

"I'm not going to make you sleep on the hard tile, Tommy. The bed is big enough for both of us."

I was surprised by how confidently those words came out of my mouth. It felt like someone else had taken over my brain for those few seconds. Normal Maggie never would have suggested sharing a bed with an extremely hot man that she had developed strong feelings for. That was a recipe for disaster. I'd seen practically every romantic comedy movie that existed. I knew how this ended.

"I'm going to go get changed." I swiped my bag off the bed with my overnight clothes and dove into the bathroom before Tommy could say anything or the red spreading across my cheeks could give me away.

Before I attempted to get out of that stupidly expensive dress, I grabbed my toiletry bag to unpack my skin care routine. Just because I wasn't in my apartment didn't mean I was going to miss a chance at relaxation while giving myself clean skin again. It wasn't until my skin was bare that I felt like myself again and not some version of myself that was used for a photo op. The second I went to reach for the zipper behind me, I knew I was in trouble. It was too high for me to get on my own.

I sighed before calling out to the one person I had been trying to avoid as much as possible. "Tommy, can you help me?"

Tommy walked into the bathroom to find me struggling to grab the zipper on the back of my dress. A smile broke across his face as he slowly approached me and pushed my hands away. His eyes met mine in the mirror as he stood behind me. His hands slowly pulled the zipper down. His fingers brushed against the bare skin of my back. Sutton completely disappeared from my mind as Tommy finished unzipping the dress and it fell down around my waist, leaving me standing in the bathroom with only tape covering me.

My gaze was still locked with Tommy's in the mirror, the two of us frozen as we waited for the other to make the next move. His hands gently pulled the rest of my dress down to pool around my ankles. I was now standing in nothing but a pair of panties and tape with my back still facing him.

The jealousy was still building inside me, and I desperately needed Tommy's reassurance that everything would be okay. That our real relationship wasn't going to be over right when it was beginning because of Sutton James.

"Do you still want me?" I asked him, my eyes still locked on him in the mirror.

"I don't think it's possible for me to want you any more than I do now," Tommy told me. "But I know I'll wake up tomorrow and prove myself wrong."

MAGGIE

Tommy's hands slowly moved up my back, his hands taking their time to feel every inch of my body. His fingers trailed up the back of my neck before tangling in my hair and pulling me forward so his mouth could brush against mine. My body sighed into his as my own hands worked at the buttons on his dress shirt. My palms skated across his chest after I was able to rip his shirt open, exposing one of the best sets of abs I had ever seen. As I began to work on his pants, Tommy kissed my jaw with slow, heavy kisses. I had never done any kind of drug before, but in that moment, I swore I was high from the pleasure wracking my body.

He stepped out of his pants as soon as they hit the floor and shrugged off his jacket and shirt without even pulling away from our kiss. Then, in one motion, he reached down and lifted me out of the puddle of dress I was still standing in and walked me back out of the bathroom and toward the bed.

Every fiber of my being wanted this to be everything he and I needed. It was clear now that we had both avoided relationships for very different reasons because of the hands that life had dealt us. Tommy had been played, leaving him with trust issues, and I had had a love that had been torn away. But as Tommy gently laid me down on the bed, I only hoped that I was filling a piece in him like he was in me. For now, I lost myself in the moment with Tommy and the way he was looking down at me like I was the most beautiful thing he had ever seen. He gazed at me like he had all the time in the world and simply wanted to take his time looking over every inch of my body.

"You are incredible." Tommy's hands trailed down from my shoulders to the sides of my body, following the curve of my waist to my hips. As I lay underneath him, I could finally take in Tommy the way I'd always wanted to, unabashedly, without feeling embarrassed about it. My eyes hungrily devoured the sharp edge of his jawline and how his eyelashes were so long they almost brushed his cheeks when he closed his eyes. It was one of the most intimate things I had ever done in my life, to simply stare at another with the sole intention of appreciating their beauty as the other person did the same.

"Hold on." Tommy gave me a cheeky, apologetic smile as he slowly pulled off the tape covering my nipples. I flinched as he pulled, and he mouthed *sorry* at me as he tried to gently pull the last one off.

"Just rip it off like a Band-Aid," I told him, steeling myself for the sharp tingle of pain.

"Are you sure?"

"Just do it, Mikals."

A hiss of pain left my lips as he pulled the last piece off and Tommy quickly covered it with his own. He pulled me flush against him as an overwhelming need flooded my senses. My hands wrapped themselves in the band of his underwear and yanked them down. Tommy's hands gripped my own and pulled them down my legs. Then he was on me, his mouth everywhere, kissing the inside of my thighs, my stomach, my chest, my neck, and then my mouth. His mouth wanted to devour me, and my body arched up to meld every inch of me to him. I gasped as his hand cupped me, and every nerve in my body exploded like a firework.

My legs wrapped around his waist as the desperate urge to get even closer to him raced through me. My hips moved against him on the desire and need building inside me. Tommy groaned at the feel of us. His arms wrapped around me, and his fingers dug into my back.

"You are unreal," he breathed into my shoulder.

"Do we have a condom?" The words came out breathy, like I was someone other than myself. I was someone who was desirable and worthy of affection. It was like Tommy's touch had unlocked another piece of me that had been hidden away.

He peeled himself off me and went to dig around in his suitcase. Tommy found a foil package in one of the pockets and ripped it open.

"What? You just keep those handy?" I asked.

"Part of me was hoping for the opportunity to present itself with you." Tommy slid the condom on, and within seconds, he was back on top of me. "I've been dreaming about this moment with you for a while."

With that, Tommy was pushing into me, his hands digging in to find a grip on my waist, his mouth leaving kisses on every inch of me that he could reach. His breath tickled my ear as my hands threaded through his hair and pulled him closer. His name passed through my lips like a whisper, and my own rolled out of him like he was riding a tidal wave of pleasure.

Tommy held me as the pressure cascaded through us and continued to hold me after everything had subsided. He only rolled off me once the two of us had caught our breath again, but he kept his arms around me and pulled me flush against his chest, his chin resting on top of my head. I never wanted to leave this hotel room and face the reality that would lie on the other side. For now, the world was perfect.

We had sex three more times that night before we fell asleep in each other's arms. It felt like we were making up for lost time, all of the tension that had built up between us driving our needs. When we woke the next morning from the sun streaming in through the curtains that we didn't do a good job of closing the night before, our bodies were still tangled together. Tommy's fingers lazily moved through my hair, which was mussed from sleep. A lazy smile crept across his face as I stared up at him.

"Hi." His voice was thick still from sleep, and I was shocked that I could find any part of Tommy even sexier than before.

"Good morning." I let my hands run up his back, feeling the muscles in his shoulders stretch as he lifted one hand above his head.

"We have a flight to catch," he reminded me.

"Do we have to?"

He chuckled as he looked down at me; his hand smoothed down the side of my face and traced the line of my jaw. "I wish we didn't, but I'm in the lineup tonight."

"I know. May would kill me if I missed my actual job just for something Monica wanted us to do."

Tommy slipped out from under the covers and made his way to the bathroom to shower. I propped myself up on my elbow to watch him. The sound of water interrupted the quiet silence that had filled the room as Tommy turned the handle. He turned around to look at me.

"You coming?"

A smile broke across my face as I yanked the covers back and hurried after him.

———

Tommy drew circles on the back of my hand with his fingers on the flight back to Chicago. The sun was rising outside the plane's windows. Vibrant pinks and oranges stained the sky like a watercolor. This flight back almost felt like we were leaving our little wonderland to return to reality, and a thick blanket of silence hung over us as we drew closer to it. I was becoming a different version of myself, but this version I actually liked. This version wasn't staged or lying for a photo op. It was me, but the happiest I had been in a while. The Tommy I had next to me was someone else too. He was carefree and unbothered. A piece of me would be okay if the second we landed in Chicago all of this disappeared, because that one night with Tommy felt worth it. Because, for a moment, I was a girl who was worth loving again. For one moment, I felt alive again.

As I fell asleep the night before, part of me had wondered that if when I woke up everything that had happened would disappear. Tommy would be gone and all that would be left would be a memory. It all felt too good to be true, and he would have regretted it as the sun rose in the sky. But instead of waking up to find it was all a dream, Tommy snuggled into me like a little kid as he begged for a few more minutes in my arms before we had to escape to the airport. Our hopes were high for what could happen in the future.

But the closer we got back to Chicago, the more it seemed that the tension was weighing heavier on us; however, it seemed to be weighing on Tommy more than it was me. It had me wondering if maybe I had misjudged how he had been feeling about the situation, like I had potentially misread everything about him and he really was a one-time kind of guy.

"Are you happy?" I asked him.

"Of course I am," he replied as he lifted the hand he had been tracing to his mouth and pressed a kiss to it. "Why would you ask that?"

"Because something seems to be bothering you other than the fact that our stolen night away is ending."

Tommy sighed and dragged both of his hands over his eyes. After a moment, he dropped his hands away from his face and turned his head to look at me again. "I'm nervous about the game."

"Why?" It wasn't like Tommy had something to worry about. He had been playing well.

"My parents are in town to watch."

Then it all made sense. I remembered how he had gotten when we had visited his parents in California. He had been on edge around his dad, wanting desperately to make him proud, but at war with his dad's disapproval for his previous actions. I truly believed that he would be okay if his career ended tomorrow, but only if he had finally done something to make his dad proud. Tommy was on a redemption mission with the Cougars. This was his opportunity to rewrite the story of his professional career and make up for the stains that mottled it.

"You'll do great, Tommy." I reached back over to grab his hand and gave it a reassuring squeeze.

"It feels like I have to do more than great to get my dad to think I'm doing anything with my career." My heart ached as I watched the pain on Tommy's face.

"Your dad loves you. I'm sure he is beyond proud to see his son as a professional baseball player living out his dreams."

"I'm sure he's proud of that," Tommy agreed. "I'm not sure if he will ever get over my actions from those first few years."

At that moment, I knew that nothing I could say to Tommy would help. He didn't need reassurances that he was doing the right thing or that he was a good person. He needed to hear from his father's mouth that he was proud of his son, and I would be damned if Tommy never got to hear those words.

MAGGIE

That night was the crosstown rivals game. The Cougars would be playing the Eagles, and the city was alive with energy. The rivalry ran deep between the north side and the south side. Every year when this game happened, families would draw the line of family members that were fans of the team they were cheering for and those that weren't. Social media was on fire with fans debating who would win that night or who was the better team.

As the team bus drove across town, I watched people dressed in both teams' jerseys walking the streets as they went in and out of bars near the Eagles' stadium. The team was bouncing with nervous excitement. They had been waiting for this game on their calendar, wanting to take back the title. Last year, the Eagles had slaughtered them in a brutal outing. The energy on the bus was pointing toward a night of payback. The only thing I wanted to see tonight was a smile on Tommy's face by the end of it. He deserved to be able to revel in the good moments when his parents came and not have to worry about whether his performance had been good enough.

Olivia sidled up next to me as we followed the team through the stadium and to the field. She hadn't texted me to ask about the ESPYS yet, and I knew that was because the interrogation would be done in person.

"That dress was stunning," she told me. "Please tell me that Tommy lost his mind."

I stayed quiet as I tried to keep a smile off my face. Olivia studied me for a moment before her mouth dropped open and her eyes widened.

"No!" she exclaimed. "Was it mind-blowing? It was mind-blowing, wasn't it?"

My eyes slid over to Tommy, who was walking with Adam and Jamil toward the back of the group. It was like he could feel my eyes on him because he glanced back over his shoulder and gave me a small smile.

"Oh my God," Olivia hissed as she watched the interaction.

I pressed my lips together as she stared between the two of us.

"Tommy Mikals is smitten. Like, completely smitten over my *best friend*."

Just the thought of that being true made my insides feel like a big bowl of soup. "I'm not sure he's smitten, necessarily."

"Are you kidding, Maggie?" Olivia asked me incredulously. "He would be insane not to be."

The two of us continued toward the tunnel that would take us out onto the field while the team dove into the locker room to change for the game. Tommy was the last to go in, and as we passed by the door, his hand reached out to brush against mine before he disappeared after his teammates.

"Totally smitten," Olivia told me smugly.

Part of me wished that Tommy and I could teleport back to the hotel in Los Angeles for a few more stolen moments together.

———

The energy in the stadium grew as the game drew longer. It was tied going into the top of the seventh as the Cougars went up to bat. Tommy was leading the team in runs batted in and hits. He was having a phenomenal night. But even with his performance, I watched him scan the crowd with a strained face and heavy shoulders. My eyes followed his line of sight to see what he was looking at. His parents were sitting behind the visitors' dugout.

I knew in my gut that even if Tommy had the best night of his career, it would mean nothing if his dad wasn't proud of his performance. I looked between Olivia, Tommy, and Tommy's parents. Olivia was in the dugout with me and had barely moved her camera from her face all night. Tommy was busy putting on his batting gloves and preparing for his at bat that was coming up. I debated for a couple of seconds if what I was about to do was out of line, but something in me told me to do it anyway.

A stadium worker was standing in front of the gate that blocked off our dugout from the rest of the stadium. He pulled the gate open as he saw me approaching. I gave him a quick nod before I dove into the busy stadium, angling toward Tommy's parents. His mom wore a shirt with his number on it, and his dad wore a Cougars sweatshirt with a hat pulled down over his eyes. The two watched Jamil's at bat with anxious eyes, just as invested in the game as any diehard fan. I stayed back for a moment longer as I watched the pair. It was clear how much this win meant to them too. I could practically imagine them in the stands at Tommy's games when he was younger, cheering loudly for him as he got a hit.

His father shouted out encouragement for Tommy as he approached the plate for his at bat. Jamil had gotten a double, giving Tommy the perfect opportunity to give the Cougars the lead. I watched as his dad sat forward in his seat, wringing his hands together as he watched his son take the first pitch. With the crack of the bat on the next pitch, Tommy's dad was on his feet as the ball sailed toward right center, nowhere near an outfielder. It was the perfect hit for Jamil to score. As Tommy slid safely into second and Jamil had crossed home, Scott's hands lifted above his head triumphantly.

I knew that it wasn't that Scott wasn't proud of his son. It was that he did a terrible job of showing that he was proud for his son to see. The seat next to Scott was open, and I dodged around cheering fans to slide into it.

"Maggie!" Linda exclaimed when she saw me. "It's so good to see you."

She reached over to squeeze my hands.

"That was awesome," I told them, sharing in the joy they were feeling for their son.

"Yes, it was," Scott agreed, his eyes still glued on Tommy standing on second. "He's had a great night."

I hesitated as the words I wanted to say weighed heavily on the tip of my tongue. The moment they left my mouth, I could ruin any chance of a relationship with Tommy's father depending on if he took what I said poorly. But my feelings for Tommy and how much I cared about him outweighed the risks.

"You should tell him that."

Scott turned to look at me, his eyebrows pulled together. "I'm sorry?"

"You should tell him," I repeated. "I've watched your son stress about his performance this season because he wants to make you proud. This game was all he could think about on our plane ride home this morning. I don't want to cross any boundaries. I just want you to know that I think it would do Tommy wonders to hear it."

Linda's eyes shone as she watched the interaction between me and Scott. She wasn't appalled by my gall. Instead, she looked thankful that I was brave enough to express what her son needed from them.

Scott looked back toward Tommy, who was now standing on third after his teammate had moved him. My body felt tense as I waited for his response. The last thing I wanted was for this to worsen Tommy's relationship with his dad. But Scott surprised me when he turned back to look at me.

"Okay."

My eyes found Linda's, shocked at Scott's simple response. Her eyebrows were raised in surprise, mirroring my own emotions. But it didn't seem that Scott was going to supply an explanation for his quick agreement.

I excused myself back to the dugout as another Cougars player punched a ball past the infielders, bringing Tommy safely home. The two of us entered the dugout at the same time. Tommy's teammates offered him high fives, and he made his way down the dugout toward me, returning every high five that was offered to him.

He stopped right in front of me with the biggest grin on his face, one that I couldn't help but return. Without any hesitation, he bent down and wrapped his arms around my legs, right under my butt, and lifted me into the air. A surprised laugh pushed out of me as he spun me in a circle before setting me down on the ground. It was almost intoxicating to see that kind of joy on his face.

"Wait for me after the game." His mouth was inches from my ear and sent shivers down my spine. "We have to celebrate."

All I could do was nod because I was sure that if I spoke, no sound would come out anyway. He turned away from me to put his helmet and batting gloves away, leaving me breathless as I watched him retreat. My eyes caught on Olivia who was looking at me knowingly.

Smitten, she mouthed. I rolled my eyes at her, but a small part of me was desperately hoping she was right. Because I was past the point of telling myself that hoping was dangerous. I had firmly jumped right off the deep end of my feelings for Tommy. With every second that passed, I was sinking farther toward the bottom and becoming more enveloped within the sensations of him.

After the game, I waited outside the locker room for Tommy. The team was slowly trickling out and walking toward the buses that would take us back across town. Olivia had left me to board the bus, but not after wiggling her eyebrows at me suggestively and telling me that I better not be sleeping alone tonight. I waved her off dismissively, trying to hide the fact that I was hoping for the same thing.

Tommy was the last to leave the locker room, as per usual. He looked like he had taken a quick shower. Water droplets fell off the ends of his hair as he turned to look at me. The smile that had been on his face in the dugout was still there, lighting him up. The Cougars had managed to hold on to the lead that Tommy had given them, securing a win against their crosstown rival. The media team had named him the game's MVP, which was rightfully deserved.

"Congratulations," I told him. He dropped his travel bag from his shoulder and scooped me up, like he did in the dugout. My body sizzled as he twirled me around. Before we had made our fake relationship a very real one, it was like my body wanted to avoid feeling anything that

Tommy's touch made me feel. But now there was nothing to stop my body from experiencing an entire fireworks show.

"What a night," Tommy breathed as he set me down. His eyes immediately flickered down to my lips, and without any hesitation, he covered my lips with his own.

I wasn't sure I would ever get used to kissing Tommy this way, without cameras and with each and every kiss meaning something. His arms wrapped around my waist and pulled me closer to him, his strength keeping me from melting on to the floor at his feet. Too soon, though, the kiss ended and Tommy slowly pulled away from me. His arms stayed around my waist as he looked down at me with a softer smile.

"Want to come over to my place when we get back?"

"I'd love to." I tried making my response seem casual, because I had been hoping that Tommy would invite me over to his place to extend our time together after Los Angeles.

"Maybe we can go for another few rounds," Tommy whispered in my ear as the two of us started to walk back through the stadium to where the bus would be waiting for us.

I was too busy ducking my head to hide my blush to see who was in front of us to make Tommy stop in his tracks. When I glanced up, I saw Linda and Scott waiting by the bus. Linda waved excitedly when she saw us, and I was surprised to see a smile break out across Scott's face when he saw his son. But Tommy stayed rooted to the spot.

"Come on." I gave his arm a gentle tug and was relieved when he followed me toward his parents. It was clear that Tommy was worried about being around his father. He didn't want to hear any judgment from Scott tonight. I could tell that all Tommy wanted to do was revel in the performance he had delivered tonight.

"Tommy!" Scott's voice boomed. "What a game."

Scott reached out and wrapped Tommy in his arms. I could see the look of shock on Tommy's face as he stared at nothing in particular over his father's shoulder. But after another moment passed, he wrapped his arms around his dad. I wasn't sure if Scott was going to take my advice and tell Tommy how proud he was of him tonight, but even if he didn't, that hug seemed to shave some of the hurt and tension from Tommy's shoulders.

"I am so proud of you." Scott pushed away from Tommy and held him at arm's length, making sure that he was looking his son in the eyes as he said the words. My own heart seemed to feel lighter watching the interaction. I caught a glance of Linda's eyes and they looked like glass as she watched her husband and son. She peered over at me, gratitude all over her face.

Thank you, she mouthed. I nodded at her in return.

I knew this was something she had been hoping to see for a while, both her husband and son happy together again. But all that mattered to me in that moment was watching the smile that broke out on Tommy's face. He reached out and offered his father his hand. His father took it, before pulling his son in for one more hug.

I wasn't sure what came over me—maybe it was the fact that I didn't want this moment to end for Tommy—but I found myself saying, "Tommy and I are going to go back to his place to cook dinner after we get back to the field. Maybe you guys can meet us there?"

The part about cooking dinner may have been a little bit of a fabrication, but I wasn't about to tell Tommy's parents what we really had planned on doing, and the look on Tommy's face was all I needed to know that my suggestion was welcomed by him.

"You guys haven't seen it yet," Tommy added. "I have stuff to make pasta and homemade garlic bread. That was one of my favorite meals you used to make me as a kid," he told his mom.

"We would love that." Linda looped her arm through Scott's and began to steer him toward the parking lot.

"I'll text you the address," Tommy called after them.

The two of us filed onto the bus, the last people to get on. We found an empty seat together toward the front, and once we were both situated, Tommy turned toward me.

"Why do I have the oddest feeling that was your doing?"

All I could do was give him a smirk and a quick shrug of my shoulders. "A true mastermind never reveals her ways."

"You're amazing," Tommy breathed, his hand wrapping around

mine as a quick squeeze was the only thing that wouldn't draw any attention from his teammates around us.

It was weird that we had gone from making sure we were seen holding hands by someone to not wanting anyone to see. These small moments felt even more special than anything the two of us had done before, like they were too important to share with anyone else.

MAGGIE

Tommy and I showed up to his house about an hour later. His parents were parked out front, waiting for us. The four of us walked inside together, Scott and Tommy chatting back and forth about the game. They were dissecting Tommy's at bats and discussing what had worked for him tonight that he should practice on replicating. It was a completely different experience watching him interact with his dad than what had happened the first time we traveled to California.

Linda and I left them to continue chatting while we headed toward the kitchen to start dinner. I dug through Tommy's cabinets to find the pasta and ingredients for the garlic bread. Linda began heating up a pot of water. The two of us let Scott and Tommy's conversation fill the space, just enjoying the camaraderie between the two men.

Scott pointed out all of the paraphernalia that Tommy had kept and displayed proudly on his shelves in his living room. I watched the two of them as I helped Linda roll the dough out for the garlic bread and begin cutting them into shape.

"I feel like I owe you more than a simple thank-you." Linda broke the silence that had filled the kitchen. Her eyes were also locked on the two men in the living room. She had barely taken her eyes away from them since the stadium.

"I don't know about that," I told her as I dumped the pasta into the now boiling water. "All I did was say what Tommy needed."

"I've been telling Scott to be more vocal about how he feels about Tommy for years. He's listened, but ultimately, he's always fallen back on tough love. His father did it with him, and then Scott thought it was what he needed to do for Tommy. I had tried to break that generational pattern, but with very little luck." Linda slid a sheet pan full of the garlic bread we had made into the oven.

"How was what I did different?" I asked.

"You are clearly someone Tommy cares about very much and I think hearing it from you, Scott felt like he was hearing it straight from Tommy. You are the first girl that Tommy has ever brought home to us, so we knew it was serious with you."

I stared at Linda incredulously. "He's never brought anyone else home?"

Linda shook her head.

"What about Sutton?" The two of them had dated for over a year. I found it hard to believe that Tommy never brought her around his parents when they were all in San Diego at the time.

"We never met Sutton and probably for the better. I don't think that girl wanted to hear what I had to say about her choices when it came to my son. She never put him as a person first, only his money."

I glanced over to Tommy as I thought about what Linda had told me. I found it hard to believe that the first girl he would bring home, after never having brought anyone home before, would be a girl that he was fake dating. He hadn't even brought a girl that he had been seeing for over a year home to his parents. Why me?

Tommy caught me looking at him over his shoulder, and he flashed me a quick smile before rejoining the conversation with his dad. Part of me wondered if he had wanted Monica's contract to work so badly that he would toss his previous morals out the window. Or maybe there was something more that I was missing. Because Tommy didn't seem like the type of guy that would forgo everything he stood for simply to fix his past wrongdoings.

"It's like I'm watching my son morph into who I knew he always was. But I would be naive to think he had done that all on his own." Linda's voice brought my attention back to the kitchen. Her eyes were flitting between me and Tommy, taking in the way I had been looking at her son.

"I'm sorry?"

"You don't seem to fully believe that you are important to Tommy in the way that I have been saying. Tommy knew he would have to change some of his habits when he moved to Chicago, but I don't think he knew how to at the time. He's grown up and has become more of a man. A man's strength is in how gentle he loves a woman. And he treats you like you are the most precious gift this world has given him yet." Linda wrapped a hand around my forearm. "A mother can tell when her son's in love."

Love?

My mouth grew dry as my brain tried to process what she had said. Linda thought her son was in love with me, and her evidence wasn't the press photos or when we were staging for the cameras. Her evidence was moments that were for the two of us, with no expectations or obligations making us do anything.

Was she right?

Did Tommy love me?

It felt like there were too many obstacles in play for that to matter, even if it were true. Tommy was trying to regain control over his life and his career. I was trying to pick up the pieces of mine. We were both under contract for the rest of the season to publicly be linked as a couple. Meanwhile, I was getting paid to do so. The idea of us loving each other—despite all of it—felt impossible.

I looked back at Tommy, who was now walking over toward us with his eyes locked on mine. He gave me a small smile, one that was for only us. I couldn't help but return it as he and Scott joined me and Linda at the kitchen island.

Even if the possibility of a relationship with Tommy felt doomed from the start, that didn't mean I couldn't enjoy the time we had left with each other before everything would go back to normal. Because wasn't that what was going to happen? When the contract was over, he would move on with his career with a shiny new image and I would go back to trying to make a name for myself in my career.

"We could have helped!" Scott exclaimed, making me want to chuckle. It was the ultimate dad catchphrase after having missed all of the work while they were off doing something else.

"That's okay." I waved him off.

"So, Maggie," Scott started. "I was meaning to ask Tommy about this when I saw it, but now seems as good a time as any."

Tommy's eyes narrowed, like he still didn't quite trust his dad enough to not say something terrible following that sentence.

"Linda and I saw those horrible articles that were put out about your late fiancé. We wanted to make sure you were okay." Tommy's eyebrows shot up in surprise. I was expecting my heart to clench at the mention of those dreaded articles that had photos of me and Luke plastered all over them, but it didn't. Instead, I felt grateful that someone was asking if I was okay first and not digging to find some version of the truth that fit whatever narrative they had made up from the article.

"I'm okay," I told him. "It wasn't a lot of fun when I first saw it, but I've since realized that I owe them a thank-you for posting it. It let me close some doors that I had left open."

Tommy gave me a soft smile. It was one that was full of care and support, like if something were to be said next that I wouldn't be able to handle on my own, he had my back. I drew comfort from the feeling that gave me. Not even Olivia or my parents knew the extent to which I was still trying to heal from Luke. It had always been a journey I needed to take on my own. Until Tommy. His steady presence gave me the confidence to unburden some of my guilt and share it with someone else. Someone that would help me finish this path of healing I had taken.

"We're here if you need anything, sweetheart," Linda added.

It was an odd feeling the moment it seemed like your family was growing. Linda and Scott were checking on me like they would a daughter, like someone they cared about. It reminded me of Luke's parents. The loss of Luke had rocked my village more than just losing the love of my life.

Having Tommy's parents care about me was like filling a hole that I didn't realize had existed.

The conversation over dinner flowed. Scott and Tommy chatted easily about the season and Chicago, catching up over topics that previously had been off-limits to avoid arguments in the past. As the night wore on, I could see Tommy grow visibly lighter.

After dinner, Tommy walked his parents to the door. Linda reached up to give him a kiss on the cheek and whispered something in his ear before she followed Scott out into the night. Tommy closed the door behind them and paused for a second before he turned back around to look at me. There was a slight flush to his cheeks, and I wondered if that had been a result of whatever Linda had said to him.

"So I've been thinking about something all night." Tommy started walking slowly toward me. "Either my father was abducted by an alien and they replaced his brain, or somebody talked with him in a way that actually got through to him for once."

I turned away from him quickly and walked toward the living room to hide the nervous smile that was trying to spread across my face. What I had said to Scott was not done for appreciation from Tommy. I did it with his happiness in mind, not for selfish reasons.

"So what did you say?" he asked as he sat down on the couch next to me. His arm immediately rested on the couch cushion behind me, his fingers rubbing circles into my shoulder.

"I wasn't going to say anything to you," I told him.

"Did you think I wouldn't figure it out?" The smile on his face was quickly becoming my new favorite accessory of his.

"I wanted your dad to see all of the amazing things you've done this year. You've been trying to pave a new path for yourself, and you've done a damn good job."

Tommy didn't say anything right away. That smile stayed on his face, though, while he looked at me, his fingers now rubbing circles on my lower back. His head began to shake slowly from side to side as his eyes roved over my face.

"What?" I asked.

"I think you're amazing." The look he was giving me made a pressure fill inside me. My mind flashed back to what his mom had said earlier at dinner, that she knew when her son was in love. I wasn't sure if that was necessarily accurate, but the look on his face was making me wonder if Linda wasn't too far from the truth.

"You're pretty amazing yourself," I told him.

"Stop doing that." Tommy sighed.

"What?"

"Stop brushing off my compliments. You are an expert at dodging them and reflecting them back onto me. I want you to take them. Just take the compliment, Maggie." Tommy's arm encircled my shoulders and pulled me into his chest.

An awkward laugh rumbled out of my chest as my body curled into his. He had called out one of my worst qualities: my inability to graciously take any compliments anyone ever gave me without feeling extremely awkward.

"Will you let me call you amazing?" Tommy continued. "Because I think you are fantastic. You exude such passion for your career, you've got one of the biggest hearts I've ever seen, and you are always taking care of the people around you."

The intensity in his eyes as he told me what he thought about me practically took my breath away. There wasn't a single sign of him being insincere. Silence fell over us as we looked at each other. Tommy's fingers traced down the side of my face before they hooked under my jaw and drew me closer to him. His lips brushed mine before he pulled back, now inches from me.

"I never want to let you go." The words were barely loud enough for me to hear, making me wonder if I had heard him right.

Tommy's arms wrapped around my waist to support me as he slowly lowered me onto the couch. My body sank into the cushions before his body covered me from above. Every inch of me was yearning to be pressed against him, like Tommy was the other half of me and I was desperately trying to make us whole again.

His mouth covered mine again and it was like his kiss had me running on all cylinders. I was tired of feeling hesitant about giving in to my feelings for Tommy. Everything about him drove me crazy. The way he kissed me, the way his hands seemed to want to feel every part of me, the way his eyes crinkled when he smiled, and how all of these were quickly taking root in my head as some of my favorite things.

Our movements grew frantic, like we couldn't keep up with the need that was running through us. Fingers were digging into skin, pulling at clothing, tangling in hair. I was sure the emotions I was feeling would consume me if they weren't expressed in some way, and it seemed that Tommy felt the same way.

He made quick work of my clothes, leaving me naked as I undressed him. As Tommy held me in his arms, it felt like he was making a mark on my heart in the shape of him, and I was terrified that I'd have to cover it like a bad tattoo. But a much larger part of me pushed that thought away, too concerned with how perfect he felt nestled there in the spot beneath my rib cage.

MAGGIE

The sun coming in through the curtains of Tommy's room the next morning woke me up from my deep sleep. I pulled the comforter up around my body, trying to keep any chill away from me. My clothes still lay in a pile on the living room floor downstairs. I reached out a hand toward Tommy, only to feel a cool, empty bed.

I pulled the covers back and padded over to his dresser. The first drawer had a stack of his T-shirts and some sweatpants. I grabbed one of each and threw them on. The shirt came down to mid-thigh and I had to cinch the sweatpants as tight as they would go so they wouldn't fall off my hips. As soon as I walked out of the bedroom, the smell of food hit my nose. My mouth instantly watered. Tommy was stationed in front of the stove, a pair of pajama bottoms slung low on his hips. His chest was still bare, and just the sight of it made me want to go for round two on the kitchen island.

"Good morning," I rasped, sleep still clinging to my voice. Tommy turned around in surprise, spatula in hand.

"I was hoping to bring you breakfast in bed." My heart melted at the disappointed look on his face.

"I can go back." I pointed a thumb back up the stairs, a playful smile on my face.

"Then I'd miss this view in front of me." Tommy set the spatula down and came over to lift me onto the kitchen island.

Maybe my daydream might actually come true.

"You look so sexy in my clothes," Tommy growled into my ear, sending butterflies flying all over my body.

He went back over to the stove to flip the pancake he was making, giving me the perfect view to watch him at work. My eyes roamed over the strong muscles of his back that were covered in black ink. The tattoo sleeves on his arms flowed into the tattoos that spread across his chest and upper back. They were bold, full of thick lines and sharp patterns. His body was a true work of art.

"When did you start getting tattoos?" I asked him as he flipped another pancake onto a stack next to him.

"When I was eighteen, right after I got drafted. I started on the sleeves first."

"How did you decide on them?"

"I designed them myself, actually. I created the patterns in high school and desperately wanted them tattooed on me." My eyebrows shot up in surprise. I definitely hadn't expected him to tell me that he had made them.

"They're amazing." My eyes traced each line, curve, and design that flowed effortlessly into the next. They helped define the hard planes of his muscles that made my mouth water just looking at them.

"Thank you," he told me as he brought a plate of pancakes over to me. A bottle of syrup was already on the counter, and I dumped an unhealthy amount onto the stack of fluffy goodness in front of me.

"Shooting for a sugar high?" Tommy asked as he leaned against the kitchen counter across from me, digging into his own stack of pancakes.

"How could you not want to smother your pancakes in an absurd amount of syrup?" Tommy shook his head at me with a smile on his face as he stabbed another piece of pancake with his fork.

"So how do you think the season is going?" I asked him.

"I feel really good about everything right now." Tommy set his plate on the counter next to him and crossed his arms over his chest. "I think

I've done enough to really cement myself as an asset for the Cougars, and I feel good about this season. I've kept to myself, kept my head down, worked hard, and tried to focus on baseball."

"With extenuating circumstances," I added with an awkward smile. He could have had less stress in his life if he hadn't offered to take me home from the club those few months ago.

"I don't see a single thing I'd change about this season." His eyes stayed glued on mine and again made it feel like I was glowing from the inside out. "I have a lot to thank you for with how this season is turning out, honestly."

I waved him off, busying myself with the pancakes that were left in front of me. "What about you?" he asked me after a moment.

"What about me?"

"Do you feel like this season is going well for you?"

I had to actually stop and think about what he had asked me. How had this season gone for me?

Of course, I had aspirations for my career and was trying to gain as much experience as I could to achieve them, but had this season actually moved me toward those goals? Photography was my passion in life and always would be, but it had opened my eyes to different directions mys career could take me. After a few years in professional sports, I knew this was where I wanted to be. But the idea of running my own media department one day and becoming a mentor for other young photographers and media experts excited me.

"I know I've taken some great shots this season."

"You definitely have," Tommy agreed. I chewed on my thoughts for a minute longer before I finally spoke the truth of my desires.

"But I think eventually I want May's job," I told him.

"Okay, so what're you going to do about it?" Tommy asked me.

It was refreshing having someone who challenged me like that. He wasn't jumping in to give me his advice; he was simply asking me to think outside my own box, come up with my own answers. But I knew that if I needed someone to brainstorm or strategize with, he would make a step-by-step guide for me to achieve my goals.

"I definitely need to speak with May."

"Probably," Tommy agreed. "But I'd like to say that your season *has* been phenomenal. You've taken some killer shots that have been featured, and you've done all of that while dealing with me."

"You're not that bad to deal with."

"Even if that were the truth, the paparazzi that like to follow me definitely are not easy to deal with."

I couldn't find it in me to tell him that wasn't the truth, because this season had been emotionally exhausting for me. The side effects of the contract had weighed heavily on me. I was on edge when I went out in public, waiting for someone with a camera to jump in my face. But I knew that if I told him that, he would never forgive himself for allowing the contract to happen in the first place. If I had learned anything about Tommy in the past few months, it was that he would have rather given up his contract with the Cougars than force me to be in that situation with him if I didn't want to do it at any point.

I couldn't tell him any of that because everything that had happened between him and me would have never happened. I never would have figured out that I was falling fast for him.

After breakfast, Tommy dropped me off at my apartment. It was a much-needed day off for the team and for the staff after the big win. The long stretches of multiple games without a break were starting to take a toll on everyone. People were dragging, trying to get to the All-Star break, and hoping that we'd all have enough energy to get us through to the end.

It was time off that I desperately needed to get my life together. I had laundry to do, an apartment to clean, and groceries to buy. But none of those things seemed to occupy my interest as I sat on my couch in my tiny apartment. The only thing I could think about was what Linda had said the day before.

Did Tommy really love me?

If that were the case, could I handle a relationship with him in the spotlight?

Every fiber in me was screaming that it didn't matter because I was irrevocably, madly in love with him. I had known it for some time. Hell, I had probably been in love with him longer than I had realized.

I was pacing my apartment, trying to burn off the feeling that was building inside me. But it seemed like with every step I took, the urge inside me was growing. A thought had occurred to me that I needed to tell Tommy how I felt or I'd surely do something stupid if I didn't. I could practically imagine myself chickening out of ever telling him and figuring out some way to self-sabotage the one good thing that had happened to me in years simply out of fear.

Without letting myself think too much on what I had decided to do, I started to pick up my purse and bus card. But when I got to the door, I hesitated. I remembered Tommy telling me that he would probably be heading to the clubhouse this evening to work out and take some extra swings. If I took the bus, I would miss him at his house. The only problem was, I still didn't have a car.

I cursed myself as I debated what to do. It seemed that there was only one thing I could do. Mrs. Adams's soap operas were blaring through her door, and I was worried she wouldn't hear my knocks over the sound of Fabio breaking up with his current fling. Didn't she know that I had my own love story to secure?

My knocks grew a little more persistent before I was full on banging my open hand on her door. I heard the television turn down and then slow footsteps making their way toward me. Mrs. Adams pulled the door open. She was an older woman with gray hair that she liked to keep in curlers. Her glasses sat on the bridge of her nose or hung from her neck on her glasses holder. She always had a matching sweater set on, even at the height of summer, and rarely smiled.

"Hi, Mrs. Adams. I have a favor to ask of you," I told her.

"I don't have any sugar." Her voice was crackly, like sandpaper.

"Oh, no. It's not that," I tried to tell her.

"I don't have any eggs."

"I'm not here for food, Mrs. Adams." I glanced down at the watch on my wrist. "I was wondering if I could borrow your car."

Mrs. Adams stared at me for a few minutes, her eyes narrowing as she looked me up and down. I was beginning to grow uncomfortable when she finally spoke again. "But you don't drive."

I was surprised that she had noticed. "I've been getting comfortable with driving again. I just don't have my own car yet."

"What do you need it for?"

Part of me didn't want to tell her the truth. I wondered if I should make up a lie about something more important than telling a guy that I was falling in love with him. But something inside me told me to tell her the truth.

"I need to tell a guy that I'm in love with him." It was weird speaking the words out loud. I hadn't even told Olivia yet how I felt.

She pursed her lips as she watched me. Without saying a word, she shut the door in my face. I jumped, startled at the loud sound the door made. Of all the ways I had expected Mrs. Adams to react, I had not expected her to slam her door in my face. I stayed there a moment longer before I turned to head down the stairs, deciding that I could at least give the bus a shot and wait on his steps until he got home. Then the door opened again and Mrs. Adams reappeared, holding her car keys in her hand.

"Go get him," she told me firmly, handing her keys over.

"Thank you!" I breathed, gently taking them from her hands.

Her door slammed in my face again, and a few minutes later, her soap opera was blaring once more. I wasn't going to wait for her to come back and change her mind. Mrs. Adams's car was an old Buick that had been kept in immaculate condition. It made me only slightly worried about getting behind the wheel with the little practice I'd had, but I wanted to tell Tommy how I felt. Even if that meant doing something that terrified me to get there.

I hit the unlock button on the key fob and pulled the driver's-side door open. The inside of Mrs. Adams's car smelled like Chanel perfume and cinnamon Altoids. It flooded my senses and sent my gag reflex reeling. I punched the button to roll all of the windows down after I turned the key over to start the engine.

My chest clenched as I wrapped my hands around the steering wheel. Every part of me wanted to wait for the bus, but I knew that true growth came when there was a battle to be won. Tonight, the battle would be driving across town in Chicago traffic. I hoped the prize at the end would be worth it.

Without giving it another thought, I put the car in drive and pulled out of my apartment complex's parking lot. The traffic on the side road that I was pulling out onto was slow, and I eased myself onto the road, making sure to check my mirrors and drive precisely the speed limit.

It'll be fine, I told myself.

I let out one more breath as I drove out onto the busy road, keeping in the right lane so people could pass me because I'd be damned if I was going to keep up with the flow of traffic tonight. There was one thing I didn't miss about being behind the wheel and that was the honking. When you were in the passenger seat, it didn't feel as jarring as someone laying on the horn behind you, cutting around you, and flipping you the bird as they did so.

Tommy's brownstone was a good twenty minutes across town, and before the accident, I would have turned on some music to occupy the time. Tonight, I didn't want any distractions. The drive might have been slow, but it was still faster than taking the bus, and it gave me the time to think about what I was going to say to Tommy. I knew I wouldn't be capable of coming right out and telling him exactly how I felt. But I also didn't want to make a complete fool of myself trying to beat around the metaphorical bush that was my feelings.

My knuckles had turned white from gripping the steering wheel so hard. I would need to merge onto Lake Shore Drive next, and my anxiety built at the idea of being surrounded by so many other drivers. With one more breath, I merged onto the road and prayed that my instincts would take over. Like driving was like riding a bike.

A car honked at me as I merged in front of it with plenty of space between us. I mumbled a curse word under my breath, not missing the road rage that came with driving. There were only a few minutes left in my drive when I pulled off toward Lincoln Park. I kept my eyes peeled around me, refusing to look away from the street. I was sure I would have driving habits that would stay with me for the rest of my life after that night. Some would only be around for a while until I was comfortable again, while others I would keep with me as a reminder of the night that sent me down a fork in the road that I had not expected.

I pulled off onto Tommy's road and drove by his house to try to see if he was still home. On the first go-around, I noticed that his lights were still on, so I continued driving around the block to find a parking spot. My heartbeat started to quicken with every second that passed. Every question I had started to race through my mind.

Did I hold a boombox above my head?

Should I give him some grand speech?

Did I propose a new contract for a *real* relationship?

But no, none of those felt right. None of those were me and Tommy. As I mulled over what to do, I walked up to Tommy's brownstone with every intention of standing out front until the solution came to me.

The light inside Tommy's apartment was still on when I stopped in front of it. His front curtains were pulled back, giving me the perfect view inside. I saw Tommy pacing near the windows, dressed in workout clothes. He looked like he was talking to someone, but I didn't see his phone in his hand. A second later, someone else stepped into view.

My heart dropped all the way to my feet as I recognized who was in Tommy's home.

Sutton James.

Tommy was articulating something to her while using his hands, and she was reaching out to him, trying to grab on to him. Every part of my brain was screaming at me to leave as quickly as possible. It would only save me the pain of watching whatever was about to unfold between them. But it was like my feet were becoming part of the concrete sidewalk below them. My eyes were glued on the scene in front of me, like I was watching the part of a rom-com where the main character didn't get the guy. The only sad part was the main character was me and it seemed like I was most definitely *not* getting the guy.

Whatever speech Tommy had given her must have been over, because the next thing I knew he was wrapping his arms around Sutton, his face buried in her neck like he did with me. I wanted to cry and throw up all at once. I couldn't rip my eyes away from Tommy with his arms around his ex-girlfriend even if I tried.

A part of me had always known I would end up the fool in this situation. This whole mess started because of Tommy's previous actions, and like they always say, leopards don't change their spots.

TOMMY

As soon as I had dropped Maggie off this morning, I cursed myself that I didn't tell her how I really felt. The second I realized what Maggie had done to help get my dad and me to communicate on the same level, I knew I was a goner. I wanted to tell her over breakfast, but all the feelings I had for her seemed to clog my throat, unable to be voiced.

The entire ride back to my brownstone consisted of me debating turning back around to tell her or trying to figure out some big gesture I could do to prove it to her like one of her favorite romantic movies. My planning continued once I got back inside my apartment to tell the girl that I love exactly how I felt about her. Except my planning was interrupted by the sound of my doorbell.

Could it be Maggie? Maybe she feels the same way and came back to tell me?

I hurried to the front door and threw it open without bothering to check who was on the other side. A smile spread across my face at the expectation of seeing the girl of my dreams on the other side, only to be knocked off when the girl of my nightmares stood there instead.

"Sutton?"

"Can we talk?"

"Why are you in Chicago?"

"I'm here on a brand trip." She pushed past me into my apartment, not even bothering to wait for an invitation. My mouth remained open in shock as I shut the door behind her.

"What are you doing here?"

"I miss you." Her words struck me in the gut harder than a sucker punch.

"You what?"

"You heard me." Sutton began to reach out for me, but I took a step back, putting distance between us.

"When I saw you at the ESPYS, I realized how big of a mistake I made letting you go," Sutton continued on, like me trying to put as much distance as I could between us didn't bother her. "You're turning into the man I always knew you could be, and I thought maybe we could give us another shot."

"No."

"What?" Sutton asked, her eyebrows drawing together. It was a word she didn't hear often, so I wondered if she remembered what it meant.

"I don't want to be with you, Sutton." I began to pace the room, the feelings that I had for Maggie filling back inside me. "I'm in love with someone. Someone who never wished I was a different person. She saw me for the man I am. She never brought the worst parts of me out to exploit."

"I would never do such a thing." Sutton gasped. She was putting on an Oscar-worthy performance just for the two of us.

"Sutton, you were only with me for my money. Don't act like you and I both didn't know the truth." Sutton began to step toward me again, trying to reach for me. "How about we agree that we're better off as acquaintances?"

"Acquaintances?" Sutton asked incredulously.

"I don't think being friends is on the table either, Sutton." Pride rushed through me for standing up for what I needed. In the past, I would have folded for what she wanted. Now I had the power to put my foot down and it all stemmed from the confidence that Maggie helped me remember I had.

"I'm sorry to hear that." The act that Sutton had been putting on before dropped. "I'm sorry I took up so much of your time. I should go."

I knew that I couldn't let this woman walk out of my house without telling her I was grateful. Because I was. She was one of the people who helped push me to be the man I am today. She wasn't a positive catalyst, but she was a catalyst nonetheless.

"Thank you for helping push me to be better," I told her as I pulled her in for a hug. "I will always be grateful for that. You helped me find my home with the best person that has ever walked into my life."

Sutton nodded her head, clearly wanting to end this conversation as quickly as she could to spare herself the embarrassment.

"The next time you're in San Diego, feel free to reach out," she told me as we headed out onto the street toward her car. "I promise I can still give you a good time."

"Thanks, but no thanks," I told her, a small laugh shared between us at her last-ditch effort. "Have a nice life."

My patience was thinning. I had moved on, started a new life, and had a fresh start. I wasn't about to let her taint any of this. We walked in silence toward her rental car that was parked on the side street by my building. I reached to open the driver's door for her, ready for her to be out of my life for good. With a little more force than necessary, I shut the door behind her once she climbed in. The sound of her window rolling down filled the night around us.

"You deserve happiness, Tommy," she told me. Anger coursed through me at her words. Who was she to tell me what I deserved? All she ever did was use me. My eyes dropped to my feet as I fought to keep myself from exploding. She didn't deserve anything else from me, not even my anger. She would only relish the fact that she could still pull that sort of a response from me. I gave her a nod to acknowledge that I heard her before I stepped back from her car. She rolled her window back up and slowly pulled away from the curb. I watched the car until the lights disappeared around the corner. The weight on my chest I felt the second I saw her finally lifted away.

Movement grabbed my attention out of the corner of my eye, and I looked down to see Maggie, crouched behind a random car.

"Maggie?" I called, walking closer. The despair on her face was evident, and it twisted a knife in my gut. Something had happened to her, and everything in me wanted to make it better.

She stood up and looked around, clearly searching for a way to escape. But my steps were able to catch her before she could leave. She looked like a trapped animal, and I didn't want to spook her.

"When did you get here?" I continued my line of questioning, trying to get her to tell me what was going on. My eyes shifted down to the keys dangling from her fingers and then to the car behind her.

"Did you drive here?" I was now a few paces from her and close enough to take in the smeared mascara and red eyes. "Are you okay?"

Seconds later, Olivia's car came to a stop next to her and she rolled down the window to catch Maggie's eye. Without giving me another look or even a response, she pulled open Olivia's door and dove inside.

"Maggie!" I called as Olivia's car sped away from me. There was a sinking feeling in my gut that something had happened between us, something I wasn't aware of. I realized she and I might be on a sinking ship and I didn't have any sort of life preserver to get us out. I knew I needed to do something or we'd be lost at sea forever, drifting apart until there was no hope left.

MAGGIE

I had stayed out in front of Tommy's brownstone five minutes longer than I needed to, watching him talk with Sutton. I don't know what made me stay there, but I think part of me was hoping I'd blink and Sutton would suddenly not be there anymore.

It would just be Tommy.

My Tommy.

Alone.

But every time I blinked and opened my eyes again, I saw the two of them talking with each other. I saw Tommy smiling about whatever Sutton was talking with him about, and I felt every shred of my recently repaired heart obliterating inside my chest.

Before I did anything embarrassing, I hurried back toward Mrs. Adams's car with tears in my eyes. A small voice in the back of my head warned me that driving right now probably wasn't the brightest idea, but all I wanted to do was get far away from Tommy.

I slid inside the safety of the car, feeling like the four walls were enough privacy to let a few tears slide down my cheeks. Somehow, seeing Sutton in Tommy's arms didn't feel like a complete surprise. It was almost the perfect twist of fate to let me believe my luck had started to change, to let me believe that I was finally worth finding love again, and then take all of that away from me in the blink of an eye.

Even though every part of me wanted to stay parked on the side of the road and throw myself a pity party, I didn't want to risk Tommy or Sutton coming around the corner to see me parked there like a fool. So I slid the key back into the ignition and turned the engine over.

To hear nothing.

I tried again.

Nothing.

My mouth dropped open in surprise at the sheer audacity that fate was testing me with in that moment. I tried the key one more time to make sure that this was really happening, and when the car stayed silent, I pushed my head back into the headrest of the seat.

"Are you kidding me right now?" I groaned up at the ceiling. "Can someone up there give me a break for once? Have I not been good?"

With no other choice, I pulled my phone out and dialed the only lifeline I could think of.

"Hey, girl! How's your day off?" Olivia's voice came over the line.

"I need you to pick me up somewhere. I don't care how long it takes." I didn't bother with any small talk. All I wanted to do was curl up into a ball on my couch and eat an entire tub of ice cream. The faster I could get there, the better.

"Where are you?" She didn't even bother asking me if I was okay, which was why I loved her. Her priority was getting to me first to make sure I was safe before she asked what happened. I gave her the address where I was before we hung up the phone.

As soon as I refocused on the quiet space around me, the only thing my brain could think about was Tommy with his arms around Sutton, and I knew that if I stayed inside the car any longer, I would surely explode into a mess of tears. Before I could watch Sutton in Tommy's arms for probably the hundredth time in the past five minutes, I threw the door open to Mrs. Adams's Buick and leaned against the side of the car. My breath was coming in heavily like I had run a marathon as I tried to prevent myself from experiencing any kind of anxiety episode.

I raked my hands over my eyes, sure that I had smeared my mascara but not really caring. All I wanted to do was pull these overwhelming emotions out of my body and distance myself from them as much as possible. But before I could attempt that form of exorcism, I heard the one voice I really was hoping to avoid.

Before I risked getting caught standing around the corner from Tommy's house with raccoon eyes and snot smeared on my shirt, I dove behind the trunk of the car with the hope that I could avoid being spotted. A few seconds later, Tommy walked around the corner with Sutton. The two weren't walking particularly close to each other, but they were both laughing at something that had been previously shared.

Envy raged within me. My heart desperately ached for me to be in Sutton's place, sharing a conspiratorial laugh with Tommy. I hated the fact that she was getting the opportunity to do that, and I hated the fact that I felt such a thing. Logically, I didn't have the right to be jealous over who Tommy shared any sort of emotions with, only because he had never been mine in the first place.

Their voices grew closer and I drew into myself, hoping to make myself as small as possible. The closer it sounded like they were, the more I slowly edged to slide around to the opposite side of the car. Tommy walked Sutton to what looked to be a rental car and opened the driver's door for her. She rolled the window down after she pulled the door shut, and luckily they were close enough that I could hear what she said to him.

"You deserve happiness, Tommy." Tommy dropped his eyes toward his feet and gave her a reluctant nod before he backed away from the car and gave Sutton enough room to pull away from the curb. My mind raced with the worst-case scenario.

Did Sutton convince him that he wasn't happy here in Chicago?

Did he want his old life back?

Was she what he wanted?

Was *she* the happiness he deserved?

A small part of my brain recognized the irrationality of the thoughts flying through my head, but they felt too consuming at the moment to ignore. A stupid tear snaked down my face, and I swiped at it with the back of my hand.

Tommy's eyes shifted over to me, crouching behind a car, clearly trying to avoid being caught.

"Maggie?" he called, walking closer.

I shot up and looked around, desperately wishing for Olivia's car to magically appear. But Tommy quickened his pace, seeing my resemblance to a trapped animal and not wanting me to bolt.

"When did you get here?" His questions kept coming, but my brain wasn't able to process any answers to them. Tommy's eyes shifted down to the keys dangling from my fingers and then to the car behind me.

"Did you drive here?" He was now a few paces from me and probably close enough to take in the smeared mascara and red eyes. "Are you okay?"

Luckily, it seemed like life had taken pity on me and given me a break. Olivia's car came to a stop next to me, and she rolled down the window to catch my eye. Without giving Tommy another look or even a response, I pulled open Olivia's door and dove inside. I heard him shout my name again as Olivia pulled away, leaving him disappearing behind us in the rearview mirror.

After a few minutes of silence, Olivia finally turned to me. "What happened?"

"His ex was here." I didn't add anything else. Olivia knew Tommy's history and she could connect the dots from prior knowledge.

"Are you two done?" The question made me pause. I thought about the contract that we both had signed.

Can we be done?

"I'm not sure we can be done," I told her truthfully. I didn't care that Monica wanted nobody to know the truth behind the origin of Tommy's and my relationship. All I wanted was to talk through my very real feelings for a boy with my best friend.

"What do you mean you're not sure you *can* be done?" Olivia asked.

I let out a breath before I looked back over at her. "I haven't been telling you the truth."

Olivia's eyebrows shot up in surprise. I was not the type of person who would lie or *could* lie very well, so the fact that I was telling her I had lied to her and she hadn't already suspected it was probably catching her off guard.

"My relationship with Tommy didn't start off real." The words felt weird coming out of my mouth, like my brain was finally registering what I had gotten myself into. Olivia didn't ask me to elaborate. The deafening silence between us spoke the words for her.

"The night the two of us left the club was innocent. I wanted to leave, and Tommy offered to take me home. When the paparazzi posted the photo they took of us, it didn't go over well with the PR team for the Cougars." Olivia turned south on Lake Shore Drive, driving toward my apartment. "Monica, the head of the PR team, gave Tommy only one option, which was to fake date me. She offered us a contract. Tommy would get to keep his job with the Cougars, and I would get a fat bonus."

Olivia coughed next to me, her eyes widening. "Are you serious?"

"Yeah," I told her. "Monica told us no one could know. I was too afraid of telling you and risking your job, so I kept it to myself."

"Maggie Redford!" she exclaimed. "Shut up! You hustler!"

A smile spread across my face at Olivia's outburst. I knew her mind was probably reeling. This was completely uncharacteristic of me.

"So what happened?" Olivia's voice was insistent, like she was now invested in the story.

"I caught feelings." I ducked my eyes down toward my hands, not wanting to see any disappointment on my best friend's face. "I'm pretty sure I'm in love with him."

"In *love*?"

"I was actually going over to his place just now to tell him, but when I got there, I saw him hugging Sutton James, his ex-girlfriend."

"Why is she coming out of the woodwork?" Olivia's support for me was exactly why I loved her.

"She must have decided she wanted Tommy again when she saw us at the ESPYS, but the reason we are in this mess in the first place is because of Tommy's reputation. So who's to say he hasn't been playing me the whole time?"

Olivia pulled up to my apartment, and the two of us got out to head inside. I was dreading having to tell Mrs. Adams that her car was stuck in Lincoln Park, but I was going to handle that later. Right now, I wanted to give myself time to grieve a relationship that may have never been real before I had to face her again.

"Were they just hugging?" Olivia asked as I unlocked my apartment door.

"That's all I saw."

"Are you sure it wasn't an innocent hug?" Olivia pressed.

"Olivia, are you serious?" I threw myself down on the couch and pulled a discarded blanket around me.

"Maggie, I need you to listen to me for a second." She walked over to sit next to me on the couch. "Even though I may not have been in on the whole charade, I know my best friend, and the girl I saw with Tommy Mikals was someone I hadn't met before. She looked alive. I also may not know Tommy very well, but the way that boy looked at you when there was no one to fool or cameras to capture something was like you were turning into his whole world."

It was like fate wanted to rear its head again because my phone went off and Tommy's name flashed across the screen. Olivia and I stared down at the phone. A small part of me wanted to pick up the call and hear what he was going to say, but a bigger part of me was too scared that he was going to lie to me again and I wouldn't be able to tell the difference. The phone continued to go off for a few more seconds before the call went to voice mail.

Olivia reached over to take my hands in hers. Her thumbs rubbed up and down the back of my hand as she looked at me. "Babe, you have effectively blocked out every potential for a relationship in your life. This is the first time you did this on your own. You willingly got into this relationship with Tommy, whether it was fake or not to begin with. I think you need to give him a chance."

What she said was logical. Tommy deserved to either explain or defend himself. But I wasn't ready for that conversation. I knew I couldn't tell Olivia that though, so I nodded my head, pretending to agree with her in the moment.

"Listen, I really need some alone time right now," I trailed off.

"Of course." Olivia stood up, but not before wrapping me in a hug. "I'll check on you tomorrow."

I walked her to the door, giving her one more wave as she left. As soon as the door closed, I threw myself back down on the couch and flipped the television on. The previous movie I had been watching was paused and I clicked play, transporting myself into someone else's happily ever after and away from my own disaster.

MAGGIE

I never thought my fake relationship with Tommy would get to the part where I was considering leaving my job with the Chicago Cougars, a job I loved, just to get away from him. But the ache in my heart was so deep, I thought I'd surely never be able to look him in the eyes again, much less continue to take his photo. My heart felt like it had been ripped from my chest the moment I saw Sutton James wrapped in Tommy's arms like a leech.

My computer balanced on my legs as I multitasked between scrolling through jobs halfheartedly and watching *The Proposal*. Part of me wondered if watching something that was a little too closely related to the situation that was causing me so much pain was actually good for my mental health, but I couldn't boycott Ryan Reynolds and Sandra Bullock just because of a heartbreak.

As I was shoving my mouth with popcorn and debating if my previous thought about JCPenney hiring me would look like a down-grade on a résumé, my apartment door opened and Olivia barreled inside. She looked around at the sight in front of her. I had spent the night hunkered down and hadn't bothered to clean up the takeout boxes and dishes I had used last night and today.

"I'm here to check on you. You haven't responded to any of my texts, Maggie," Olivia said as she looked around in partial awe at my ability to turn my apartment into something similar to a landfill.

"And your point is?" I asked around my mouthful of popcorn.

Olivia took in what I was watching, the remnants of snacks around me, the empty bottle of wine from the previous night, and the fact that I was still in my pajamas.

"Is this really what you want for yourself?" she asked me.

"What do you mean?"

"Do you really want the only form of happiness you ever feel to be from movies?"

Ouch.

"What I had with Tommy is over, Olivia. There's no happiness coming from that relationship anymore. Honestly, was it even a relationship to begin with?"

Olivia walked over to my coffee table and swiped the remote to my television. She clicked the off button before tossing the remote on the couch next to me.

"What are you doing?" she asked, waving her hands at my computer.

"Looking at jobs," I mumbled.

"You're joking, right?" Olivia looked at me like I had grown three heads. "You're going to get a different job just because a guy you really like did something you're not even sure he actually did?"

I shrugged because I knew that if I opened my mouth to defend myself, nothing logical would come out, because there was nothing logical about what I was doing.

"I know my best friend is stronger than that."

At that moment, I felt anything but strong. The image of Tommy's arms around his ex-girlfriend had been replaying in my head all night.

"Has he tried to contact you?" Olivia asked as she reached for my phone. When she flipped my screen around, her eyebrows shot up. I knew what she saw. There were about thirty unread text messages from Tommy and a handful of ignored calls.

"Did you not pick up any of these?"

"I don't want to talk to him."

"You don't even know what actually happened, Maggie. You're

assuming!" Olivia threw her hands up in the air, giving me a look like she couldn't believe what I was doing.

"Our relationship wasn't even real," I told her.

Olivia sighed and sat down on the couch next to me. Her hands gripped my shoulders as she turned me to face her.

"Maggie, you're a terrible actor," she told me. "You can barely make it through lying to May when you want to take a sick day to grab brunch when you're not really sick. You're trying to tell me that all of a sudden you became the best actor I know and convinced everyone, including your family and best friend, that you weren't head over heels for a guy?"

"I never denied that I didn't catch feelings. That's why I'm in this mess, Olivia."

"I wasn't done." She pointed a finger at me, warning me to stay quiet. "You're also trying to tell me that Tommy Mikals, the guy that used to go through girls like toilet paper, all of a sudden was willing to be monogamous because of a fake relationship? And that all of the times I caught him staring at you like a lovesick puppy at practices or on the bus or on the plane or at any time when there were *no* cameras around meant he didn't really like you?"

"Even if that were all true," I replied, "he told me that at one time he would have forgiven Sutton for everything she did if she would have chosen him. That may have been that moment."

"You will never know for sure until you find out for yourself." Olivia's gaze softened as she watched me. "I've seen you grow significantly this season because of that man. I don't want to see you regress. You are so close to fully moving on and allowing yourself to be happy."

Olivia wasn't far from the truth. With each passing day, I felt lighter than ever before. It was like I was detaching a piece of baggage with every thread I tied. I knew I wasn't done yet, but Tommy had been a big reason for the progress that I had made this year.

"I'm not saying you need to forgive him." Olivia pulled me into a hug. "I'm just saying that you have the opportunity to be happy again and you're letting it slip from your fingers. I'm saying you need to *try*."

A small part of me knew that what she was saying was the right thing to do. I had effectively cut Tommy out again after I had seen

Sutton in his arms. I was too scared for my biggest fears to be confirmed, so suspending it in time forever with no answers was better than getting the answer I didn't want. But the realistic part of my brain realized that I deserved to hear Tommy out. The rate with which he was trying to get ahold of me proved that he wanted to talk to me. I had to be strong enough to listen to what he had to say.

"Okay," I told her.

"And a shower. You definitely need a shower."

I laughed into her shoulder as she continued to hug me. My arms tightened around her waist as I held on to one of my biggest lifelines for the past few years.

"Something is still holding you back." Olivia didn't say it like a question. She knew me well enough to know the truth.

"I think there is something I need to do before I talk to Tommy."

Olivia held me at arm's length as she studied my face. "Do you need me?" she asked. I shook my head in response. I knew this was something I needed to do on my own.

"Promise me you'll talk to him?" Olivia asked as she gathered her purse. "And shower. You *have* to shower."

"I promise," I told her, and meant it. I wasn't sure when I would talk to Tommy, but I knew I would eventually.

Olivia pointed at me as she backed out of my apartment. "Call me if you need anything."

"Always."

Olivia gave me one more smile before she closed the door behind her, leaving me in the mess that was my apartment with a completely different mess inside my head. I lifted my armpit and took a whiff. The first thing on my list was definitely to take a shower. Then I would deal with my apartment once I didn't smell like I'd been avoiding taking care of myself.

I took my time with tidying my apartment. It was therapeutic and gave me the chance to think about what I had to do next. There were a couple of things on my list I needed to do before I could talk with Tommy. As I cleaned off the mountain of dirty dishes from my kitchen counter, a piece of paper slipped to the floor.

"Shit," I breathed before reaching down to snatch it off the ground.

It was the check I received for the contract, only now it had a stain on the corner from the pizza I had the night before.

I stared at that check before reaching for my purse and sliding it inside.

The bus ride to the stadium allowed me to rehearse what I was going to say to Monica enough times in my head that I only hoped it would come out from memory. The stadium was relatively empty today. There were a few people cleaning and getting ready for the next home game coming up this week, but it was practically a ghost town. The C-suite was the complete opposite of the stadium below it. People in suits were hustling from room to room, making the wheels turn behind the scenes.

Monica's office was toward the back of the floor, and the trek to it was the longest hike of my life. I had to remind myself that what I wanted to tell her wasn't something that I was dreading doing. It was something I should have done the moment I had started developing feelings for Tommy.

I knocked on Monica's door, drawing her attention from where she was sitting at her desk. The woman was the epitome of a boss bitch. Her suit was perfectly tailored to her body, not a single hair was out of place, and the look of a shark stayed firmly on her face. She pushed back from her desk and rose when she saw me.

"Maggie! What a surprise," she exclaimed. Her arms swept toward the chair on the other side of her desk. "Please have a seat."

Once the two of us sat in our respective seats, Monica turned to look at me. "What can I help you with?"

"I need to talk about my contract with Tommy." Monica pursed her lips and sat back in her chair. She didn't say anything, only allowed me to continue. "I will understand if I can't terminate the contract, but I don't want the money that I agreed to. What I would like to do is to give back the payment agreed upon. It doesn't feel right anymore to take it."

I slid her the check that May had given me weeks ago, still untouched. Monica's eyebrows shot up, but that was the only sign of her surprise. Her eyes searched my face, trying to discover whatever it was I wasn't saying.

"You actually love him," Monica concluded.

Was I that easy to read? I opened my mouth to say something and then closed it. Opened it to try again before closing it once more.

"Can you do what I'm asking?" I decided to avoid acknowledging what Monica had said and instead confirm what I wanted to be done.

"Are you sure?" she asked me.

"Yes."

"Oh, and one other thing," I told her.

Monica waited patiently.

"Never speculate on our future together with the press again. That was never a part of the contract. Stick to the terms of the deal or I will walk away from this, and if it's not clear already, I'm done with all of this once the terms of our agreement come to a close."

Monica frowned, but she gave me a short nod of acknowledgment.

I had never been more sure about a decision. I had spent the entire night staring at that check, thinking about how it could change my life. I could afford a nice high-rise apartment for many years with that money. I could buy myself a new car. I could get a new camera, expand my portfolio, and take classes. The possibilities were endless. But none of those things seemed worth it if it would put at risk any potential for a relationship that Tommy and I had. I wasn't sure where he and I stood, but I couldn't live with myself if I cashed that check. Even if Tommy turned me down and told me that maybe we weren't the best decision—I knew my heart would be broken, but I would at least be able to look at myself in the mirror. I couldn't monetize the time we shared together. It would only taint the happiness I had while we were together. My time with Tommy was more than a bunch of zeros on a check.

I stood up quickly, wanting to leave her office as fast as I could. There was still one more thing I needed to do before I could talk with Tommy, and it was probably the most important thing on my list.

MAGGIE

I found myself standing in front of Luke's gravestone. It was the first time I had mustered up the courage to visit, which was mostly due to Tommy's encouragement and Olivia's pep talk from the day before.

It was four years since the accident took him from me, and the first year when it didn't feel like my heart was dying inside my chest from guilt and loneliness. The past three months had given myself back and more. I wasn't a shell of myself living out in the world and hiding behind my camera. This Maggie was the version I knew Luke would be proud of.

I sat down with my back against the gravestone and let out a breath that had been pent up inside me for the past four years.

"Hi," I started. "It's been a while, I know. But I'm not going to apologize for that because I know you've been around these past few years. I see you everywhere. I feel you when the crowds at the games get excited. I see you every time I fold my pizza because you were the first person to teach it to me. I hear you when I queue up our favorite album when you used to sing every word to me off-key. You're never far, I know that.

"But I know it's about time that I make the effort to meet you where you are. So here I am." I patted the ground beneath me, feeling my chest start to constrict. "I promised myself I would get through this with no tears, but let's be honest, that was a bad promise.

"After you left, I was different. I wasn't me. I was so angry at the world because what happened to you wasn't fair. And I know how angry you would have been with me if you watched the person I became. I'm sorry for that. I hope you're proud of the person I grew into. I feel like I've been a phoenix rising out of the ashes."

I swiped at a couple of tears that fell down my cheeks.

"I met someone . . . and I guess that's the reason that brought me here today. Not to tell you that we're happy or anything like that. We're not even together. I guess it wasn't really meant to be. But I really think you would have liked him. He's a big reason why I came today. He made me realize that what happened wasn't my fault. I felt guilty, and that guilt kept me from you these past few years. I'm sorry for what happened that night because it wasn't fair. But I thank you for putting me on the path I am on now."

With each word that left my mouth, it was like a weight was lifted off my chest. I had finally realized that I would never let Luke go. He would always be a part of me, but I had to learn what life looked like after him and I never would have done that if it weren't for Tommy's encouragement. He was the only one who understood that Luke couldn't be this taboo thing that happened to me. The narrative had to change, and the only way to do that was if I finally faced the fear I had of dating and being truly happy with someone else after Luke. I had made up this irrational fear in my head that if I found another guy attractive or he made me laugh, I was disgracing the legacy Luke had left. But that would never be the case. Luke had taught me how to love and love hard. It was time I showed that to someone else.

My phone buzzed in my pocket, and I pulled it out to see a text from Olivia.

Olivia: You're late!!!

I sat up like a bolt of lightning had struck my body.

> Olivia: You have that event to shoot at the
> field. Don't you remember?

I obviously didn't remember the event because if I had, I wouldn't be sitting in a cemetery instead. My legs were Jell-O as I pushed myself to my feet and took off toward the bus. I couldn't afford to lose my job over being scared. I had just told Luke how much I had grown; it was time to suck it up and prove it.

The bus ride was agony as I watched the minutes tick by, making me even more late for whatever I had forgotten about. Whatever event I had so conveniently forgotten, I was in deep shit if May was here for it. I grabbed my camera bags from the seat before sprinting into the stadium, not even bothering to say hello to the usual people. My footsteps echoed as I ran down the tunnel, cursing myself every step of the way for having neglected any form of exercise for the past few years. The tunnel opened up onto an empty field, making me stop in my tracks.

Do I have the right place?

I pulled my phone out to check the texts that Olivia had sent me, telling me where to be. She did, in fact, say the field.

I glanced around, trying to spot either May or Olivia anywhere in the stadium. But nobody was there. I started to walk toward the infield, thinking that maybe they were waiting for me in the dugout and I couldn't see them. Suddenly, the Jumbotron turned on and a series of press pictures of me and Tommy started to flash across the screen. They were then followed by the selfies we had taken in Tommy's home, on the pier with Olivia in California, at the ice cream place right after I managed to get us there unharmed after my first time driving. It was like my eyes couldn't tear themselves away as I relived some of the best months of my life. But then the slideshow ended and I was left alone on the field again.

Or so I thought.

Someone cleared their throat behind me. I spun around to see Tommy standing there by himself in a pair of jeans and a simple black T-shirt. The dressed-down Tommy was my favorite.

My heart had slowed down to a dangerous rhythm in my chest as I stared at the man that I had fallen in love with. The man that had ripped my heart out and crushed it, shredded it into a million pieces, unable to be repaired.

Or so I thought.

Because the way he was looking at me right then felt like it was slowly mending it back together, piece by piece. It was the same way he had looked at me the first time I had met him.

"Maggie." My name came out of Tommy's mouth like a whisper, like he was afraid if he spoke it too loudly, I would break again right in front of him and float off in the breeze.

"What are you doing?" I breathed.

"I need to say something." He held up a hand to try to silence me, but I was beginning to question if I really did have the strength to stand here and listen to whatever it was that he had to say. What if this was some cruel way of saying goodbye?

"I have work to do though, and I should really go." At this point I had put the pieces together that I did not in fact have work to do and I really didn't have anywhere to go. But my heart was now beating at a speed that terrified me, and I thought anywhere but here would be a safer option.

"Maggie, will you shut up for one second?" Tommy raised his voice slightly, silencing me in one fell swoop. Even though the pain inside my heart that had started the night I saw Tommy through the window of his house with Sutton was making it unbearable to stand there in front of him, the look on his face kept me rooted in place. He looked like he was hurting as badly as I was.

"When we first met, I thought you were ridiculous." *Okay, definitely not where I thought this was going.* "You were this shy girl, too afraid to put yourself out in the world because you were too frightened the world would hurt you even more than it already had. So you shut yourself off from everyone and refused to show anyone how special you are."

Okay, this is better.

"But then you, quite frankly, upended my life by ruining everything I thought I had built the night we left that club."

And back to ground zero.

I started to speak, but he shook his head, taking a step closer to me.

"You're frustrating, a perfectionist, never on time, and quite particular about your pizza. Your hair is always on everything, and you never seem to go anywhere without your camera. You cackle when you laugh like a crazy person and insist on watching romance movies instead of anything else. But I love you despite all of those things."

With each word, Tommy took a step closer to me. My heart was beating so fast that I was sure I was going to need the defibrillator in the dugout if he didn't stop soon. There was a part of me that didn't want to believe what he was saying or acknowledge the way he was looking at me as my mind replayed the last time I had seen him, hugging Sutton.

"I love the way you eat your pizza because it's ridiculous. I love watching the way you melt apart at the same movie scene you've watched a million times. I love the way your eyes are always dissecting a moment like you are trying to figure out the best way to capture it in a picture. And I love that when anything good happens to me, I look for you, because I want to share all of those moments with you. I love you, Maggie Redford."

My heart felt like it may very well burst from my chest and land on the ground between us. *Love?* Did he just say he loved me? I wasn't sure if I wanted to cry, scream, or laugh.

"What about the contract?"

"I will be damned if some contract gets in the way of what I feel for you."

He took a step closer.

"What about Sutton?"

Realization crossed Tommy's face as he put the pieces of our timeline together. His grip loosened on my hands. I thought for sure he realized that I had caught him in the act and that none of those things he had said about me would really mean anything, but then I felt his hand slip under my chin and lift my eyes to his.

"She was there to try to win me back." My heart sank as he confirmed exactly what I hoped wasn't true. "But I told her she had to leave, Maggie."

What?

"I told her that the guy she had dated didn't exist anymore. I'd stopped being that guy over a year ago, but the fact that you and I were all over social media made her think otherwise. I told her that I had met someone that felt like home to me."

"I don't understand."

But part of me did. It was soaring up within me. It was *hoping*. That feeling felt foreign. I hadn't hoped for something this much since that night I had hoped Luke wouldn't leave me. That night, I had learned that hoping was dangerous. But Tommy had taught me that daring to hope was the bravest thing a person could do.

"I'm trying to tell you that I want to take you on a date where there aren't any cameras unless it's a camera in your hands. I want to take you on a date and kiss you good night at your door with so much passion that there's no question about my intentions. And I want to tell you how much I love you every goddamn day until you don't doubt it."

"Can I ask you something?" I said after he was silent for a moment.

He nodded. "Anything."

"Why'd you sign the contract in the first place?"

"My plan was to walk away the second they offered it, but then I looked over at you and that just wasn't an option anymore. Because if I walked away, I would miss the opportunity to get to know you, and part of me knew that day in the conference room that you were worth getting to know." He took another step closer to me, and I could practically feel our breaths mingling in the air between us.

"I gave all the money from the contract back." Confusion flashed across Tommy's face. "I couldn't stand to even look at it. It felt dirty. I didn't want to be someone who took advantage of you. You've already had so much of that in your life."

"Maggie, you could never do that. But I appreciate the gesture, even though you definitely didn't have to do that. I feel like you've gone through so much this season so far that's completely unfair." The guilt that Tommy felt over our predicament was all over his face.

"I wanted to do it," I told him. "For you."

Tommy sucked in a breath at my confession.

"I'm scared," I breathed, tears filling my eyes.

"I am too," he whispered back. Then his hands reached down to take mine in his. "Maggie Redford, I am madly, deeply in love with you. You've been in my head from the moment that stupid baseball almost took you out at practice. If you give me the chance of dating me for real this time, I promise I will spend the rest of my life honoring the woman that you are and being the man that you deserve."

As I stared at the man before me, I realized that this was part of the growing I had told Luke about. If I opened my heart up fully to Tommy, I wasn't disrespecting Luke. I was honoring him. Because he would want me to continue to be happy and to *live*. I wasn't living sitting on my couch watching other people get their happy endings, especially when my own happy ending could be standing right in front of me.

Love is scary. It's scary to trust your heart in someone else's hands. I had mine ripped from me four years ago. But love wasn't just trusting that someone else wouldn't break your heart. It was trusting someone would keep it safe when you did go through the worst times in your life, and they'd celebrate with you through the best. And as the man I knew I was head over heels for stood in front of me, trusting me with his own heart, I realized there were different kinds of love. Luke was the first love. It was new and exciting, like I was seeing the world for the first time. Tommy was the comfort of my favorite blanket or, in his words, like coming home.

"I love you." Tommy's eyes widened as the words came out of my mouth. Honestly, part of me was surprised too.

In an instant, I was wrapped in a pair of strong arms. My body relaxed as it moved around him. "I promise you I will try my best every day," Tommy told me as he held me against his chest.

"I know you will," I told him.

Tommy tipped his chin down, and I rose up on my toes, the two of us meeting in the middle. As soon as our lips met, it felt like the last chain snapped off me, leaving me feeling brand new.

"And the crowd goes *wild* . . ." Tommy and I glanced up to see Jamil, Adam, and Olivia in the press box. Jamil's cheeky grin was wide enough we could see it on the field. He and Adam were fist-bumping and Olivia was snapping pictures with her camera. A laugh bubbled out of my chest as I watched our friends celebrate us as if they'd just won the World Series.

"Are you happy?" I asked Tommy. He looked back down at me with a grin that I was sure I would never grow tired of seeing.

"I'm the happiest man in the entire world." He leaned back down for another kiss as the sound of "Take Me Out to the Ball Game" echoed around the park.

THREE YEARS LATER

The stadium was full of baseball lovers ready for their favorite time of year to begin with the sound of the umpire yelling, "Play ball." They had all come to see a show, a game they had grown up playing, but on the big stage. Not a single one of them noticed a short, curly-haired woman weaving effortlessly through the crowd, a camera in her hands.

To any fan, she probably looked like one of the team photographers, which may have been true at one point. She was, in fact, sporting a Cougars jersey with the name Mikals on the back, snapping pictures of various fans as she passed. What a fan wouldn't have known was that she wasn't hustling for the perfect shot anymore. She'd already achieved that.

Or maybe they'd think she was some player's girlfriend, enjoying Opening Day. Which may have been true, but it still didn't encompass the whole truth. She was clearly important to the club because her name was called out over the speakers, asking her to come down onto the field. The woman hustled through the first archway she could find that led down to the field, taking the steps two at a time. One of the ticket checkers waved at her, telling her congratulations on her new position as she ran by. She had recently been given the job of running the entire media department of the Cougars, overseeing not only their major league team, but all of the minor league teams as well.

Fans watched her run down onto the field and wondered who exactly she was. Some recognized her from the gossip magazines that were plastered everywhere three years ago. It became obvious what was happening the moment that her feet hit the dirt of the field and she was greeted by the Cougars' star player, Tommy Mikals. He took her hand in his and said some words that no one but the two of them could hear. But everyone knew what was happening the second Tommy's knee hit the ground and the girl started nodding her head yes.

The crowd erupted in cheers as they watched Tommy become engaged to the woman of his dreams on the Jumbotron. The picture that would be on the front page of the paper the next day would be taken by Olivia Thompson and would be the first picture of the couple in the news in the past three years. They had remained private after every aspect of their relationship had been out there for everyone to see. It was like all of a sudden they were the world's favorite couple to read about, and then *poof* they were gone. But after they disappeared from the public eye, Tommy Mikals stepped into a new role as the team's captain and MVP, leading the league in multiple categories. It was like his career had exploded, and many had speculated it was due to a certain curly-haired woman.

The cameraman zoomed in on the couple as Tommy swung the woman around in circles, a look of pure joy on his face. To the average person, their love looked like a storybook romance. The girl met the guy. The guy swept her off her feet. But for the few people in the stadium that knew the truth, their tale was more than a storybook romance. It was the story of two perfectly imperfect people loving each other despite it all.

How could you not be romantic about baseball?

Acknowledgments

I have many individuals in my life that I must thank that knowingly or unknowingly helped foster the creation of my debut novel. My love of reading was fostered by my parents, who encouraged my brother and me to read and read voraciously from a young age. I have memories as a kid of my dad reading every Twilight and Harry Potter book first before giving them to me. I tinkered on my parents' old computer, writing my own wild stories or doodling them in the many journals that I hoarded.

That love for reading only strengthened while I was in college, where I entered the world of reviewing. Eventually the idea of writing my own novel began to take shape and was encouraged by my fiancé for months before I finally decided to give myself a chance. I was convinced the words I would type and put together would be terrible or I'd never be able to finish such a daunting task. What I hadn't realized was how writing *First Base* would fill a hole in my heart that I hadn't realized was there. What first started as a fun project morphed into something greater. I had only ever dreamed of being able to call myself an author— that title still feels surreal to say. For that achievement, I have so many to thank.

First and foremost is Saskia Leach, my amazing and extremely talented agent. She was the first person to tell me that my words truly meant something. I remember holding back tears as she offered me representation. She truly is a wonder woman with how she has guided me through this whirlwind of a journey. There is no one else in this world that I'd rather partner with. Thank you for believing in me and this book. I am forever grateful.

To my editors, Katherine Pelz and Melanie Hayes, I was so excited from our first meeting that I would get to work on this book with both of you. Katherine, your keen eye set lightbulbs off in my head during my edits that I couldn't quite put my finger on before. Your insight has been invaluable, and I am so thankful to have someone as knowledgeable as you in my corner. Melanie, your excitement for this book was one of the first times I'd realized how my book could resonate with others. Thank you to you both!

To Erika Russikoff, thank you for being the first set of eyes on this project and being the original guiding hand to shape *First Base* into something that would eventually change my life. Your editing talent spans far and wide, and I am so thankful to have decided to have you be one of the first people to ever read my book in its earliest stages.

To my best friend, Sydney, I am so grateful for your endless amount of support through all of this. You celebrated my wins and have always been so excited for me as I navigate this journey. I am so grateful to have a friendship like yours and I love you!

To my parents, thank you for encouraging the gift of reading. It has taken me on many journeys in my life and this one may be my biggest one yet. Thank you for always being my number one fans and supporters.

To Dawson, thank you for initially encouraging me to simply just do it. Without your encouragement, this book never would have happened. Thank you for supporting me when I suddenly began dedicating months out of my year to writing a first draft, and for not complaining when we had to stay in so I could get my words in. Thank you for constantly brainstorming with me about the newest manuscript or about what the future may hold. But I am thankful, most of all, simply for you.

About the Author

Ally Wiegand currently resides in Texas. FIRST BASE is her debut novel and the first book in the Chicago Heartbreakers series. She loves her family, fall, and writing love stories that make your heart squeeze. Ally has dreamed of being a writer since she was a girl. She is a coffee addict, a classic car lover, and a cat mom to two furballs. Her dream is to make readers happy, make them sad – but, most importantly, feel something.

To keep up with Ally and learn more about the Chicago Heartbreakers series, visit her online at www.allywiegand.com.

About Embla Books

Embla Books is a digital-first publisher of standout commercial adult fiction. Passionate about storytelling, the team at Embla publish books that will make you 'laugh, love, look over your shoulder and lose sleep'. Launched by Bonnier Books UK in 2021, the imprint is named after the first woman from the creation myth in Norse mythology, who was carved by the gods from a tree trunk found on the seashore – an image of the kind of creative work and crafting that writers do, and a symbol of how stories shape our lives.

Find out about some of our other books and stay in touch:

X, Facebook, Instagram: @emblabooks
Newsletter: https://bit.ly/emblanewsletter

Milton Keynes UK
Ingram Content Group UK Ltd.
UKHW010317250424
441679UK00001B/8

9 781471 416927